hole hearted

a *Songbird* novel

Is love enough to heal a wounded heart?

MELISSA PEARL

NOTE

For previous Songbird Novels, I have placed the playlist here, but one reader suggested to me that I should put it in the back, as the song list can give too much away. So that's what I've done. If you'd like to see it first, you are welcome to flick to the end of the book to check it out.

For every artist on this playlist

Every song on this playlist stirs a memory. Thank you for giving me so many good times, emotional moments, and songs I could sing at the top of my lungs.

"Music acts like a magic key, to which the most tightly closed hearts open."

Maria von Trapp

ONE

CASSIE

Pushing the book cart down the narrow aisle, I stopped by the R section and scanned for RIO. I slid *The Lightning Thief* back into place and ran my fingers down the spine. Rick Riordan was a genius. His Percy Jackson series was my favorite. I loved getting lost in his different worlds—demigods, heroes, battles where the evil beasts were defeated.

Taking *Holes* by Louis Sachar, I housed it on the next shelf down and frowned when I noticed a few books out of order. It took two minutes to rearrange the mess before I continued shelving the remaining young adult fiction books. A few paces along, I stopped to straighten four spines out of alignment and then nodded, satisfied that everything looked neat and perfect.

Aubrey always teased me for being too fastidious. "You take twice as long to shelve as anyone else in this library."

I didn't care. I liked a job well done. Neat and tidy made me feel better.

With a satisfied grin, I pushed the cart out of the "For Teens" section and over to the adult romances. I was too busy reliving the wall of water scene from *The Lightning Thief* that I didn't even hear the moaning couple until I turned the corner and noticed them up against the wall.

I jerked to a stop, a tendon in my neck straining. I couldn't move for a moment. I was stunned still by the audacity of these lovebirds. They looked like college students. Well, she did anyway. I couldn't see his face. It was buried between her breasts while she fisted his hair and bit her lower lip. His hand was gripping her butt while he gyrated against her. Were they actually having sex…in the Pasadena Public Library?

I gripped the cart handle so hard my short nails dug into my palms.

What did I do?

My throat was thick and gummy as I continued to stare at them. Why was I staring at them? I will never know. Actually, it was probably out of some deep-seated longing I didn't understand at the time.

The woman's mewling morphed into a different

kind of whimper that haunted me. My back snapped straight, the dark memories disintegrating any kind of yearning.

I cleared my throat and the couple jolted. He whipped around to give me a coy smile, but I was too distracted by the tent in his pants to notice. His erection strained against his faded blue jeans, sending a hot fire crawling over my skin. I glanced away and stared at the books in front of me while she giggled.

I sensed her pulling down her skirt and rearranging her top while he tried to hide his tight-pant situation with his bag.

"Sorry about that," he murmured as they brushed past me.

I gave him a jerky nod, then held the cart like the world's most insipid statue until their titters faded out the door.

My hands were shaking, darkness swamping me as I pushed the cart forward. Pitiful whimpers taunted as I tried to dodge memories I hadn't unearthed in months...years, even.

The book slipped from my hand and smacked onto the floor. I bent down to collect it, brushing my hand over the cover. A strong man with bulging muscles was holding a woman against him. She was looking up at his face like he was everything, while he tenderly touched her lips like he wasn't about to slap or punish her...like he'd protect her from any man who did.

The book was probably filled with romantic dialogue and passages that made most women swoon and blush.

"This is why I only read fantasy," I muttered, standing tall and shoving the book back into place. I was quite happy to stick with my wizards and elves, a world where reality was so far-fetched I could dive into it and forget how brutal life could be.

My hands didn't stop shaking until I put the last book away. I hated that it took me so long to reclaim my composure and shove the past where it belonged—in a locked box in the farthest reaches of my mind. I was frustrated that simply spotting a heavy make-out session could bring it to the surface so easily. I'd gone such a long time without those memories touching me.

I wouldn't let him win like that.

That was then.

He couldn't have my now.

Smoothing back my hair to ensure it still sat secure in its ponytail, I raised my chin and headed to the front counter. I parked the cart where it belonged and moved behind the counter to check out some books for a waiting customer before disappearing into the break room.

I poured myself a glass of water, gulped it down, and then put it in the dishwasher.

"Hey, Cassie."

Aubrey's chipper voice made me jump.

"Oh, hi." I spun around and forced a smile, gripping the counter behind me as she hummed while making a cup of coffee.

"Greg just took a call informing us that this old

guy has requested his entire library be donated here. It was in his will. Isn't that cool?"

"Yeah, wonderful. What kind of books?"

"It sounds like a massive collection. Lots of variety. I can't wait to go through it."

"Me too." I was forcing it. My voice wasn't usually so bright and bouncy. I clenched my teeth, hoping she wouldn't notice.

She didn't. She was too busy stirring her coffee and rabbiting on about how cute Greg was.

"Do you think I should ask him out?"

I shrugged. I didn't know!

I'd forced myself to go on a date a few months back, because normal twenty-two-year-old girls went out with nice guys who asked them. It was a miracle in itself that someone even noticed me. He was a single parent, and I met him at a read-a-thon event the library ran as part of our summer program.

The date was nothing but painful. I didn't know what to say or do. The poor guy worked overtime trying to strike up interesting conversation, but we had nothing in common, and I wasn't about to shell out details of my childhood. My life was hardly entertaining, so I pretty much gave him nothing. It was awkward. He dropped me home straight after the meal, didn't even get out of the car to walk me to the door. There was no promise of a follow-up phone call, just a swift goodbye that suited us both.

I swore I'd never do it again.

As much as I wanted to be normal, like Aubrey, I couldn't. I had my routine, my structured life, and my buried secrets. It kept me safe and that was pretty much all I wanted—control and security.

My bubbly co-worker leaned against the counter and sipped her coffee. She had styled blonde curls and her makeup was subtle yet effective, highlighting all the right features to make her look beautiful. I brushed my cheek with the pads of my fingers, then turned it into a chin scratch when Aubrey glanced at me.

I couldn't imagine ever being as pretty as her. I didn't really know how to wear makeup or style my hair. A neat ponytail suited me just fine.

So why was I standing there feeling like the world's ugliest duckling?

The door swung open, making me jump. No one noticed. Aubrey's eyes lit with a dreamy smile. "Hey, Greg."

"Hi." He nodded at her but turned to me. "You do know your phone's been ringing incessantly all afternoon, right?"

"My phone?" I touched my chest. "But no one ever calls me."

"Well, they're calling you today. Would you go and deal with it, please? Either take a minute to return the call or switch your phone off."

"Uh, sure." I scampered out of the break room. My bag was stored under the front counter next to Aubrey's bright purple handbag. I still had the black backpack I'd used for the last four years at community college. Wrestling it out, I unzipped the top pouch and pulled out my phone.

Three missed calls.

One voice message.

I didn't recognize the number.

Chewing my bottom lip, I stared at the screen and wondered if I should return the call, but then the damn phone started ringing in my hand and I was forced to answer it.

"Hello?" I stepped into the back workroom, checking that I was alone before closing the door behind me.

"Hi, Cass."

I jolted, my heart nearly jumping out of my throat. I knew that voice. I hadn't heard it in over a decade, but I knew it. Even though she'd only spoken two little words, I'd recognize my sister's voice anywhere.

I didn't know how to respond.

I'd settled with the idea that I'd never see her again.

"Um...it's Crystal." She filled the silence. "I know this is really out of the blue, but I have to see you."

I opened my mouth but still couldn't make a sound.

"It's important."

Licking my lower lip, I shrunk in on myself, backing up until I hit the solid, immovable wall. "Uh..."

"Please." Her desperate whisper cut right through me.

Closing my eyes, I tried to ward off memories of her beautiful face. She'd always been prettier than me, with big soulful eyes and a wide open smile. It was fake—too full, too sunny—but only I knew it. Because only I knew her.

"I get it if you never want to see me again, but I wouldn't call if I wasn't desperate. Please, Cassie, I need to see you."

My lips quivered as I tried to rein in my emotions. I wanted to shout at her to never call me again, to hang up the phone, throw it on the floor and smash my heel through it.

But I wouldn't do that.

I needed control, composure. Sniffing in a breath, I tried to unclench my teeth but wasn't quite capable. Of all the days to call me. When I was already fighting the memories, she had to throw me into a pit of turmoil, make it a thousand times worse.

But in spite of the earthquake in my chest, I still couldn't say no to her. I never could. "Where are you?"

"Hannah Home in Fox Hills."

"Hannah Home?" I frowned. "What's that?"

She paused with a beat long enough to instill a sick sense of dread.

After a weak sigh, she finally murmured, "It's a hospice."

I nearly dropped the phone. The pause, the way she said it...

My sister didn't work at Hannah Home. Crystal was dying.

Her important message was obviously a goodbye.

After all that time, she was finally going to say

something she should have said years ago.

TWO

FELIX

Mom's hands shook as she placed the phone down beside her.

"Hey, sweetie. How was school?" Her pale eyebrows rose, wrinkling her forehead. I couldn't buy her smile—it was too wide and tense.

"Good," I murmured, not having the heart to ask who she'd been talking to.

She looked more tired than usual...more fragile.

The panicked beat inside my chest kicked in big time, and I had to look away from her, sliding the backpack off my shoulders and laying it at the end of the bed. I glanced back and my heart wouldn't calm the hell down.

Mom pursed her lips and started blinking fast. I didn't see her cry much. She saved up that kind of thing for a locked bathroom when she didn't think I could hear her.

I stepped around the bed and sat in my usual spot. Taking her hand, I rubbed my thumb over the back of it. Even her fingers were skinny now. Two years ago, the doctor told her she had breast cancer. Since then she'd fought it...until about three months ago when they told us it had moved into her brain and there was nothing more they could do. They used a bunch of big words I didn't understand, like masking the reality would somehow make it less brutal.

It didn't.

Cancer was eating my mother alive. They should have just said that, because it was the truth. Mom used to be like the sun—bright and vibrant, shining with a warmth you couldn't escape from, even if you were in a bad mood.

Now she was a soft glow. Her heart was still big and beautiful, but she didn't have the energy to beam anymore.

She spent the first year denying it. Swearing that chemo and radiation and operations would cure her. They did for a while, but the cancer always came back, more pissed off than before.

Adjusting her thick glasses, Mom sniffed and gave me a smile.

It was one of her closed-mouth ones, which meant she was doing everything she could to keep it in…to hide the pain.

I couldn't say anything. I just held her hand and stared at her.

She'd been making a lot of phone calls lately. She always tried to hide it, but the last couple of days when I arrived after school she was finishing up a call. I wanted to yell at her to stop planning for the future, but I wasn't stupid. She was getting prepared.

I swallowed.

The day before, she was saying goodbye to her lawyer as I walked in. I knew it was him because she said, "Thanks so much, Gerry." And I only knew one Gerry.

I didn't know who she'd just finished talking to, but it'd made her kind of emotional.

Usually she told me everything, but something was off. Whoever she told this address to was someone she hadn't seen in a really long time. I could tell by the jittery way Mom pinched her lower lip into a V shape.

She hadn't told me much about her past. I knew her dad died when she was five and her mom died when she was ten. Then she was put into foster care. I knew she had a sister, but they were separated before I was born. I didn't know how. I'd never met my Aunt Cassie, so either Mom couldn't find her or they had some bad blood running between them.

I wondered what it'd be like to have a brother or sister. For the last twelve years, it'd been me and Mom. I didn't mind so much. But when I found out she was going to die for real... I haven't stopped feeling lonely since. When she went, I was gonna have no one, and I'd be an idiot to try and pretend like that didn't scare the crap out of me.

Mom wouldn't tell me what foster care was like. I asked once, and her skin went so white I thought she was going to pass out. She managed to stutter that it was tough and she didn't like to dwell on it—whatever the hell that meant. I never asked her again, but I hoped my time in the system would be better than hers.

The system.

I shuddered, imagining how awful it was going to be.

"Are you okay?" Mom squeezed my hand. "Do you need a drink or something to eat?"

I shook my head, trying to hide what I'd been thinking. "Nah, I'm good."

She gazed at me then, her hazel eyes starting to glimmer. "You know what you do need to do?"

"What?"

"Smile." She touched my cheek, forcing my mouth up at the side.

I couldn't do it.

How was I supposed to smile when all I felt like doing was crying?

"Remember how lucky we are, baby." Mom's voice shook with conviction. "Promise you'll never forget it. Never stop being grateful for what you have. No matter where you go or what you end up doing with your life, there's goodness in everything. Even if it's just the smallest spark, I want you to find it."

I'd heard the speech so many times before, but I couldn't roll my eyes like I wanted to. I just stared at her and promised, "I will, Mom."

Gently shifting away from her touch, I stood from the bed and walked to the window. I didn't want her to see my eyes. They were stinging pretty bad, and if I kept looking at her, I'd cry. I didn't want to do that. She needed me to be strong.

Mom cleared her throat and then "My Favorite Waste of Time" started playing from her phone. I closed my eyes and couldn't help a snicker.

She always used music to change a mood. It didn't matter how bad things got, she was always able to find a song that would make my lips twitch.

Glancing over my shoulder, I saw her mouthing the words, her bony limbs trying to dance as she tempted me to give in.

Her head bobbed with the beat, a sweet laugh coming out of her as she got the lyrics wrong. Covering her mouth, she giggled and then spread her arms wide.

I couldn't resist.

Shuffling back across the room, I sat on the edge of the bed and rested my head on her shoulder. She kept singing, brushing the hair off my forehead and holding me like I was five again.

I didn't mind so much. When you knew your mother's hugs had a time limit, you didn't care that you were twelve going on thirteen and it wasn't cool to do that kind of thing anymore.

You took it.

Because it made you feel better.

Because you never knew which one was going to be the last.

THREE

CASSIE

The hospice smelled clean. It was quiet, people's movements hushed and respectful. I gripped my bag strap and headed down the hallway the receptionist told me to take. My emotions were everywhere. It was a struggle to contain them. In the car, I let out what I could, yelling at Crystal for leaving me, cursing her for being so damn selfish.

I didn't cry...I managed to pull myself together before that happened.

But by the time I reached the hospice, I was mentally exhausted. I hoped I had the strength to hold up around her. I had no idea what to say. Did

I tell her everything I screamed in the car? She deserved my anger after what she'd done.

Rounding the corner, I spotted the room Crystal was living…dying…in.

My stomach clenched.

Dying.

She was only twenty-seven. In that second, I didn't care what she'd done to me. No one deserved to die so young.

Biting my lips together, I slowly approached the room. A boy with dark hair and pale brown eyes stood at the drinking fountain, eyeing me up. I glanced at his cautious expression, not understanding it. His wide mouth dipped at the edges, his soulful gaze tugging at my heart.

He reminded me of someone I once knew…a sad, lonely girl who'd just lost her mother.

I'd only been six at the time. He looked much older than that, but the expression was still the same—uncertainty, tinged with a low-lying fear that your life was about to turn to shit.

I glanced away from him. I didn't know who he was, and it wasn't actually my problem. I had my own battles to face.

Pausing outside Crystal's door, I drew in a breath and held it. My hand shook as I raised my knuckles and rapped once on the door.

"Come in." Crystal sounded weak and tired, so I pushed the door open gently, telling myself to breathe as I turned to face my long-lost sister.

She was not at all like I remembered her. She'd cut her hair. I didn't remember her having curls, but her scalp was covered with them—short, tight ringlets. Last time I'd seen her, she'd had waist-length locks, fine and straight. They'd fly in the wind when she ran.

I threaded my fingers together and gripped until it hurt.

Crystal gazed at me. Her eyes were glistening with affection. They shone with a peace and beauty I hadn't seen since Mom died. If I were honest, I couldn't remember seeing it...ever. I was so young and she'd been my tower. But then that tower started to crumble and disappeared altogether.

My nostrils flared as I fought my raging emotions. I wouldn't let them show. I was not broken. I was in control.

"Hey, sis." Crystal's wide mouth lifted into a grin.

I couldn't smile back.

"It's been a long time." Her voice was husky and shaking a little.

I kept mine flat and even...controlled. "Thirteen years."

"I'm sorry it took me so long to call you."

She looked like she meant it. The regret in her gaze nearly undid me, so I looked to the white blanket covering her skeletal body. "H-how'd you find me?"

"I started with a social worker in Bakersfield. She helped me track where you ended up." She paused, filling the space between us with such thick emotion it nearly swallowed me whole. "In the end I spoke to um... a...Michelle, is it?"

I bobbed my head. "The Kellermans were my last family."

"She sends her love."

Working my jaw to the side, I shooed away the guilt that niggled. I hadn't spoken to the Kellermans since I graduated. As soon as I had my diploma, I left Bakersfield and never looked back.

"She was very kind and helpful. I'm so glad you—"

"What do you want, Crystal?" I snapped, not caring that I'd interrupted her. My breaths were getting punchy. I couldn't talk about the Kellermans. So, they were kind and sympathetic, but they didn't really know. I had to get away…to separate myself from all that had been before.

Crystal let out a soft sigh. It sounded sad and defeated so I looked up. Her face crested with pain as she whispered, "I'm dying. Cancer. It's, um…spread to my brain now, and there's nothing more to be done. I've spent the last two years exhausting all treatments, and according to my most recent doctor's visit, I have maybe three weeks left."

I couldn't breathe for a moment. I just stood there, gaping. Part of me wanted to wrap her in a hug and cry with her, the way we used to when we were kids.

But she'd left me. She'd left me with *him*…and I couldn't cry with her anymore.

Anger spiked through me, bringing out my inner bitch. "So, you brought me here to cleanse your conscience before you go?"

Crystal rebuffed my scathing tone with a soft smile. "I'd love your forgiveness." She looked up, staring at me with a peace I didn't recognize. "I'll understand if you don't want to give it to me. It's not like I deserve it." She glanced down, gripping her hands together. "Just saying sorry will never be good enough."

"How could you just leave me like that?" I wanted my words to come out sharp and snappy, but instead they got strangled and I ended up stuttering, "Y-you just left without a word!"

Crystal drew in a shaky breath. "I'm not saying it wasn't selfish, but I wasn't just thinking about me."

"Who else were you thinking about?" I frowned.

She turned to look at the door. Her smile was beautiful as she softly murmured, "My son."

"What?" I barked. Shock was making me sound like an ogre. I cleared my throat, crossing my arms tight and glaring at her. "What son?"

"I was pregnant." Crystal swallowed. "That's why I ran."

My lips parted but I couldn't make a sound.

"Davis would have killed me. If he'd found out I was knocked up, I don't know what he would have done."

I clenched my jaw, my skin crawling at his name. How could she say it aloud like that?

"So, he's not the father?" I gritted out.

Her eyes sparked as she growled, "I refuse to believe that. You never say that again!"

The raging fear flooding her expression made

me wonder if she was lying.

If Davis the Devil was the father of my child, I wouldn't be able to accept it either.

I let her have her fantasy and quietly asked, "Who is the father, then?"

"I never got his name." She shrugged. "It was at a party. Just a bit of fun."

"Fun?" I closed my eyes, repulsion coursing through me. "How could you call it that? It's…" I shook my head. "How'd you even get away with that?"

"Davis was out of town that weekend. I snuck out after you were asleep. I needed to get out, do something normal." She looked so sad and beat up. "I honestly can't remember the guy's name, but he had a sweet smile and one thing led to another." Gazing across the room, her voice grew distance. "It felt good because it was my choice, and… and he has to be the father! I can't believe anything else, Cass. It *has* to be him." Her eyes were wild and wide when she whipped back to stare at me.

All I could do was bob my head and whisper, "Okay."

Crystal closed her eyes, scratched her forehead and sighed. "I was so terrified that Davis would find out. He would have seen it as cheating. In his warped mind, we were in love with each other. Forcing someone to say that to you doesn't make it true, but he wouldn't understand that." She let out a disgusted scoff. "When I found out I was pregnant, I was so scared. He couldn't afford for anyone to know what he was doing to me, but he wouldn't be able to stomach the thought that someone else had touched me either. In his mind, I was his."

I hated all this talk of our sick, twisted foster father. I had fingernail marks on my skin and my hands were trembling from gripping so hard.

"I know I shouldn't have left you, but he barely noticed you in the house and I figured..."

Her eyes slowly traveled to mine, searching for the truth.

No way in hell I was giving it to her. I was *not* unlocking that box. It was gone. Buried. That night never happened!

Crystal gasped, her eyes popping wide. She shook her head, breaths spurting out of her. I obviously wasn't hiding things very well. The realization in her eyes was ugly and brutal. "No, he was in love with *me*. He wouldn't have touched you. You were only ten!"

I glared at her remorse, despising it for a second. What the hell did she think would happen when she left? The man was a deranged monster.

"No, Cassie, no," she whimpered, covering her mouth with trembling fingers.

I couldn't say anything. For one, my throat was constricting, making it hard to swallow let alone speak. And two, I wouldn't admit it. Not to anyone.

"Did he make you say 'I love you'?" Her whisper was pitiful.

My whisper was hard and metallic when I finally found the voice to respond. "He tried."

Crystal sucked in a sob, her entire body shaking. "I'm sorry. I'm so sorry."

I stood beside her, cold and unflinching. I was struggling to breathe. I didn't think it was possible to reach forward and take her hand. Instinct was telling me to comfort her but I couldn't move.

"I shouldn't have left you behind, but I was desperate." Tears spilled from her eyes. "I had this window of time. It was my only chance, so I took it. I convinced myself you'd be all right, that he'd ignore you like he always had. I couldn't be pregnant and looking after you at the same time! I just..." The agony on her face was ugly...forgivable, but still I couldn't say anything. "I wasn't strong enough."

I swallowed, her torment making me relent just a little. Pulling a tissue from the box, I held it out for her. "You were only fourteen. If we'd had normal lives you would have been starting high school, not running away pregnant."

She slipped off her thick glasses and dabbed her eyes. "How'd you get out?"

I turned away from her question, my skin prickling as memories tried to decimate me. Squeezing my arms tight against my stomach, I dug my nails in and counted to ten, grappling for control. I didn't speak until I could talk without my voice shaking. "I'm past all that now. I've moved on. It's been years, and I'm over it."

I glanced over my shoulder, checking that she believed me.

She didn't.

I spun back to face the window.

The silence that followed was filled with so much potential. I had the chance to wound with the truth, to lay it on thick and make her realize just how much I had to forgive her for. But I couldn't. She was dying, and in spite of everything, I couldn't help putting myself in her shoes. If Davis had found out she'd had sex with someone else…

I shook my head, not willing to imagine his wrath. If I hadn't lost her like I did, I may have lost her to a hole in the ground.

A shudder shook my spine.

"Cass, I need your help," Crystal said.

My first reaction was an indignant prickle. Thirteen years of radio silence and she was only calling to use me. I didn't have any money. I wasn't rich. I couldn't bail her out of medical bills and—

"I need you to take care of my son."

My heart hitched and I spun to face her. "What?"

"They'll put him in the system if you don't. Please, please, you have to make sure that doesn't happen." Her voice pitched high. "He's a good kid. He's kind and sensitive. The system will rob him of all of that."

"I-I can't raise a kid! I'm not…" I squeezed my eyes shut. "No! Crystal, you can't ask that of me!"

"Please, Cassie!" she practically screamed. "He doesn't have anyone else. You know what the system did to us. I can't…I can't go until I know he'll be safe. Please." Her panic turned to gut-wrenching sobs. "Save him," she pleaded. "*Please*."

Her tone made my skin crawl. I remembered it, that pathetic begging.

"Stop. Please, stop."

He never did.

I backed away from the sound, the memories set on destroying me. I couldn't. I couldn't lose control. With a firm shake of my head, I grappled for the door handle. "I can't. I'm sorry, Crys. I just... I can't."

Flinging the door open, I rushed out, avoiding the kid in the armchair outside Crystal's door. Her whimpers continued to haunt me as I rushed to my car. Covering my ears, I tried to escape the sound of her crying, his grunts, the demands.

"Say it, Crystal. Tell me you love me."

I tripped out the door and stumbled to my car. My stomach was trembling and jerking, wanting to unleash a torrent of ugly tears. I slapped my hands against the roof of the car.

Crystal's tiny voice did what he wanted, giving in so he could have his filthy way.

She did what he asked because she was terrified.

I didn't because I was just as scared.

Fear kept me silent.

Fear got me beaten and isolated.

The smell of the dank basement seared my nostrils, the memories strong enough to cripple me.

But I never gave in.

I never once said, "I love you."

And I never would.

My life was set, orderly...controlled. I couldn't disrupt that with a kid. Especially one who reminded me of what it was like to lose everything that made me feel safe.

FOUR

TROY

"Don't Leave Home" by Dido was playing on the radio. I pulled my car into the parking lot and hummed the song as I made my way into the office.

"I will be your safety," I sang quietly, unlocking my door and shouldering it open.

I didn't see anyone on my way in. I shared the small building with three other counselors. It was actually an old house that had been converted into a counseling center. Most of us were in and out quite a lot. I spent most of my time hanging out in classrooms, and sometimes homes to make sure they were safe for the children. My goal was to help families communicate, resolve their issues, and find a way forward.

The job was tough, but satisfying. There was nothing more rewarding than seeing a family work through their pain, learn to communicate and love again. I'd seen so many cases of success. A few failures too, but the success stories kept me going.

Pulling out my laptop, I placed it on my desk and dropped my bag on the floor behind me. My butt wasn't even in the seat when my phone started ringing. I dug it out and flopped into my chair before answering.

"Good afternoon, Principal Turrell. How are you today?"

"Fine, fine." His tone was always so clipped and busy.

I grinned and opened my laptop. "What can I help you with?"

"I'm having trouble with one of my seventh graders. Kid keeps getting into fights. We have a strict policy at this school. Fighting will not be tolerated under any circumstances, but yet again he's in my office. I've told him this is the last straw. If he throws one more punch, I'm going to expel him."

I rolled my eyes at the guy's hard-line attitude. From my experience, kids didn't kick and punch without a good reason.

"I'm happy to come and chat with him if you like."

"Yes, well, his mother's asked me to contact a counselor for him."

I raised my eyebrows.

"She's dying. Cancer. It's just a matter of time now and he's probably acting out because of that. He's a very quiet, morose boy. Was a star student in elementary school but has been struggling for the past couple of years."

"Does he have any family support?"

"No, it's just the two of them. When she dies he'll become a ward of the state. It's very sad and we've tried to accommodate him as best we can, but I won't tolerate any more fighting." His voice crescendoed, giving away just how exasperated the situation made him.

I winced. "I understand. If you'll send over his details, I'll look into it right away."

"Thank you, Troy. I'll send the email now."

As soon as he hung up, I set my phone down and opened up my mail account. Sounded like a tough case. Poor kid was facing foster care. He was probably terrified, plus heartbroken over losing his mother. If it was just the two of them, she was probably his everything.

My inbox dinged. I skimmed the message and double-clicked the attached file.

"Felix Grayson," I murmured, scrolling down the screen until I came to his image.

He was a sweet-looking kid—a mop of dark hair and these pale brown eyes that did something to my heart. He looked sad yet resigned. Had he known about his mother's cancer when the picture was taken?

I scanned down and read the history, quickly

working out that his mother had been battling the disease since he entered the fifth grade. The photo was taken when he started middle school, no doubt terrified with everything that awaited him.

"Poor kid," I muttered, slowing down and reading the detailed reports from his teachers and principals. I looked through his grades and quickly built an idea of who the kid was.

I liked to get a full scope before going in to meet someone.

The more I read, the more it reminded me of my younger brother, Jimmy. He was a wild piece of trouble when he started middle school. I shook my head at the hell he put me through. I'd basically been raising him since my dad split and Mom became obsessed with her cleaning business. I'd been six years older than him, and for some reason that made me capable of parenting him. I don't know how the heck my mother came to that conclusion, but there it was.

I did okay, I guess. Jimmy turned out pretty good in the end. His life was on track—taking him to the stars, actually—but it'd been a tough road to travel.

Scrolling back up the screen, I gazed at the picture of Felix.

He didn't have an older brother to cover for him, fix his messes, get him out of trouble. He had a mom, and he was about to lose her.

I honestly didn't know what I could say to make him feel better about the situation. I always prided myself on being able to fix things, heal...restore.

But how did you help someone whose future looked so bleak and hopeless?

All I could pray for was a good foster home for the guy...to be with someone who could love and care for him the way every kid deserved.

FIVE

FELIX

I waved to Nurse Miranda as I walked past reception. She looked at my eye and winced. "You want an ice pack, honey?"

"Not today," I muttered, stopping by the counter so she could grimace at my red knuckles.

"Hope you won."

I shrugged. It kind of depended on what you qualified as a win. Did I deck those idiots who tried to wedgie me?

You bet.

Did I end up getting busted by Principal Turrell and told I had one chance left?

Pretty much.

I cringed, flicking the hair off my face and wondering what Mom was going to say.

"Don't worry about it." Miranda rubbed my arm. "You know she loves you more than anything."

I nodded and headed for Mom's room. I kind of hated that she'd moved into the hospice. But the staff took good care of us. I had a bed beside hers, and they served extra meals each night so I could eat too. Mom was too weak to look after herself and I couldn't do it on my own. It was the right move for us...even though I didn't want to do it.

I was living in a death house. Every day reminded me that the clock was ticking.

With a heavy sigh, I pushed the door open and dumped my bag on the chair. I didn't want to look at Mom even though that's all I could think about doing.

"Come here, sweet boy." She beckoned me with her fingers. I shuffled to her bed and took a seat on the edge. Her hands were cold yet gentle as she lifted my chin and brushed her thumb over my bruise. "Did you start this one?"

"I never do, Mom! It's self-defense! Not that Principal Dickhead ever wants to hear my side of the story."

She smiled at my insult. "I love the way you fight."

"What?" I frowned. "Mom, I could get expelled."

"I know," she croaked. "I just mean I love the

way you stand up for yourself. You don't let anybody push you around. You're a fighter...just like your Aunt Cassie." Her voice trailed off, that sad look swamping her again. "She was always so much stronger than me."

I sat back and gazed down at her, forcing my voice to be bright and upbeat. "You raised a kid on your own. You're strong, Mom."

"I'm not strong enough to beat this, kid." She looked so sad again. I wanted to shake her out of it, tell her to give me a little sunshine, but I couldn't move. If I shifted, I could shatter. If I spoke, I could fall apart.

Touching my cheek, Mom gave me a tender smile. It was so full of love that I thought I might cry. "I don't know what your future holds, baby. If I'm one hundred percent honest, that scares me. I want you to have a good life full of love and sunshine and happiness."

I forced a smile. "You've given me that, Mom."

"You have to keep shining for the both us when I'm gone, okay?" She held her hand against my other cheek as well, so I couldn't look away. Her voice was thick with emotion. "You have a beautiful soul. Don't hide it from the world because you're sad or scared." Fear skittered across her face, stark and disconcerting. "No matter where you end up. You keep fighting for a good life, because that's what you deserve. Don't let anyone hurt you or take advantage of you. You're better than that." I went still at her fierce voice, the pleading in her eyes. "Promise me, Felix."

"I-I promise."

She studied my face, making sure I was telling the truth.

"I promise," I whispered again.

She relaxed with a smile, then pulled me into a hug. Her arms trembled as she held me against her. I gently rubbed her shoulder, and "The Lucky Ones" started playing on Mom's phone. We both went still, locked in an embrace and listening to a song we made ours years ago. Mom wanted it to be our theme song, and we went through a phase of listening to it every day.

Mom's grip loosened and I sat back, grinning down at her as the music swirled around us.

"Guess what?" She smiled.

I snickered and raised my eyebrow at her, already knowing what she was going to say. "What?"

"I love you."

"I love you too, Mom."

And I went back in for another hug.

SIX

CASSIE

The pavement felt good beneath me. My stride was full and steady, my pace good for this far into my run. I was going faster than usual but I needed to. Running was the only thing that came close to the peace I so desperately strived for. Running was an escape. *The* escape.

Sweat trickled down the back of my neck, soaking into my sports bra. I focused on my breathing as I powered up the hill. I was on my seventh mile. I usually ran about nine a day, but I wasn't tired. I didn't want to stop. If I stopped, I'd think.

I'd have to face the problem looming ahead of me. I couldn't distract myself with rhythm and breathing, the sounds of traffic around me, the color of the sky.

Wiping a finger under my nose, I veered off my normal route. The hill descended quickly, and I was soon in a busy part of town. I didn't mind so much. It gave me more things to look at and helped me dodge the inevitable faces dancing in my brain.

Crystal's sobs had been tormenting me for a week. Seven nights of dreaming about her. Seven days of obsessing over her pitiful plea to take her son when she died.

I'd fought against it night after night, hour after hour, yet still she came back to me.

My brain and heart were at war, but they kept switching sides.

Logically, I should take him. He needed a home, and I knew from experience that there were no guarantees in the system. Before Davis and Mindy McCoy, we were with a lovely family—the Thompsons. They were fun and smart and kind. But then she got pregnant and they decided they didn't want foster kids anymore, so off we went, discarded like a piece of recycled cardboard. We then got dumped in a home with three other foster kids. It was a noisy, chaotic place that I hated. After that was the grumpy lady who we used to call the Gingerbread Witch. We had fun playing tricks on her, hiding mice in her fridge and ants in her cereal. She got rid of us after only four months and then came the McCoys.

We thought we were set. Davis was a nice guy with a loud laugh. He told great stories and constantly made us giggle at his silly jokes.

But after five months…when we'd been lulled into a sense of safety…the nighttime came.

I clenched my fists and pumped my arms a little harder.

Rounding the corner, I ran toward the setting sun. The golden rays cast an orange glow on the buildings around me. I dipped my head against the bright glare and that's when I noticed her.

She looked about my age. Her hair was long and ratty. Her feet were bare. Hollow cheeks and wild eyes gave away her drug addiction. She sat at a bus stop, twitching and muttering to herself. Her hands trembled as she tucked a lock of greasy hair behind her ear. I got a whiff of her stench as I jogged past.

It stayed with me, a lingering torture that only added to my unrest.

Jogging past a shop, I then got hit with the strains of a song Crystal used to play on our stereo—"If That Were Me." The tune was slightly haunting, the lyrics totally confronting. Mel C sang about how cushy her life was while those on the streets suffered the cold and their despair.

I slowed my pace, my limbs complaining at the change-up. Eventually I dribbled to a stop, standing on the corner of a busy intersection and holding my sides. My chest heaved while my heart rate found its usual pace.

Staring back down the road, I strained to see the bus stop. I couldn't make out the girl anymore…instead I was faced with a mirage.

Crystal, pregnant and alone, sitting on a park bench. She would have been dirty and homeless, no doubt terrified, constantly looking over her shoulder for Davis's retribution. He always promised that if we left him, he'd hunt us down and make us pay. His fingers dug into my cheek, threatening to bury me in the backyard if I ever told anyone what he did to Crystal.

"It's okay because we love each other. It's a private thing. You don't tell anyone, you understand me?"

Even at the age of nine, I knew he was full of shit. But I nodded anyway because I didn't want to be buried alive.

My mind flashed to the boy waiting outside Crystal's door. That was him…her son. It had to be.

I tried to picture him in my house, taking over my ordered space—disrupting it, pulling me to the edge. I couldn't handle chaos. I needed order…control.

But then I pictured him in another house.

Davis McCoy had died nine years ago, but there would be other men like him. Rough hands, iron fists, chilling threats that kept you awake at night.

Crystal's son with his soulful eyes… She was right. The foster system would rob him of something beautiful.

Unless I did something about it.

When Crystal left me, I didn't think I'd survive. I'd never felt so lonely, so desolate.

Would her son be feeling that way? I couldn't stand the idea of *anyone* facing such a terrifying future. It didn't matter who his father was. That boy had a sweet face, kind eyes. I hadn't thought *Davis McCoy* when I looked at him. Crystal didn't want to believe that man was the father, but the chances were high. Could I handle living with his offspring?

I had to.

I had to be strong enough.

I couldn't say no to my sister. I couldn't say no to that kid!

Spinning back to the lights, I pressed the pedestrian button and raced across the road as soon as the green walking man appeared. Sprinting through the foot traffic, I double-timed it back to my place.

I'd be a ragged, exhausted mess when I got there, but it didn't matter. I had to get to Hannah Hospice as soon as I could. I had to rescue Crystal's son.

SEVEN

FELIX

It'd been a long, quiet day at the hospice. I'd done my homework because Mom made me, and then I'd sat and read to her. She was one of those girls who had been born in the wrong era. That's what she always said anyway. Although she'd only been a baby in the '90s, her favorite type of music was '80s and '90s pop and rock. She loved reruns of *MacGyver*, *Full House*, and *The Cosby Show*. Her favorite books were Sweet Valley High. She'd never outgrown her love of those blonde twins, and so I spent most of my Saturday reading about Elizabeth and Jessica Wakefield.

Yeah, it was painful, but it made Mom happy so I waded through pages of romantic crap and teen angst that felt over the top and silly.

"Chapter fifteen," I murmured. Flipping the page of the tatty book, I was about to launch into the next scene when the door flew open.

The lady from last week rushed in. She was kind of skinny but had a round face. I had to admit she looked like Mom, but not as pretty. Her long hair was a shade darker and pulled into a military ponytail—not one hair was out of place. She had big eyes...brown, kind of like mine, except darker and more intense. There was something really uptight about her.

She stared at me and I couldn't tell if she was about to cry or get mad.

It was really off-putting and I leaned away from her gaze, looking to Mom instead. Her eyes were stuck on her sister.

Yeah, I knew.

Mom told me last time that my aunt Cassie was coming to visit, but I didn't want to believe her. After all the years of never knowing the woman, I wasn't expecting her to show up, but then she did. The way she stared at me while I poured a drink from the cooler was weird, and then my chest deflated when she walked into Mom's room.

I didn't like the idea that I was somehow related to a crazy lady. I'd been all set to meet her, because that's what Mom wanted. I'd psyched myself up for the big intros. I'd waited outside the room until Mom asked me to come in, sat through the snappy exchange wondering if I should burst in anyway. But then Crazy Chick just took off. I'd walked back into the room and found Mom lying there, bawling her eyes out.

I'd been seriously pissed off. That woman made my mom cry.

Gripping the Sweet Valley High book, I glared at my aunt and then turned to Mom. I was about to say, "Should I ask her to leave?" but Mom's face was practically shining. Her eyes were bright with hope, her lips pulling into a grateful smile.

"I'll do it," Aunt Cassie whispered.

Mom let out a shaky laugh, her body quivering. "Thank you." Tears lined her lashes as she reached for her sister's hand. "Thank you."

My eyebrows dipped low as I watched the exchange. Aunt Cassie was hesitant to take Mom's hand but finally slipped her fingers in for a very brief squeeze. Mom started crying and smiling.

"Thank you." She said it again before turning to me. "Felix, I'd like you to meet your aunt Cass."

"Hi," I mumbled.

"Hello." She raised her hand in this awkward wave. She looked like such a geek with her shirt buttoned all the way up. Her cable-knit sweater was a drab beige. She looked like a librarian from the 1950s. I bet she never wore her hair down. Before chemo stole Mom's hair, she used to wear it down all the time or had it up in these cool braids. She was a cool mom, always looked stylin'. I was happy to hang with her in public.

Aunt Cass looked like she didn't belong in

public.

Taking my hand, Mom gave it a little shake and softly dropped a bomb in my lap. "Aunt Cass is going to look after you...when I'm gone."

I flinched away from the news.

"It's gonna be okay, baby. She's a really kind person and she'll take care of you. Everything's set."

I pulled my hand out of Mom's grasp and glared at the woman across the bed. Her smile was weak and forced. She looked about as happy with the news as I did.

"You'll be safe with her," Mom whispered, bright hope flaring in her eyes.

I didn't know what that meant or what she was trying to tell me. Aunt Cassie was blinking, chewing on her lower lip, and looked about ready to pass out. Her white skin was pale, the way Mom's sometimes went when she'd gaze out the window at nothing.

Mom gave me another reassuring smile, and all I could do was swallow my disbelief.

*****

Aunt Cassie came back the next day, along with Gerry the lawyer. Troy was already there when they arrived.

I liked Troy. He'd been to check on me at school and visited Mom once before. He made her smile, and for a second I wished she had married a guy like him. Then I'd have someone cool to take care of me instead of my weird aunt.

She shook Troy's hand but I could tell she didn't want to. Her cheeks were kind of pink and she wouldn't look him in the eye when he introduced himself. It was kind of funny seeing them stand next to each other. Her in a knee-length polka-dot dress that looked like it'd survived the seventies, no makeup, hair in that standard low ponytail. Troy towered beside her in this cool brown leather jacket, faded and worn. His jeans were dark and he had these big boots on. He could pass as a model with his sharp features and blue eyes, but he didn't ooze an arrogant vibe or anything. He was just a good-looking guy who was nice. I bet he didn't have any problems with the ladies.

That's the kind of guy I wanted to be when I was older.

Troy kept his eye on me while the adults signed stuff, making decisions about my life that I had no say in. His smile was sympathetic and it started to get to me. I turned away from him and kept my eyes on Mom instead.

She seemed more and more relieved as each sheet of paper was scribbled on and filed away. Aunt Cassie seemed more and more nervous.

I stayed silent the whole time. I didn't want to upset Mom. I wasn't ready to answer Aunt Cassie's lame questions like "Where do you go to school?" "What's your favorite subject?"

She didn't care. She just didn't know what else to say.

Man, she was uptight. Everything about her was

tense and closed off. Her facial expressions were always minimal, her answers soft and emotionless.

Dread seeped into me, making it hard to breathe. Mom couldn't leave me with this woman. I'd rather go into the system. I could luck out with a cool family that listened to music and knew how to smile.

As soon as she left, I was going to say something to my mother, beg her to reconsider.

But when Gerry and Troy left, Aunt Cassie stayed.

The minutes ticked by. Mom made me read more Sweet Valley High. Aunt Cassie listened, her lips twitching with the odd smile. Mom would glance at her and murmur, "Do you remember this part?"

Aunt Cassie would nod but say nothing.

I finished the book and set it down. Mom's eyes were closed. She looked tired and pale. Leaning over her, I kissed her forehead and gently brushed the curls away. I missed her long hair, but the curls were cool too. She'd even been beautiful bald.

Her eyelids fluttered and she stared up at me, her smile soft and affectionate. "Do you remember everything I told you, baby?"

I nodded and grinned. "Yeah, Mom."

"We're the lucky ones." Her voice was so weak and croaky. It was hard for me to hear. I leaned in closer as her lips parted to say more, but all I felt was a soft breath in my ear...and then nothing.

My smile faltered and I moved my face a little closer.

Still nothing.

"Mom?" I shot back, gaping at her, expecting her eyes to pop open. "Mom!"

Aunt Cassie stumbled out of her chair and rushed to the bedside. Hovering her fingers over Mom's lips, she stared at her sister...and then her expression crumpled. She shook her head and looked at me.

"No," I snapped. Grabbing Mom's shoulders, I gave them a little shake. "Mom, wake up. Mom!" I shook a little harder until Mom's head started to wobble on the pillow. It drooped to the side and Aunt Cassie touched my hand, a brief brush of her fingers, warning me to stop.

"Mom," I whispered again, my voice broken and hollow...just like my insides.

A cold numbness took over my body. Icy fingers of realization cut off my senses until I was standing by Mom's bed, a lifeless statue. I couldn't move. I couldn't speak. I couldn't do anything but stare at my mother's beautiful face and wish her back to life.

EIGHT

TROY

My feet were heavy as I walked up the path to Cassie Grayson's place. I'd only met her twice and I couldn't believe my first home visit was straight after a funeral. It sucked on so many levels, but I had to check out the place. Even though Crystal had signed for Cassie to be Felix's guardian, it was still my role to ensure she'd do a good job with her nephew.

I was hoping to make a real connection with Felix before his mom died, so that I could be someone safe to turn to. But I hadn't really had the time and now I was just another stranger, someone else he had to deal with while he mourned the loss of his everything.

The funeral service was two days ago. It had been a small affair with fewer than thirty people in attendance. Felix stood by his aunt, acting like a morose statue. He didn't cry once. Cassie shed a few tears, but they were silent, her lips fighting to stay in line as she held herself together.

It was painful to watch them standing at the front of the church, both so lost and scared.

I tried to speak to them after the service, but neither was up for it.

With a heavy sigh, I stepped onto the wooden porch and knocked on the screen door.

The house was a neat little bungalow—olive green with dark red trim. The window frames and door were painted the same red as the trim, and everything about the house looked meticulous and well-kept.

I knocked and waited, listening for the sounds of footsteps. They were quiet and unhurried as they approached the door. The net curtain shifted behind the glass panel, and I caught a pair of cautious eyes.

I smiled. Cassie's face disappeared and then came the clicking of three locks. The door opened, and she greeted me in her soft way.

"Hello, Mr. Baker."

"Please, call me Troy."

She nodded and stepped aside, allowing me entry.

"So, how's everyone doing?"

Smoothing a hand over her hair, she ran it down her ponytail, then closed the door behind me. "It's a challenging time. He hasn't cried once. Is that bad?"

I shrugged and gave her another smile, trying to reassure her. "People express grief in different ways. It's a journey, and his path might be different than yours."

"I haven't cried much either," she murmured.

"Well, maybe your paths will be similar, then." I winked and smiled again.

Her lips twitched but then fell back into a tight line. "I'll let Felix know you're here."

"Thanks for letting me pop by to visit. I just wanted to quickly scan his new environment and talk to him about how we can make him feel at home here."

She paused, resting her hand on the archway into the kitchen. I looked past her shoulder and spotted a pristine cooking space. Every surface gleamed. The counters were clear of clutter.

"Not much of a cook, huh?" I pointed behind her.

She frowned and glanced behind her. "No, I cook every day."

"Oh." I gave her a sheepish grin. "I just... It's so clean and tidy. Sorry, I shouldn't assume."

"What's wrong with clean and tidy?"

"Nothing. I've just never seen such a... It's practically sparkling."

She adjusted her shoulders, eyeing me up with those big brown eyes of hers, trying to judge if I was insulting her or not.

I smiled, hoping to relax the straining tendon in her neck. "I wish I could keep my kitchen that nice."

"I like it clean. I need—" She smoothed a hand over her head again. "There's nothing wrong with being neat and orderly."

"No, there's not," I assured her, bobbing my head to back up my words.

She looked to the floor and shuffled off to get Felix.

I puffed out my cheeks and expelled a quick breath, my eyes bulging a little. I didn't get such a tense vibe from Felix's mother, which meant the kid was going to struggle adjusting to a neat-freak house and a twitchy aunt who obviously had issues.

Stepping into the living room, I glanced around the space. It was pretty spartan. There were no pictures on display, no evidence of family or friends. A small TV was nestled in the corner, opposite a two-seater couch and a comfy-looking armchair. Beside that were two massive bookshelves stacked with novels. I walked over to peruse the titles. They were all fantasies. Huge, fat spines held together pages of dragons and knights, witchcraft and magic spells.

She obviously liked to escape reality, which told me her reality wasn't always what she wanted it to be. Running my finger along one of the shelves, I noticed that each book was lined up perfectly.

Yet another indicator that Cassie Grayson liked

order…control.

But she didn't seem the dominant type, not with her quiet voice and shy demeanor, so that meant the control wasn't driven by a need to be in charge. Maybe it was self-preservation?

I flipped open my file and scanned the second page, looking for history on Felix's mother. It didn't say much, just that the girl ran away from foster care when she was fourteen. She went off-grid until Felix was born, and the two were put under the care of Arthur Winter. He was an older man and passed away four years earlier.

Ran away from foster care.

My forehead wrinkled as I toyed with a few scenarios. She must have been miserable if she'd run away…and she must have taken off without her sister; otherwise, it would have been stated in the file.

Cassie cleared her throat, pulling me away from the myriad of questions exploding in my brain.

I spun with a smile.

"Hey, Felix." I kept my voice bright but soft, hoping to coax a reaction out of him.

It didn't work. He remained blank-faced.

"So…" I slapped the file closed. "I just wanted to pop by and see how you're doing."

Felix shrugged. Cassie stood nervously behind him, about as confident as a kid lost in a department store.

"Uh, Cassie, would it be all right if I had a glass of water?"

"Sure." Her head bobbed erratically and she

scuttled off, obviously relieved to have something to do.

As soon as she was out of earshot, Felix's shoulders relaxed.

"I'm guessing life is one big suck-fest right now."

"Yeah," he mumbled, shoving his hands in his pockets.

"I know it doesn't feel like it right now, but things are going to get better and eventually, once the pain's not so bad, you'll be able to remember so many cool things about your mom."

Felix blinked and nodded. I paused, giving him time to say something, but he didn't.

"So, Principal Turrell asked me to check in with you today as well. He wanted you to know that there's no rush to come back to school. Just take your time, and you can return when you're ready."

"What about my work?" Cassie appeared, the glass of water trembling in her hand.

I took it before she dropped it. "Thanks."

"Don't worry," Felix muttered. "I'm going back to school."

"Are you sure you're ready for that?" I asked, slightly annoyed with Cassie for being so worried about her job. Felix needed her support, and I was sure her boss would understand her taking a few extra days.

"I just want to get on with life. Moping around this place isn't going to make me feel any better. I might as well be in school, distracting myself with learning stuff."

I narrowed my gaze at him. "Is that really what you want? According to your grades and the incident reports I've read, you're not doing much learning. Sounds like fighting's more your style."

"What?" Cassie's eyebrows popped high.

Felix rolled his eyes and started to leave the room.

"Hey, buddy." I called him back. "I wasn't trying to offend you. I just want to have an honest conversation."

"You want honesty?" Felix spun, his brown eyes flashing. "I hate this place! I hate my school! I hate the assholes who go there! But I don't have a choice! My mom's dead and I should be grateful not to be in the system. For some reason that seemed to scare the crap out of her. So I'm doing what she wants. I'm gonna live here and I'm gonna go to school and I'm gonna tell myself I'm lucky." His voice cracked. Clenching his jaw, he turned and fled back to his room.

The door slammed shut.

Cassie flinched and then worried her lip, blinking fast while she threaded her fingers together.

"It's okay," I said. "He's doing his best, and it's better that he gets some of it out of his system. Bottling things up only makes it worse." I went to pat her shoulder, but she shied away from my touch.

She gave me a tight, closed-mouth smile, then dipped her head. So she didn't like being touched. Interesting. I was guessing that Crystal and Cassie

Grayson had an awful experience in foster care. I'd been doing this job for five years, and it didn't take much to conjure up a bunch of ugly theories.

I sealed my lips against the questions wanting to break free and instead thought of Felix.

"Cassie, I get the sense you didn't ask for this gig."

She shook her head.

"Doing this for your sister is really amazing, but I know it's a big ask."

"I don't know what I'm doing." She looked up at me, her expression full of fear.

"You'll figure it out along the way." I smiled. "I can see how much you want to help Felix. Even though you're feeling lost right now, the fact you agreed to this shows how much you care. These things take time. Don't put pressure on yourself. Just take each day as it comes."

"He said he hates this place." She sighed.

"He just needs to get used to it." I looked around. The house reeked of single-womanhood. "Um, maybe you could give him a space that's his own. You know, give him total ownership of his bedroom or something."

Her shoulders tensed. I wanted to spin her around and knead those muscles, whisper in her ear to relax, but I could already tell that would freak her out big time.

I had to fight a smile. She was like a wound-up doll that had never been released.

"Try to relax. I know it's hard, but the more tense you are, the more tense he'll be."

"I'm not tense." She shook her head.

I gave her a dubious smile.

She dipped her head and relented with a small snicker. "I'm twenty-two. I'm not old enough to be a mother. Seriously, I don't know what I'm doing!"

"All he needs right now is someone to take care of him. Feed him, talk kindly to him, give him ownership of his room. Let's start with those and we can build from there." I dug into my pocket and pulled out my card. "If you need anything, night or day, just give me a call."

She gazed at the card I held out to her, pausing for a moment before reaching forward and taking it. She read my details then looked up with a skeptical frown. "Night or day? Is that really part of your job description?"

I grinned. "My job is to help people deal with their pain and find a way forward. If I'm reading you right, I'm not the only one who wants that for Felix. But you look scared as hell right now, so please, call me if you need *anything*. We'll find a way forward together, okay?"

Her head bobbed again, a little more controlled this time. Slipping the card into her pocket, she walked me to the door and then gave me a tentative wave before I stepped off the porch and walked to my car.

I couldn't help a soft chuckle as I started the engine. Oh man, what I wouldn't give to unlock whatever shackles were holding her tight and see what she looked like with her hair down and a carefree smile on her face.

Turning out of the street, I drove away from the Grayson home and started praying. I didn't know how it was going to happen, but I couldn't help thinking that those two needed a miracle. And I wanted to be a part of that transformation.

NINE

FELIX

I couldn't sleep. Every night I tossed and turned in my little bed, chasing something that wasn't there. I'd dream weird dreams, then open my eyes a groggy mess. Mom had died less than a week ago, and I felt like a steaming pile of useless.

I slipped out of bed and went to use the bathroom. Everything in the house was so clean and tidy. I was afraid to do anything. The water dripped off my hands and onto the vanity. Aunt Cassie would no doubt hate it, but I walked away and headed for my room. A few drips on the vanity never killed anybody.

I shuffled down the dark hallway, not expecting to see my aunt coming toward me. I nearly jumped out of my skin.

We both did.

She patted her chest and tried to smile at me. It didn't really work.

In the end she mumbled, "Sorry for scaring you. I thought you'd be asleep."

I shrugged and shook my head, then looked at what she was wearing. I couldn't see details in the dim morning light, but I could make out sneakers, yoga pants, and a big Nike swoosh on her T-shirt.

"I wrote you a note." She waved a piece of paper in the air, then handed it to me.

Felix,

Hopefully you won't have to read this because you'll still be asleep. I'm just out running. Will be back soon. Don't unlock the door for anyone.

Aunt Cassie

"I go every day. I can't miss it."

"Okay." I shrugged, scrunching the note in my hand.

"Will you be all right here on your own?"

I nodded.

She studied me in the dim light, obviously trying to read my mind or something.

I raised my eyebrows and gave her a pointed stare. "I'll be fine."

"Good. Okay. Well, I'll only be an hour, so just stay in your room. I'll lock the front door behind me and uh…" She scratched her forehead, really unsure. "I looked it up online and it said you're old enough to be home alone for a little while, so, I mean, did your Mom ever…"

No, but that was only because she'd been pretty much housebound since I turned twelve. Mom started feeling bad that I was the one going out to do the grocery shopping and taking care of *her*. She always went on about how it was supposed to be the other way around.

It wasn't long before she moved us into the hospice.

If I could handle buying groceries on my own, cooking, cleaning, and taking care of our little apartment, I could handle hanging out in my aunt's house for an hour.

"I'm fine. Go for your run."

"Okay." Her smile was relieved. "We can get you ready for school as soon as I get back."

I nodded again then walked past her and into my room. She'd reluctantly told me after Troy's visit that I could make the room my own. My boxes were still piled in the corner. The only one I'd opened was Art's CD collection. He was the guy who looked after us when I was born. When he died he left us everything…including his epic CD collection.

Flopping onto my bed, I pressed play on the stereo, and because Aunt Cassie wasn't home, I cranked up the volume.

"Semi-Charmed Life" thumped through my room. Lying back on my pillow, I stared up at the white ceiling and drowned in a sea of guitar riffs and drumbeats, then started singing along.

One day, when I had control over my own life, I was going to play the guitar. I was going to rock out on a stage, singing my throat hoarse and playing to a bunch of screaming fans who thought I was the hottest guy on the planet.

One day…

I held on to that dream as the song kept playing, and tried to ignore the fact that it was still years away and I had a lot of suffering to do before then.

*****

Aunt Cassie's knuckles were white as she drove me to school. I kept looking at her out of the corner of my eye. She was one uptight chick. Everything about her was tense and uncomfortable. Was it just me or was she always like that?

It looked exhausting to live that way.

Mom wasn't like that at all. She laughed, shouted, cried, danced, cheered…everything about her was spontaneous and loud.

Everything about Aunt Cassie was eerily calm and robotic.

I almost couldn't wait to get to school, which was insane because I hated school.

So which was worse?

An uptight freak or a bunch of bullies I could smash?

I squeezed my eyes shut and reminded myself that I couldn't do that. Mom wouldn't want me to.

I'd get kicked out, then be stuck at home with a neat freak and her spotless counters.

The car lurched to a stop outside school. "Is this the right place?"

"Yeah, here's fine." I unbuckled my seatbelt and got out without any drama. I didn't even say goodbye, just hitched my bag onto my shoulder and hurried away.

She took off just as fast, no doubt wanting to retreat to the safety of her work.

A library.

I scoffed and shook my head. It was the perfect job for her—quiet, neat, tidy, and where all the geeks hung out.

Walking through the main entrance, I kept my head down, avoiding the whispers that seemed to chase me.

"His mom died." I heard that one a couple of times.

My shoulders bunched and I gripped my bag strap.

An anger I didn't even know I had simmered inside me. I wanted to turn around and scream at them for even talking about her.

Clenching my jaw, I kept shuffling forward, not realizing I was about to crash into someone before it was too late.

Big Bad Bryson lurched and stumbled forward, finding his balance while I grimaced and tried to move around him. The eighth-grade beast had been hounding me since the day I started at this stupid school. I didn't know why he couldn't just drop it.

We'd scrapped plenty of times, and he always came off worse. He was obviously a sucker for punishment, or maybe he had something to prove.

"Where the hell do you think you're going?" He grabbed my collar and yanked me back.

I pushed him off me. "It was an accident, man."

He scowled and lunged back, grabbing my collar again and slamming me against the lockers. I tried to remember my mom, I swear I did, but when that bull started snorting in my face, I just lost it.

I was already feeling beat up, and I wasn't going to let that ass-face push me around.

With a feral growl, I attacked with my foot and then with my fist. The guy was a fat ogre with a powerful right hook, but I scampered around him, doing damage where I could.

It didn't take long for a quick circle to form around us.

Shouts, cheers, gasps, one scream.

Fists.

The taste of blood in my mouth.

And then a teacher hollered at us to stop.

Neither of us listened. We just kept hitting, and I totally forgot everything my mother had told me.

TEN

CASSIE

I was late for work. Having to drop Felix at school first ended up adding forty minutes to my trip. I hadn't taken into account how far away it was or how heavy the traffic would be on my return.

I hated being late for anything, and my stress levels were elevated as I busted through the door.

"You're late," Greg reprimanded me.

I avoided eye contact and slid my backpack away. "I know. I know. I'm sorry. I had to drop my nephew at school and traffic was a nightmare on the way back."

As I stood up and smoothed down my skirt, Greg's hard expression morphed into a sympathetic smile. "I know it's a challenging time."

He reached forward to pat my shoulder but I tensed, giving him a closed-mouth smile and thanking him before shuffling into the back room.

Piles of books were waiting to be logged. They were the new additions to our fiction section, and I couldn't wait to see what was available. I'd had a little say in the selection, but Aubrey was the one who'd put the final order in.

Rushing to the table, I waited for the excited buzz to hit me. I was about to handle brand new books…nothing gave me greater pleasure. But I couldn't stop thinking about Felix.

His sad little face as he left my car that morning. He hadn't even said goodbye.

Things were so awkward in the house.

His room was a total mess. I nearly died when I knocked on his door and got a glimpse of the disarray he was leaving behind—clothes on the floor, CDs stacked in crooked piles, tissues scattered around the trash can.

I swallowed and tried to remind myself that everything would be all right. My house was clean. Dirty rats wouldn't invade because of a few bunched-up tissues on the floor. I closed my eyes. The clicking of rat claws on a concrete floor made my skin prickle. I tried to forget that dark, dank space…and then I had to talk myself out of the urge to rush home during my lunch break and clean up.

The room was Felix's. I had to respect that.

But maybe I could institute some kind of tidy-up Saturday policy or something. Surely he'd be okay with that. A little dusting and vacuuming on the weekend never hurt anyone, right?

"Cassie." Greg's voice was quiet, but it still made me jump.

I spun around.

"Your phone's ringing."

"Oh." I turned my back on the shiny new books and walked to my backpack.

I didn't like ringing phones. It was never a good sign.

I missed the call and didn't recognize the number. I was tempted to put it on silent and ignore all communications until my break, but what if it was to do with Felix?

Since becoming an adult, I've never had to think about anyone other than me. It was weird to suddenly have this extra person at the forefront of my brain. But then I thought about his sad eyes, and I slipped into the break room to return the call.

It rang five times before the receptionist at Felix's school answered.

My muscles pinged tight, and my voice was no doubt strained. "Yes, hi. It's Cassie Grayson speaking. I just missed a call."

"Of course, Miss Grayson. Let me put you through to Principal Turrell."

"Thank you," I squeaked.

Nerves attacked me from all sides as I tried to figure out why the principal was calling me.

"Please let it be something good," I mumbled.

"Miss Grayson?" The principal's voice was clipped and firm.

"Uh, yes. Hello."

"I'm sorry to disrupt your day this way, but I'm afraid you're going to have to come and pick up your nephew."

"Why?" I frowned.

"I warned him about fighting. Told him if he couldn't control himself that I'd have to expel him. Well, I'm sorry to inform you, but he's crossed his last line. I'm making the arrangements now to have Felix removed from our school."

"What!" My body snapped straight. "No, wait. You can't do that."

"I'm sorry. I know he's had a really hard time and I don't envy the family situation, but he's had so many chances already. I think what your nephew needs is a couple of weeks at home to recover, and then a fresh start somewhere new."

"No, please."

He ignored my begging and clipped, "If you could please make your way to the school as soon as you can."

And then he hung up. I pulled the phone away from my ear and gaped at it. I couldn't quite wrap my head around what the hell had just happened.

Walking back out to the main desk, I caught Greg's attention and told him in a numb monotone that I had to go. "There's a problem with Felix at school."

He took one look at my ashen expression and

immediately told me to take the rest of the day. "Better yet, take the week. I'll see you back on Monday, all right?"

I nodded, too shocked and disappointed to argue with him. There went all my annual leave days. Some vacation.

Shuffling out to my car, I slumped into the driver's seat.

"Shit," I whispered, resting my forehead against the wheel and resisting the urge to cry.

Felix needed me. I had to go.

But I felt so freaking unprepared for this.

Kicked out of school?

What the hell was I going to do?

A thought came to me—tall and handsome, wrapped in a faded leather jacket. With trembling fingers I pulled his card from the front pouch of my backpack. Rubbing my thumb over Troy's name, I bit my lip and wondered if this was one of those times he was talking about.

"If you need anything, night or day, just give me a call."

Did I need him?

I didn't want to need him, but the thought of going into the school by myself and dealing with an angry principal terrified me.

Pulling out my phone, I glanced at the card, my insides warring.

Did I bring Troy in on this one or battle it out on my own? After Crystal left me, I swore I'd never rely on anyone ever again.

But this wasn't just about me. I had a twelve-year-old to think about.

I closed my eyes, nausea rolling through me.

I was not cut out for this.

ELEVEN

TROY

"Jovi! C'mere, boy," I yelled across the dog park, bending down and slapping my knees. "Come on. That's a boy." He scampered across the grass, his short, pudgy legs taking a while to cover the distance.

He was a British bulldog with a grumpy-looking face and a heart of gold. I got him when he was a pup, his tan fur wrinkled and too big for him. He'd since grown into his skin but was still just as cute as the day I got him.

"You're a good boy, aren't ya." I rubbed behind his ears while he panted from exertion. His pink tongue hung out of his mouth.

I laughed as I attached his lead, then walked him out of the park. Lifting him into the car, I patted his head and drove him home. I was due for an appointment in an hour, and I wanted to get the guy a drink before leaving. He was pretty self-sufficient and would no doubt spend the afternoon napping in his bed. I tried to take him out at least once a day for a walk.

I started up the car and "You Give Love A Bad Name" by Bon Jovi started blasting.

Jovi immediately barked and wagged his stubby tail.

"That's right, buddy. It's the legend himself." I laughed and started singing along.

By the time I got home and gave my bulldog some eats and drinks, I was in a really great mood.

And then my phone rang.

Pulling it out of my bag, I glanced at the screen. I didn't know the number, but I got calls from new people all the time so it wasn't a big deal to answer it.

"Troy Baker speaking."

"Troy, it's Cassie." Her voice was soft, making it hard to hear...but then she drew in a shaky breath.

"Is everything okay?"

"It's Felix. He's being expelled." Her voice pitched.

I closed my eyes, not at all surprised, but wishing it hadn't happened so soon.

"I'm on my way to the school now to get him. What am I going to do? I don't even know where to start looking for a new school, and how do I convince a school to take him when he's been kicked out for fighting! Or should I be arguing with the principal to let him stay? And what am I supposed to say to Felix? Do I tell him off or be sympathetic? I don't know what to do!" I'd never heard her say so many words at once. Her volume rose with each sentence, which oddly enough, made me smile. It was nice to hear some genuine emotion out of such a closed off person.

"I know it's stressful, but we'll work it out. I'm coming. I'll meet you at the school, okay?"

She let out a slow breath as if she were trying to calm herself then softly muttered, "Thanks, Troy."

"Anytime. See you soon."

I glanced at my watch, then quickly texted to reschedule my appointment. The family I was bailing on had their own crisis to deal with, but this one took precedence. I'd squeeze them in later today.

Patting Jovi on the head, I said a quick goodbye and raced out the door.

Traffic was light for LA, so I made it in good time and was parking the car just as Cassie was walking into the building.

"Wait up," I called.

She paused on the step, glancing back with a worried frown.

I jogged across to her, not missing the scent of her perfume. She smelled like blossoms.

"It's going to be okay." I rubbed her lower back without thinking and felt her stiffen beneath my touch.

I quickly shoved my hands in my pockets and walked up the stairs beside her, pretending to ignore how uptight she always was.

Principal Turrell was quiet when we were ushered into his office, but his expression was grim. Felix sat despondent in the chair by the window. His knuckles were red and he had a swollen lip, nothing too bad. The worst thing about him was the defeated look on his face. If I couldn't win over the principal, then poor Felix would have to face another upheaval.

"Hi, Mr. Turrell." I extended my hand and he gave it a firm shake.

"Nice to see you again, Troy," he muttered and took a seat.

"This is Felix's aunt, Cassie Grayson."

"How do you do?" The principal nodded, his hard eyes boring into her.

She shrank away from him, shuffling over to Felix and bending down to get a better look at his face. "Does it hurt?" she murmured.

"I'm fine," Felix grumbled, crossing his arms and angling away from her.

She stood up and flashed me a desperate plea for help.

I put on my best smile and turned to the principal. "You sure we can't resolve this? I'm pretty confident we could—"

"Forget it," Felix snapped. "I don't even want to stay at this stupid school. The kids here suck!"

Principal Turrell's nostrils flared as he pointed a

finger at the defiant boy. "Watch your mouth, young man. It's no wonder you're friendless with an attitude like that."

Felix shot out of his chair, snatching his bag and glaring at the principal. "Let's go," he growled to his aunt before storming for the door.

"But, Felix..." Her voice petered out. She knew she'd already lost the battle and almost seemed relieved. Giving the principal a tight-lipped smile, she clutched her bag and raced out the door.

I followed quickly so as not to lose them.

"Cassie!" I called, double-timing it down the stairs and stopping her before she got in the car. Felix's door slammed. She closed her eyes, obviously fighting tears. Letting out a slow breath, she gazed up at me, refusing to let her emotions win.

I resisted the urge to reach for her, something that seemed instinctual. She was so fragile yet controlled. The paradox fascinated me, and I wanted to draw her near, wrap my arms around her, and assure her that I'd fix it all. She didn't have to be so afraid.

Resting my hand on the roof of her car, I went for an easy posture and tone. "I know this sucks and you're feeling totally overwhelmed right now, but maybe it's for the best. Felix obviously hates it here, so let's find him a place he can fit in. I have contacts in schools all over this city. If you like, I can even aim for something closer to home. Give me a few weeks and I'll look into it for you."

She rubbed her forehead and closed her eyes

again. "Isn't that *my* job... I mean, I—"

"Cassie," I softly interrupted. "I'm here to help you and Felix. Please let me. This is something that will be easy for me. Why don't you take a few weeks for you and Felix just to find your way at home, and then after Christmas he can start somewhere new."

"Christmas," she whispered, her skin paling to a sickly white.

"What's the matter?" I reached forward and lightly touched her elbow.

She didn't stiffen or shy away. She was too shocked to even notice it. Her eyes were bugging out and starting to glisten. "I haven't celebrated Christmas since I left high school. I don't...do Christmas." Her face crested with an agonized emotion I wanted to figure out.

I must have narrowed my eyes trying to read her, because she snapped her chin up and stared straight at me to prove she was fine.

I pushed out a smile and looked away from her. She was trying so damn hard...and doing such a bad job. I couldn't help a pull of affection for her. There was something so broken yet determined in her stance, like she wasn't going to let her demons beat her but the battle was almost too much.

I needed to get her talking. She'd never move past it if she didn't. And she'd never be able to fully help Felix if she didn't loosen up and let her emotions have a say in the relationship. He needed a mother figure who could love him. I didn't doubt that Cassie was trying, but whatever was holding her back needed to be broken down.

"You know, if you ever need to talk about..." My voice trailed off.

She wasn't listening. Her eyes were downcast, her shoulders slumped.

"Crystal would have," she murmured. "I bet she had a tree and everything."

I responded without a second thought.

"Then so will we." I waited until she glanced up at me before winking and inviting her to my place for Christmas dinner.

Her face wrinkled with disbelief. It only made my smile grow. "Of course, if you want to pull it off on your own instead of taking the help of a veteran like me." I puffed out my chest, putting on a show to try to get a smile out of her.

Her eyebrow arched. "A veteran?"

"You better believe it." I nodded. "My mother was a workaholic and my father was a clueless loser, so I had to make Christmas happen for me and my kid brother. I've been doing it most of my life."

Her lips parted with surprise. But then her head jolted back and her wonder changed to skepticism.

I raised my hands and laughed. "I swear it's true. But if you want to know for sure, come to my place on Christmas Day and I'll prove it to you."

She scratched the side of her neck, looking dubious. "Will, uh, anyone else be there?"

"Not if you don't want them to be."

She chewed her lower lip. "I'm just not great with big crowds."

"Then we'll keep it small. You, me, and Felix…and Jovi."

"Who's Jovi?"

"My—"

A shrill bell rang, interrupting my answer.

"Aunt Cassie!" Felix's head popped out the door. "Please, can we just go."

His request was so desperate Cassie turned for the door without even saying goodbye. I stepped back so she had room to reverse, then smiled and waved when she pulled away.

Watching her tiny car putter out of the parking lot, I couldn't help yet another grin. I didn't understand why she had me smiling so much. The woman was obviously complex…and that shouldn't have been enticing.

But it was.

Because she needed someone to help her.

And I knew I could be the guy to do it.

TWELVE

CASSIE

My mind had been obsessed with who Jovi might be. As we parked outside Troy's white apartment block, I stared up at the second floor, wondering which window was his.

Jovi was an unusual name for a girl, but I'd settled on the assumption that she was Troy's partner. I wasn't really in the mood to meet someone new, but Christmas Day wasn't about me. It hadn't been about me since my mom died and we were shoved into the system. Like some kind of curse, something bad would always happen on Christmas Day...from the moving of one home to another—yes, on Christmas Day—to the stench of the freezing cold basement.

I snapped my eyes shut against the haunting memory, but it was only pushed aside by the aching loneliness of sitting by the window at the Kellermans' wondering if my sister was dead or alive. They were the first family to buy me gifts. They were on a mission to heal me, to help me find my voice and smile again. They forced me to celebrate Christmas…in the nicest way possible, but still, I dropped the tradition as soon as I moved to LA.

"You okay?" Felix pulled me back to the present.

"Uh, yeah. Nervous, I guess." I didn't usually admit when I felt vulnerable. The words just kind of popped out. I tensed at my disclosure but then noticed Felix's weak smile.

"It'll be all right. Troy seems like a good guy."

He did… and I hoped Jovi was nice too.

Pushing my door open, I reached in the back for the gifts I'd managed to scrounge up. I didn't have much money to spare. Even though Crystal had left plenty for Felix to live on, I didn't feel right spending any of his trust fund on myself, so I used a little from my savings to buy three gifts. I hoped they were good enough.

My legs trembled as we climbed the stairs. It annoyed me. I didn't want to be weak, nervous, or shaky. I was strong and in control. Lifting my chin, I made sure my shoulders were back as Felix knocked on door 203.

A dog barked. I flinched. Troy hadn't mentioned a dog.

I swallowed and hoped it wasn't a big one.

The lock clicked and two seconds later Troy appeared with a panting bulldog at his heels.

"Hey." Felix grinned. It was a genuine smile that was nothing but beautiful.

My lips parted as I watched him crouch down and greet the dog. Its stumpy tail wagged like crazy, its tongue lolling out while Felix scratched its head.

Troy chuckled and moved aside to give Felix better access. The dog barked happily and jumped up, making Felix laugh.

My heart hitched. He sounded just like Crystal, and without my say-so, warm tendrils of affection spread through my core.

I swallowed and glanced up to find Troy's gaze on me. It was warm, and told me he saw how sweet Felix and the dog were together. I managed a half-smile then ducked my head, taken once again by how gorgeous he was. His hair was still wet from his shower. He'd brushed it back with his fingers, making him look like a model ready for a photo shoot. Those broad shoulders and the way his T-shirt hugged each curve would make any girl sizzle on the inside.

Except me. I never sizzled.

My chest restricted and I forced my gaze down. Concrete was a much safer view than Troy Baker.

"Welcome to my place," he finally said, his voice rich and comforting. "This little guy here is

Jovi." He bent down to pat the bulldog's head, and for some reason my tight shoulders instantly relaxed.

I couldn't understand why knowing Jovi was a dog made me so relieved, but it did.

"Come on, boy." Troy clicked his fingers and pointed to the living room. Jovi scampered off and we followed him into an open-plan living area. The back wall was all glass. Two massive ranch sliders opened onto a small balcony that overlooked a patch of communal grass.

I placed my presents under the fake tree, slipping the chocolate bar for Jovi into my bag. My cheeks flushed with embarrassment. Jovi was a dog. All my worry had been for nothing.

My forehead wrinkled.

I still couldn't work out why I'd been worried that Troy had a girlfriend. It shouldn't make any difference to me, but just the three of us felt a million times better.

I stood, smoothing down my skirt and asking Troy if I could help with anything.

"No. It's all under control. The turkey should be ready in about twenty minutes."

I nodded and took a seat. Felix was kneeling on the floor with Jovi, tickling the dog's stomach and looking the happiest I'd ever seen him.

Until he looked up and spotted the massive CD collection in Troy's bookshelf.

"No way." He scrambled off the floor and headed for the discs, tipping his head to scan titles. Every shelf was lined with music. I couldn't read the words from where I was, and I wondered what types of tunes kept Troy entertained.

Felix ran his finger over the CDs, his smile lighting up the room.

"Dude, you a Bon Jovi fan or what?" Felix glanced over his shoulder.

Troy laughed from the kitchen as he poured soda into champagne glasses. Cute.

"I know it's considered old school, but I just can't resist a little rock 'n' roll." He grinned. "Bon Jovi, Def Leppard, Poison, Twisted Sister." He caught my eye. "The list goes on."

I smiled, then found a spot on the floor to focus on. His eyes made me think of cloudless skies—those days where you looked up and it was so clear you could almost believe that anything was possible.

"Wait a second." Felix pointed at the bulldog who had parked it next to his feet. "Did you name your dog after Jon Bon Jovi?"

"You better believe it, man." Troy's smile took over his whole face as he walked into the living room and handed out drinks.

"Thank you," I murmured, taking the glass and feeling far more sophisticated than I should have. I sipped the sparkling lemonade, then licked the sweetness off my bottom lip.

"Put something on if you want." Troy took a seat beside me and rested his elbows on his long legs. They looked strong...capable. Everything about him did.

That should have scared me.

Hard muscles could hurt and bruise.

But something about Troy's eyes told me they wouldn't.

I looked away from his face and out the ranch slider. Eyes could lie. It would be unwise to trust them, even if my heart was telling me I could.

The CD player clicked and whirred. Suddenly the room was filled with a blasting anthem.

"Yeah!" Troy laughed and made the rock 'n' roll sign as the band started yelling a bunch of na-na-nas. "'Born To Be My Baby'!"

Felix took Troy's enthusiasm as permission to crank up the volume, and I was soon drowning in a sea of shouted lyrics and a drumbeat that pulsed right through me.

I hadn't listened to music that loud in a really long time. It stirred up memories long forgotten…good ones that didn't hurt so bad—my mother dancing around the kitchen and laughing, turning the spatula into a microphone while Crystal twirled beside her. I'd always been too self-conscious to get up there and make a fool of myself, but I'd sit in my chair, swinging my legs and singing.

Felix continued scanning CDs, pulling out the hard plastic covers and smiling at the artwork before putting them back on the shelf. He did that until lunch was served twenty minutes later.

It smelled delicious.

I pulled my chair in, surveyed the array of Christmas food, and had to resist the urge to cry. Last Christmas I sat by myself in my cute little bungalow and ate a pepperoni pizza while watching the Lord of the Rings trilogy…the extended versions.

It wasn't a bad thing to do…it was just really un-Christmas-y.

"So, shall we pray?"

I didn't really do that kind of thing but didn't want to be rude, so I bowed my head while Troy said a short and simple prayer, thanking God for the food and for letting him share Christmas with a couple of very cool people.

I couldn't help a grin. He really was a sweet guy.

Felix ate like he hadn't touched food in months, wolfing down turkey and potatoes like a glutton. At one point I murmured for him to slow down. He blushed and grinned but kept chomping.

At my place he'd only nibbled. We'd sat together in painful silence, both picking at our food and wondering what to say to each other.

But Troy's place was different. There was a relaxed friendliness about him that brought out Felix's words.

Or maybe it was the music.

Whatever the reason, Troy managed to coax a whole conversation…out of both of us. He even had us laughing over a few Christmas stories about his brother and the mischief he got up to as a kid.

My stomach quivered with an unfamiliar feeling. It was warm and bubbly, something so unchecked and natural. I actually had to rub my tummy and remind myself I'd been drinking soda, not wine.

Felix sat back in his chair, looking ready to pop, and let out a loud belch. My eyes bulged and I frowned at him just the way my mother used to frown at Crystal. I remembered it really clearly because it always made me giggle, and then Crystal would belch again, which would get her giggling too.

It'd been well over a decade since the car crash that killed her. I tried really hard never to think about her, but sometimes it blindsided me and I was struck by how much I still missed that beautiful woman.

"Excuse me," Felix mumbled, and I couldn't help a little snicker.

I clamped my lips together and dipped my head.

Troy chuckled and rose from the table, dumping his napkin next to his plate. I followed suit, gathering dishes, set on cleaning up.

"Let me do that." Troy touched my arm and I instinctively shied away, nearly dropping the plate. "Whoa," he murmured, steadying it and mercifully stepping back.

I closed my eyes. I hate the way I did that. It wasn't intentional. I just...didn't like being touched.

Damn Davis McCoy—his fists, his threats, his dark warnings. He'd ruined me for life.

"Let's clean up later." Troy's bright voice made me open my eyes. "I'm kind of keen for presents right now."

"You got us presents?" Felix stood from the table.

"Of course I did." Troy laughed.

I set the plates down. It was a major effort to walk away from the table. I was used to cleaning up and setting things straight right after eating. I couldn't relax otherwise. But Felix was already sitting on the floor beside the tree, and I didn't want to keep that eager face waiting.

Being here seemed to bring out a whole new side of Felix. He was smiling, relaxed, enthusiastic. I really liked it and was already worried that the second we left, he'd return to his quiet, morose self. I wasn't enough to bring out his happiness. Maybe Crystal was wrong to leave him with me. She should have found a kind family in the system to take him in.

I gripped the back of the chair, reminding myself that kind families in the system didn't last forever, and the risk of him ending up with someone like Davis McCoy… I shook my head. I'd take morose and safe. It was the only way.

Tucking my skirt beneath my legs, I took a seat on the couch and nervously bobbed my knee as Troy handed Felix his first present. "This looks like it's from your aunt Cassie."

Felix's smile was broad and infectious, but I couldn't return the gesture. He was ripping the wrapping off my gift, his excitement quickly petering out as he gazed down at the books in his hands.

"Percy Jackson," he murmured, his forehead

wrinkling.

I swallowed. "They're really great books."

He nodded and forced a polite smile. "Thanks."

"You're welcome." I pursed my lips. "You like to read, right?"

"Yeah, it's okay." Felix shrugged and set the books aside.

I sank back into the couch, feeling so useless I nearly shouted for Troy not to open my gift. But I was too late. He was already ripping open the envelope and pulling out the Amazon gift card.

"I didn't know what to get you, so…"

"No, this is great." He beamed. "I love gift cards. I can get whatever I want." His wink made my stomach curl. I smoothed a hand down my ponytail and mouthed my thanks. He was being very sweet over my totally lame gift.

Clearing his throat, he rubbed his hands together. "Right, my turn."

His wiggling eyebrows made Felix snicker.

"Ladies first." He pulled out a small box and passed it over.

The paper was blue and covered with pictures of white snowflakes. There was a silvery sparkle, which I ran my finger over before carefully peeling off the tape. I took my time. I hadn't opened a gift in…years, and I wanted to cherish the moment.

Inside was a long, rectangular box. I smoothed my thumb over the velvet finish before lifting the lid to discover a necklace.

My lips parted and I glanced at Troy before lifting the jewelry out like it was made of pure gold. It wasn't gold. It was a leather-bound necklace with three small pendants—an open book, a quill, and a bird.

"I figured since you worked in a library..." Troy smiled. "I just saw it and thought of you."

"It's beautiful." I swallowed, my throat thick with emotion.

"Can I put it on for you?"

I met his gaze. It was so open and sweet. If I said no, he wouldn't make me feel bad, I could sense it. Which was enough for me to bob my head and pass it to him.

Spinning around, I clenched my fists and focused on my breathing while his fingers brushed the back of my neck.

"There you go," he whispered.

I touched the pendants, giving him a genuine smile. It felt warm and addictive.

He winked and settled himself by the tree. "Right. Felix's turn."

Reaching around the back, he pulled out a tube and a square. Felix unwrapped the square first, nearly jumping out of his skin when he saw the CD. "Chaos! I love these guys." He opened the cover and his eyes popped wide. "It's signed! To me!"

"Uh-huh." Troy grinned, nudging the tube closer to Felix.

He let out a delighted laugh and ripped into the second gift. "No way!" He unfurled the large poster of a band I didn't recognize.

Four guys and one girl—five signatures.

"How did you get this?"

Jovi barked at Felix's loud enthusiasm.

Troy patted the dog's head and grinned. "I know a guy." Felix's eyes narrowed, which made Troy laugh. "Jimmy's my brother."

Felix gaped. "Jimmy!" He pointed at the guy with the sexy smirk and hot blue eyes. "This Jimmy."

"Yeah." Troy nodded.

"You're related to him?"

Troy laughed. "Yep. Known the guy my whole life."

I smiled. Felix was flipping out, so I had to ask. "Who is Chaos?"

Felix gasped and whipped his head to look at me. "You haven't heard of Chaos?"

I shook my head, then shrugged. "Oh come on, you're more shocked by that than the fact Troy's related to a famous guy?"

Troy chuckled. "They've been a bit of sensation lately. New band, top-ranking album. It's been a whirlwind."

"I can't believe it." Felix shook his head, still in awe.

Troy chuckled. "I'll see if they've got any gigs coming up. Maybe I can get us some tickets."

And that was it. Felix was completely won over by the towering counselor. I thought he was about to leap into his arms and hug him.

My chest restricted at the idea, a longing I didn't understand threading through me. Troy and Felix were oblivious to my gaze as they chatted about the band, walking to the stereo together and putting on the new CD.

It was a great view—peaceful, comforting, inspiring.

It felt so foreign yet alluring. I wasn't sure how to feel. I tended to shy away from new things—they made me too vulnerable and exposed—but there was something very sweet about the scene before me...something I must have craved deep down, in places I hadn't accessed for years. I rubbed my stomach, unsure if I wanted to go there. Dabbling with the long-buried could unearth things I didn't want to face, dark demons that I liked to pretend didn't exist in my life.

But as I sat on that couch watching the boy I'd taken into my home interacting with a man who'd been forced into my life, I couldn't help the fleeting voice that told me I might not have a choice. My life was changing whether I wanted it to or not. I just hoped I had the strength to cope with it.

THIRTEEN

TROY

I stood on the curb waving goodbye to Cassie and Felix until her little car disappeared around the corner. My lips were smiling, but my heart hurt as I watched them leave. Poor Cassie had no idea what she was doing and she knew it. She was fearful, hesitant, so afraid of doing something wrong. For someone so uptight and in control, she must have been going through hell.

Felix was a great kid. He liked old school rock 'n' roll. That in itself was enough to love him, but then he pulled out a laugh and played with Jovi. I shook my head with a grin as I jogged back up the stairs. Jovi started barking the second he sniffed out my approach. His stumpy tail went to town as I walked in the door and crouched to pet him.

"You have a good day, bud?"

He barked. I laughed and scratched his ears before standing up to gaze at my lonely apartment.

"Wind of Change" by Scorpion was playing, the song having an eerie effect on me.

It was weird. I'd never really thought of my place as lonely before, but with Felix and Cassie gone, it suddenly felt too empty and quiet.

I frowned, a little perplexed, and headed into the kitchen. Cassie had insisted on helping me clean up. I tried to refuse her, but she just walked into the kitchen and got busy. I was going to stop her, but then I noticed the expression on her face. It was almost relief, like being able to tidy my kitchen and make it sparkle was something useful she could do. It would make up for Felix barely glancing at her gift. She sat on that couch looking so dejected. I tried to make a big deal of the voucher she gave me. I mean, it was a great gift, but hardly exciting.

Instead of fighting her on the cleaning thing, I pitched in. So while Felix and Jovi rocked out to Chaos, then Bon Jovi, then Def Leppard, Cassie and I made my kitchen sparkle.

Cleaning had never been so satisfying.

I ran my finger across the pristine countertop and for a fleeting moment wondered what it'd be like to have someone to do the dishes with every night. Someone to cook for, take care of…share my life with.

I'd had girlfriends before, but all of the relationships had been short-lived and never close to the move-in-together stage. I always blamed the busyness of work, because I didn't want to admit...

My phone started ringing. I checked the number and hesitated before pasting on a smile and answering.

"Hey, Mom. Merry Christmas."

"You too, sweetheart. How are you?"

"Yeah, good." I found it ironic that she cared. Since all the hard stuff was over and I'd moved across the country, she'd become far more attentive. "How's Tom?" I veered the subject to her favorite one—her new boyfriend.

"Very well." She sounded like she was smiling. "We've just had a lovely Christmas meal with his children and grandbabies."

"Nice." I nodded. I did that a lot when I was speaking to my mother.

"Have you spoken to Jimmy yet?"

"Yeah, I called him this morning. He took Nessa back to Mississippi to spend Christmas with her family. She was a little nervous, but Ralphie and Veronica went too, so at least she's got some support around her. Hopefully they'll have a good time."

"You still keeping tabs on your brother? He's doing okay, right? Looking after himself?"

I rolled my eyes. We'd been having the same conversation since I was six. *Can you watch Jimmy for me? Can you make sure he's fed, watered, cared for?*

Because I'm too busy running a business and trying to pretend that your father abandoning us and turning into a man whore isn't killing me.

I hid my thoughts behind a voice that I hoped was bright enough. "Jimmy's doing great now, Mom. He's with Ness and she brings out the best in him. The band is doing awesome. They're working on their second album and planning another tour for the summer. You know, you could always call and ask him yourself."

"I know." She sighed. "But we've never been that close. He always sided with your father and I just couldn't…"

"It's never too late to change that, Mom. He's only a phone call away."

She scoffed. "You can talk. When was the last time you spoke to your father?"

I clenched my jaw, unable to reply.

After a long, tense beat she sighed again. "I'm sorry. I have no right to say that to you. If I don't have the guts to call Jimmy, then you shouldn't have to call your father."

"Jimmy's really changed, Mom. He hardly speaks to Dad now. He doesn't party anymore or sleep around. He's with Ness and that's it."

"I should call him."

"Yes, you should call him."

Her snicker was soft and afraid. "I follow him online, you know. Watch his YouTube clips and turn up his songs whenever they come on the radio."

"He'd probably love to hear that from you," I

responded quietly.

Jimmy never talked about Mom, but I couldn't help wondering if he thought about her. They hadn't grown apart after a big fight or bust-up. It'd just slowly happened over time. As Jimmy hit the partying scene and turned into Dad, Mom shied away, subtly digging this chasm between them that they never knew existed until the gap was too big to cross.

"You've always been a voice of reason, kid." Mom was smiling again. I could hear it in her voice. "Even when you were young, you were always the sensible one. You'd come in and calm the storm, find a way forward. You're something special, you know that? I don't know any problem you can't solve."

I was so humbled by her words I couldn't find my voice for a moment. "Thanks, Mom," I finally croaked.

"Merry Christmas, sweetheart."

"Merry Christmas."

And then she was gone, and I was back in my apartment with Jovi, my music…and no one else.

FOURTEEN

CASSIE

Christmas Day hadn't been as scary as I thought. It surprised me. I usually spent Christmas holed up in my bungalow watching movies and eating junk food. The day had been a special treasure, even if the guys didn't love my gifts. At least I was able to clean Troy's kitchen for him.

For the past two days, Felix had hung out in his room, blasting the Chaos album. I had to admit, the music had grown pretty quickly on me, and I found myself quietly singing along as I dusted the living room.

I still wasn't sure how to connect with my

nephew. We lived in the same house but not together. The only time I saw him was when he emerged to use the bathroom or get something to eat. He seemed nervous in the kitchen, probably because I always walked in to see what he was doing. I asked him what foods he liked and tried to fill the cupboards with what I could, although I'd put more fruits and vegetables on his list than he wanted. I also refused to buy the sugar-loaded cereal he liked.

He'd frowned but not said anything.

Pursing my lips, I ran my cloth along the bookshelves, wondering if we were ever going to have a real conversation. The boy that emerged in Troy's apartment had been a delight. I wanted that kid. Did we need to get a dog? Was that the answer?

My forehead wrinkled. I wasn't opposed to a pet, I supposed. But…how much mess would a dog make?

The doorbell rang, distracting me from the problem. Peeking through the curtain, I made sure it wasn't a salesperson before unlocking the bolts.

It was Crystal's lawyer.

My stomach jittered as I tried to smile and greet him.

"Sorry to bother you, Miss Grayson. I feel awful about this, but I forgot to pass these on to you."

He held out two presents, wrapped and tied with bows.

"What are these?" I took them from his hands.

"Crystal arranged it all before she passed, and I

was supposed to give them to you on Christmas Eve. With the busy rush of getting ready for my own family, it completely slipped my mind. Please forgive me."

"Of course," I murmured, staring at Crystal's handwriting on the white envelope.

The first gift was for Felix, and the one beneath that was for me.

I was so surprised to see my name, I barely managed to say goodbye to the lawyer before closing the door.

Rushing to Felix's room, I knocked loud enough for my knuckles to hurt and opened the door. He saw me coming and turned down the music. Sitting on the edge of the bed, he spotted the gift in my hand and gave me a quizzical frown.

"It's from your mom. The lawyer just dropped it off."

Felix's face went white, but then he pressed his lips together and stood, taking the present like it was the Holy Grail.

He set the card aside with an air of reverence, then took his time unwrapping the gift. He obviously didn't want to rip the paper. Inside was a black hoodie. Felix lifted it up and grinned. On the back, a white stylized electric guitar dominated. He spun it around and I caught a glimpse of the front. It said: *Keep Calm and Play Guitar.* Instead of the royal crown at the top, two guitars crossed over each other. It was pretty cool.

Felix pulled the sweater on, then made the rock 'n' roll symbol.

I smiled at his sweet face, but my lips began to wobble as he reached for the envelope. The parcel in my hand crinkled as I gripped my present and watched him brush his finger over his mother's writing. The expression on his face made my heart crack.

Ripping it open, he pulled out a card. A letter dropped out. He picked it up and read the card first, his face washing with lonely agony. I wanted to run to him and wrap my arm around his skinny shoulders, but I couldn't make myself move.

"Can I have some privacy, please?" he murmured.

I wanted to tell him that I could be there for him, but my throat was too clogged with emotion to speak. Instead, I backed away like a lame coward. Closing the door, I leaned my head against the wood and had to resist the urge to cry.

Why couldn't I be normal?

Felix needed a mother. Someone who wasn't afraid of hugs and emotion. Someone who wasn't so broken on the inside that the only way to hold herself together was by keeping every aspect of her life in full control.

The music in Felix's room suddenly escalated. I flinched away from the door. The volume scared me. A normal mother would have gone in there and told him to turn it down, but I had a sinking feeling that he needed to drown in drumbeats after reading his mother's letter. So, I backed away and walked to my room.

Sitting on the edge of my bed, I stared down at

the present on my lap.

Crystal disappeared from my life without warning. I'd arrived home from school and waited for her, like I did every day...but she never came home. Davis was livid, then heartbroken. He sat at the dining room table every night staring out the window...waiting for her to come back.

As much as I cried over Crystal, I was weak with relief that the nighttime visits to our room had stopped.

Until they started again.

I shuddered and nearly threw the present on the floor. Did I really want to unwrap something from her? She'd left me without a word! Left me with the beast.

Her weepy apology skittered through my mind. She'd honestly thought Davis wouldn't try to touch me. She honestly believed he'd been in love with her, that he wouldn't be able to move on.

But he had.

Or at least, he'd tried.

The first time he ever punched me was when I refused to tell him I loved him. Even as the pain radiated through my body I wouldn't give in.

"Tell me you love me," he'd roared in my face.

"Never!" I'd spat back.

He wouldn't rape me if I didn't say it, so he beat me instead.

The pain was worth it. The thought of being violated by him terrified me, so I took the hits, refusing to give in to what he wanted.

Days in the cellar—hunger, isolation. Then the

bruises would heal and he'd try all over again.

Mindy McCoy was the only one who knew the real truth, and she was too afraid to do anything about it. I could only imagine the threats he laid on her. She went along with it, turning her back on my bruises and tears.

I missed weeks of school. My teacher thought I had glandular fever, then strep throat, then an awful stomach bug. I was the sickest kid in her class, and she never thought to question any one of Davis McCoy's lies. His crocodile smile and smooth charm won her over every time.

I've never been able to figure out why I didn't say anything to her. Maybe I thought she wouldn't believe me. Or maybe I was terrified that I'd be moved to a new home with a meaner beast, someone who didn't need three little words in order to rape me.

Squeezing my temples, I fought my stinging eyes. Crystal's handwriting blurred on the envelope as I relived the fleeting guilt that haunted me.

She'd given in. She'd said what he'd wanted because she'd been a petrified thirteen-year-old.

And I'd done nothing to save her.

Swallowing, I tore the envelope open and read the card.

Dear Cassie,

There will never be the right words to express how sorry I am for leaving you. I was scared, overwhelmed, sick. Those are all excuses and none of them are good enough for what I did. I hope one day you can forgive me, but more important than that, I hope one day you can break free from the chains he wrapped around us.

I want you to have a good life, sister. Not just because you're raising Felix for me, but because I want you to be happy. Davis McCoy tried to destroy me. He nearly did, but I found a way through and I hope this diary will give you the strength to fight for a freedom you deserve.

I love you, little sister…always and forever.

Crystal
xoxo

I set the letter aside and unwrapped my gift. The wrapping paper dropped to the floor as I opened the cover and read:

Crystal's Diary

The first page was dated a few months after she left me.

I don't know what to do. How to get all this stuff out of me. I'm crippled by guilt, fear, loathing.
Someone told me to write it out of me. So that's what I'm gonna try…

I left my sister. I left her with an evil beast. But I can't tell anyone because they might make me go back *there. I can't do it. I'm not strong enough.*

I should have stayed to fetch her. I should have risked getting caught in order to save her, but I have a baby now. This little thing growing inside me is my redemption. I don't know why I believe that so strongly but I do.

If Davis found out, he'd make me get rid of it.

I can't let that happen.

And so I left.

Hopefully he'll ignore her. Because he's in love with me…and she's only ten.

He won't get into her bed.

Oh God, please don't let him get to her.

Clenching my jaw, I set the diary on top of Crystal's card. My hands were shaking. Gripping the side of the bed, I clutched it until my fingers hurt.

I couldn't believe she wanted me to read it. Like I wanted to relive that hell through her eyes.

Music continued to thump from Felix's room. I closed my eyes and focused on the beat, anything to get Crystal's words out of my head.

I didn't need her stupid diary.

There were no chains around me.

Davis McCoy would never touch me again. He was dead—killed himself in prison—and I was free. Squeezing my eyes shut, a screaming echo tore through the back of my brain, reminding me what a liar I was.

"It didn't happen," I whispered, desperately trying to believe it. Desperately trying to erase the night Davis broke his own rule.

FIFTEEN

FELIX

The car rolled to a stop outside Strantham Academy. It was a brick school with upper class written all over it. I didn't want to go there, but Troy worked his butt off getting me a scholarship and I couldn't refuse.

I felt sick.

I didn't want to walk into that place and have to meet people, learn names...be the new kid.

But I didn't want to be stuck in Aunt Cassie's house anymore either.

She'd let me make the room my own, but it still didn't feel like home. And after three weeks of hiding out in there, I was kind of suffocating.

Aunt Cassie cleared her throat, sounding just as nervous as I was. "Do you, um…want me to walk you in, or…"

"Nah, I'm good." Opening the door, I jumped out before she could fight me on it, but she actually looked kind of relieved.

I rolled my eyes and stalked away from the beat-up car. Someone snickered behind me, and I thought I heard them murmur, "Piece of junk."

If they were talking about my aunt's beat-up Ford Escort, they were right. The car was like a hundred years old with a dent in the back bumper and rust on the edge of the passenger door. It made a weird noise when it started up, but so far it'd gotten us everywhere we needed to go.

Too bad I wanted to duck for cover whenever I was in it. Talk about humiliation.

Gripping my bag strap, I took the concrete stairs two at a time and easily found the office. The lady at the front counter was cheerful and friendly. It kind of grated my nerves, but I couldn't say why.

I tapped out a beat on the counter while I waited for Mrs. Tindal. She was my homeroom teacher, apparently. She was probably an old hag with a bad temper.

My lips twitched as my mind conjured up the worst. I couldn't help it. Since Mom got sick, life had been one big suck-fest. Even up to the day she died Mom told me I was lucky, but I never felt it. I wasn't a lucky one. I was a cursed kid who'd just lost everything.

"Hi, Felix."

I spun around at the soft voice behind me and looked up at the red-haired teacher. She had a nice smile and gentle green eyes that seemed to understand.

It was a weird thing to think, but when she introduced herself to me and shook my hand, I couldn't ignore the real way she gazed at me. Troy had warned me she knew my story. I was pretty pissed at first, but he told me that people knowing was helpful. According to Troy, Jane Tindal was not the type to gossip. She needed to know my history so she could help me.

"So, I bet you're probably feeling pretty nervous right now." She smiled. "But from what Troy's told me, you're a really strong kid, and I know you're gonna do great at Strantham."

I nearly told her to save the speech for someone who'd believe it, but her smile was sweet and I didn't want to be mean.

"If you'll follow me, I'll show you to homeroom and pair you up with a buddy to take care of you today."

I nodded, already hating the idea.

Her heels clipped on the floor as we wove through student traffic. I kept my head down. The less eye contact, the better. I could feel people checking me out, wondering who I was. I heard a few more snickers.

"What the hell is he wearing?"

Bunching my fist, I shoved it into the hoodie pocket. I'd wear Mom's Christmas present 'til the day I died. They didn't know how much it meant to me. They hadn't read Mom's letter.

A memory of camping in our tiny living room one night flittered through my brain. Mom and I had stayed up late dreaming of rock bands and imagining a superstar life for us. Mom pretended she was my manager and I was this ace guitarist.

She'd promised to hook me up with lessons, but then she got sick and I didn't want to anymore. She couldn't fork out money for a guitar and lessons when we needed to pay medical bills. The money Art left could only stretch so far, and half of it was tied up in a trust fund that I'd get when I was eighteen.

Another snigger made my shoulders bunch. I made the mistake of looking up and caught a superior smirk from some asshole in his shiny leather shoes and a jacket that probably cost more than Aunt Cassie's car.

I gritted my teeth and looked down, focusing on my scuffed-up Converse, black marks on the toe and a seam that was coming apart on the side.

It took an eternity to reach homeroom, but things didn't get any easier when I walked in. I scanned the space and was met with more disdain and curiosity. Stupid rich kids. Entitled little pricks. They didn't know what it was like to go without.

I wanted to walk for the door and mumble, "I'm outta here." But where the hell would I go?

Back to the freaking clean zone?

Back to my room that was growing smaller by the day?

Back to Aunt Cassie with her twitchy smile and enough nervous energy to drive a sane person crazy?

I swallowed and hovered by Mrs. Tindal's desk while she typed something into her laptop, then reached for a tattered novel on her desk.

"This is the book you'll be reading for English. I'll tell you more about it this afternoon when I see you, but I figured I'd give it to you now."

The bell rang as I took the book off her. It looked boring and painful. I wasn't really into reading. I preferred magazines like *Billboard*, *Rolling Stone*, and *Q*. I didn't really give a shit about books with no color or life...just endless lines of words. Where was the fun in that?

"Okay, guys." Mrs. Tindal clapped her hands. "Take your seats quickly. We've got a lot to get through this morning."

Chairs scraped on the floor and there was a hurried shuffle as the students in 7JT did her bidding. She smiled at them and said a cheerful good morning. She then stepped up and put her arm around my shoulders. It reminded me of Mom, which made my throat start aching.

"This is Felix Grayson. He's going to be with us for the rest of the year, and you need to make him feel welcome."

I scanned faces again, catching a clump of boredom from some girls in the front corner, a smirk from the guy in the back, a predatory glare from the guy next to him. They'd be the ones I'd have to watch out for. In front of Evil Eyes was a blonde girl with full lips and eyes like sapphires. She was freaking hot with silky hair down to her waist. She looked like a model or an actress or something. My mouth went dry and my lips parted without my say-so. Her perfect forehead wrinkled as I stared at her, and it took everything in me to force my gaze to the other side of the room, where I met a curious set of eyes. They were brown like mine. This girl's hair was blonde too but it was messy, shoulder-length with these scraggly curls. She looked like she really didn't care about being pretty. Her thin lips lifted into a half-smile as she scratched the side of her nose. She was wearing black nail polish and a skull ring, so I was able to put her in my too-weird, no-fly zone.

Mrs. Tindal pointed to an eager-looking kid with a mouth full of metal. "Butler is gonna be your buddy for the next couple of days until you find your way around."

Someone snorted in the back of the room and muttered, "Nice job, BUTT-ler."

"Boys." Mrs. Tindal's warning was soft but full…enough to shut up the dickhead.

She smiled then indicated for me to head over to Butler. The guy stood from his seat, giving me a clear view of his checkered shirt and pressed pants with navy blue loafers. He had rich geek written all over him.

Dammit. I didn't belong in this place.

They weren't my people. Why the hell did Troy have to get me a scholarship to this school? I didn't ask for it.

I wanted my old elementary back. I was popular in that place. I had friends, a happy life. Before Mom got sick, everything was perfect.

How the hell was I supposed to remember my promises to her when everything was so shit?

I wanted my mom.

The little kid inside me started wailing for her.

But I was smart enough to know that my unheard cries were pitiful. Saying them out loud wouldn't do any good either. So, I forced my legs to move and shuffled across to Butler, who shook my hand and showed me where to sit.

I slumped into the chair beside his and had to fight the urge to flee through that classroom door. Walking the streets wouldn't feel any less lonely than sitting in this foreign room surrounded by strangers. I'd never felt more isolated in my entire life.

For the first time since Mom died it hit me, and I realized just how alone I was. Everything that meant anything was gone. All I had left were my memories, and they suddenly didn't feel like enough.

SIXTEEN

CASSIE

Work had been busy. The children's session in the morning was loud and chaotic. The lady who usually ran it called in sick, so I had to take her place. It was not my thing, and I muddled my way through a book reading and tried to engage the wriggling toddlers with a bright happy voice. I did a terrible job and came away exhausted.

At lunch, I realized I forgot to pack any food for myself. Getting Felix out the door on time had been enough to handle. I didn't want to spend money at the expensive cafe around the corner, so I decided to go hungry instead. That put me in a foul mood…not at all helped by the two little boys who decided to play fight in the New Year's Read-a-lutions Challenge area. They knocked over the big display Aubrey and I had spent hours making, and then they scampered away without even apologizing.

I stayed after closing to fix it up. I hated the idea of leaving the mess overnight.

By the time I dragged my sorry butt to the car I was tired, hungry, cranky, and in no mood to deal with any more crap. It was in that moment, as I gazed at my watch then unlocked my car, that I realized I had totally forgotten about Felix.

"Shit," I whispered, slamming the door shut and starting up the engine.

I had meant to pick him up from school four hours ago. The deal was that I'd collect him and he'd do his homework in the library while I finished work. I'd checked with Greg. He'd said okay. But those stupid boys with their play fighting made me forget.

I chewed my lip as I raced home. I hit the end of rush hour and it took me nearly twice as long to get there. I worried the entire way. Had he made it home without getting lost? What if he walked the wrong way? What if someone took him? Hurt him?

My stomach was roiling by the time I jerked to a stop in my driveway. I jumped out of the car and ran to the front door. It was locked. The keys in my hand shook as I wrestled with them.

"Felix!" I shouted as soon as I was inside. "Felix, are you home?"

I scanned the living room and kitchen, then darted down the hallway, flinging his bedroom door open without knocking.

He was lying on the bed with headphones covering his ears. His arms were crossed as he scowled up at the ceiling. At first I couldn't tell if he'd seen me sagging with relief in his doorway, but then his muscles grew a little tighter, his eyebrows knitting more deeply.

"I'm sorry," I called, trying to be heard above the music that was no doubt blasting in his ears.

Holding my breath, I entered his man-cave, stepping over a pair of dirty socks and accidentally kicking his book bag with my toe. I winced but didn't make a fuss as I hovered against the edge of his bed.

"Just go away." His voice was low and icy.

I reached for his headphones, intent on pulling them free so we could talk. He flinched, his brown eyes dark with anger as he glared up at me.

"I'm sorry. I got caught up at work and—"

"Whatever." He pulled the headphones off. "I don't need you to pick me up. I'm not a baby. I can walk home."

"Did someone show you the way?"

He rolled his eyes. "I found it on my own."

I wanted to ask him how long that took, but something about the tight set of his mouth kept me quiet. "Good for you." I smiled. His dark glare disintegrated it. I cleared my throat, noting the angry music blasting from the headphones. Smoothing down my skirt, I tried to think of something to ease the tension between us, but all I could come up with was, "How was school?"

"Shit!" he growled. "It was total shit! Did you expect it to be anything else?"

His sharp words felt like a slap to the face.

"I'm a twelve-year-old orphan starting at a new school. Do you have any idea what that feels like?"

I did. But I didn't have the courage to say it. I couldn't stand there dredging up my dirty past. Even if it could have helped him, or created some kind of common bond between us, I couldn't bring myself to say it. A normal mother would have sat down, taken his hand maybe, told him everything was going to be okay.

But I couldn't.

Because I wasn't his mother.

I wasn't normal.

The thought was kind of debilitating. Instead of acting like a grown-up and getting over myself, I threaded my fingers together and swallowed, bobbing my head as I backed out of the room.

He looked at me like I was deranged. I cast my eyes to his messy floor and then shut the door behind me. As soon as it clicked I bolted to my bedroom, slamming the door and staggering to my bed on legs that wouldn't work properly.

I wasn't normal.

I couldn't do the job Crystal wanted me to. How did I look after a hurting kid when I couldn't even talk to him?

Crystal's diary caught my eye. I snatched it, hoping for answers as I flicked to the second entry.

It was dated several weeks after her previous one.

I have shelter now. A roof over my head. I'm safe, yet I'm not.

I still feel afraid. Every time I shut my eyes I expect to hear the door creak open, to have that wave of sick travel through me as he lifts the covers and gets into my bed.

I feel filthy. I will never be clean enough to wash his dark soul out of me.

But I have a baby growing in my belly. A pure, innocent life. It's a boy.

Arthur took me to the hospital and I had a scan. I saw him. His little head and arms. He's so tiny. So vulnerable.

My little boy.

He'll enter this world unscathed, oblivious to the evils that exist here. I'm going to protect him. I will never let anyone take advantage of him, or hurt him.

But I'm scared.

Will I be enough?

How can a dirty wretch like me love something so pure?

I slapped the diary closed and placed it on my bedside table. Sitting on my hands, I rocked on the edge of my bed.

My skin crawled with the words dirty and filthy. I was one of the cleanest people I knew, but still, no matter how hard I scrubbed, I couldn't get his pudgy fists off my skin. The pain Davis inflicted was buried deep, invisible to the human eye but black and purple against my soul.

Just like Crystal, I never felt clean enough...whole enough.

I'd never be able to love anyone properly, because I still believed I was a dirty wretch who belonged in a basement cellar with the rats.

I forgot her son. I left him to walk home alone, no doubt scared he couldn't find his way. School was awful for him and I didn't even have the guts to empathize. Crystal feared she wasn't enough. But I *knew* I wasn't.

So, what the hell was I supposed to do about Felix?

If I couldn't care for him, who would?

SEVENTEEN

TROY

I paused outside Cassie's bungalow door and took a moment to catch my breath. I had no idea why I felt nervous. Maybe because I hadn't called and Cassie would probably appreciate a little forewarning of my visit. Or maybe it was because my insides jittered at the thought I'd be seeing her again.

Since Christmas she'd been with me, always lingering in the back of my mind. I found myself thinking of her at random times throughout the day, wondering how she was doing. I'd look for excuses to call and check in on Felix.

Which was exactly what I was doing that evening.

Felix would have had his first day at Strantham and I wanted to stop by and find out how it went. I figured I'd do it on my way home and maybe offer to buy everyone a takeout dinner or something.

There was a great Mexican place down the road.

The idea made me smile and I knocked twice, tapping my finger on the doorframe while I waited.

The security light above my head flicked on and the curtain twitched before the locks clicked. Cassie opened the door. She looked pale and sad...unnerved.

I felt an instant rush of concern. "Are you okay?"

"Yep." She crossed her arms and nodded. "What are you doing here?"

"I'm sorry to not call first, but I wanted to see how Felix's first day went."

Cassie's tight expression folded. She looked devastated.

"That bad, huh?"

"I just..." She sighed and winced, looking on the verge of tears. "I forgot to pick him up after school. He had to walk home on his own. He didn't say it, but he probably got lost or..." She shook her head. "I'm the worst aunt ever."

"No," I softly disagreed. "You're human." Stepping into the house, I gazed down at her agonized expression and tried to get rid of it with a wink and a smile. "We all make mistakes."

"This was a pretty big one." She bit her lip. "His

first day. He said it was total shit, and I couldn't even be there for him to help him out. I can't talk to him. I never know what to say. I…"

She clammed up on me, shrinking away and folding her arms. Cutting her healthy rant short was not the answer. I wish she'd just get it out. My guess was she had no idea how liberating it would be. Fear kept her in chains and I wanted to break her free. The counselor in me was desperate to unearth her demons.

"I think you need to talk about whatever's going on in here." I pointed at her chest.

She shrunk ever further away from me, her shoulders curving around so far her chest went concave. Her eyebrows dipped into an emphatic V.

"Excuse me?" she whispered.

I gave her a kind smile. "I know that looking after Felix is a huge challenge, but it's only made harder by the fact you're struggling with…something." I didn't have the courage to tell her my child abuse theories. I was supposed to draw that stuff out of her, not put words in her mouth.

Her eyes flashed with defiance. "I'm fine."

"Talking about things can make it better. Sometimes we have to verbalize and relive in order to conquer."

A tendon in her neck strained as she looked away from me. Her fingers dug into her arms. "I don't…" She forced a snicker. "You're here to help Felix. I'm…fine. I don't need…" She swallowed and pointed to the hallway. "He's in his room."

I watched her with keen eyes as she tried to avoid me then finally relented with a soft whisper. "Okay. But if you ever need to talk, I'm here. I'll listen to anything you have to say."

She gazed up at me, her dark brown eyes a thing of beauty. They held so much depth and heartache, yet she tried so hard to hide it. She reminded me of a wounded bird attempting to fly, doing her best to keep going in spite of the injuries weighing her down. She wouldn't give in...wouldn't stop fighting.

My lips curved into a soft smile, my heart squeezing with affection.

Her milky skin bloomed with color and she smoothed a hand down her ponytail, her eyes darting to the floor as she awkwardly cleared her throat.

Man, I wanted to set her free. If she was that endearing when she was locked up tight, imagine what she'd be like unhindered. I wanted to see that transformation, and I decided right then that I was going to stick around until it happened.

It'd take time. I'd have to be patient. But one day, I'd see Cassie Grayson the way she was born to be.

The thought made me smile. Her eyes flicked to mine then back to the floor. She was starting to squirm beneath my gaze, and I cut things short before doing any damage.

"Well, I better go see..." I pointed down the hallway.

"Of course." She kept her eyes on the wooden

floor beneath us, her head bobbing quickly.

I walked to Felix's room alone, not missing the way she hung back.

Poor thing. She must have felt so out of her depth. I did the math a few days earlier and worked out that Cassie would have only been ten when Felix was born. The gap between them was that of siblings, yet she had to fill his mother's shoes.

It was a tough ask. I understood that burden of responsibility all too well. I practically raised Jimmy, so knocking on Felix's door didn't seem that hard to me.

No one answered, so I knocked again. "Felix? It's Troy."

I heard a thump, then angry steps before the door flew open.

Felix glared at me, his chest heaving. The headphones around his neck still blasted music, and I could see right through the angry set of his mouth and the thumping beat he was trying to disappear into. His pale brown eyes narrowed, the sorrow within them unmissable.

I decided to play it with one hundred percent raw honesty. "So...a shitty day, huh?"

He huffed and shuffled back to his bed, slumping onto it with a defeated sigh. Pulling off his headphones, he dropped them on the floor and raked skinny fingers through his hair.

"How could you send me to that place? It's full of rich jerks."

"Yeah." I nodded and walked in. I left the door

ajar in case Cassie wanted to listen in. She probably wasn't even there. She was no doubt in the kitchen cleaning or cooking up a storm. My mom used to do the same thing on a bad day.

I took a seat on the floor in front of Felix and rested my elbows on my knees. "It's a good school though."

Felix scoffed.

"I know. I get it. You're twelve. Like you give a rat's ass about your education. Jimmy was exactly the same. He was so busy being an angry rebel he barely got his high school diploma."

"And look at him now." Felix flicked his arms wide. "He's a rock star! So, I don't need school. I just need a guitar."

I grinned. "Jimmy's been through a lot to get where he is. *Shock Wave* was a lucky break for those guys. I'm not saying they don't work hard, but there are no guarantees, and if that hadn't worked out for Chaos, they'd still be scraping by. You've got to have a backup plan for your dreams, Felix, and a good education is going to give you options."

His upper lip curled.

"Hey." I tapped his knee. "I wish I could tell you that you can forget school and just do whatever you want, but I care about you and I want you to have a good future. So, you have to go back tomorrow…and the day after that…and the day after that. You need to find a way to make it work."

"I'm not in the mood for your pep talk," he grumbled.

"You'd rather I let you sulk?"

His head snapped up, his dark glare warning me off. I faced it, not shying away from his anger. "I'm not saying you haven't been handed some pretty big shit in the last few years. I get it, okay? The fact you have survived it all is proof of what an amazing kid you are. See, that's my point, Felix. You are amazing. You're tough, strong, intelligent. You've had the worst day. You're at a school where you feel like you don't belong. Your aunt forgot to pick you up and you had to find your way home on your own."

"It took me an hour! I got totally lost!"

"But you made it." I smiled.

His shoulders slumped. "She forgot about me."

"She's trying, man. You're not the only one whose life has been turned upside down by this."

He clenched his jaw and refused to look at me, even when I ducked my head and tried to catch his eye.

"Felix, you have everything it takes to deal with this. Your mom wants you to have a good life. It's why she fought so hard to find Cassie…to make sure you stayed with family."

"She's not family! I don't even know her!"

I sighed, hoping Cassie couldn't hear his shouted words. "She's your blood, whether you want her to be or not. And she's giving you a home. She's feeding you, and she's trying to figure out the best way to take care of you."

"She's an uptight freak," Felix growled.

"Careful," I warned him. He probably didn't

mean it, but I didn't want her hearing stuff like that. Her self-esteem was low enough as it was.

Felix rolled his eyes. I guessed they were burning. They looked shiny with tears. He blinked then rubbed them, denying himself the chance to cry.

"I know this whole situation sucks, but she's trying and I know you are too. You're allowed to have a rant, feel bad, be in a foul mood for a while, but don't take it out on her, and don't let those rich kids beat you. You take advantage of every opportunity Strantham can offer. You excel, you win, you make your mama proud. Those entitled kids don't know shit. You could be the success story everyone talks about, Felix Grayson." I drew my hands wide like I was picturing his name in lights.

His lips twitched but didn't grow into a smile.

I patted his knee. "It's up to you."

With my pep talk fully exhausted, I stood and headed out the door.

"Call or text if you need anything," I murmured over my shoulder before disappearing down the hallway. I scratched the back of my neck, hoping I'd played it right. I'd intended to just go in and be a listening ear. Hopefully I hadn't pushed it too far. I wanted to inspire Felix, help him see how much strength he had. The strength of the human spirit continued to astound me, and I didn't want Felix to fall into the trap of self-pity. He was better than that.

"How'd it go?" Cassie's soft question made me

glance into the kitchen.

She was standing over a pot, a wooden spoon in her hand. Red meat sauce dripped off the end as she tapped it against the lip and set it aside. Turning down the stove, she walked over to me while untying her apron.

She pulled the apron over her head and smoothed her hair back. I wondered what it would look like if she wore it down. Those dark locks tumbling over her shoulders would be gorgeous. Not that she didn't look pretty with her hair tied back, but free-flowing hair would look...well, like she was setting herself free.

I leaned against the kitchen doorframe and smiled at her. "He's had a bad day and just needs time to process that. I tried to be encouraging, but I'm worried I took it too far."

Cassie crossed her arms. "I'm sure what you said was totally fine. It's better than I could do."

"Hey, don't be so hard on yourself. This is one of life's really big curveballs. They're basically impossible to hit out of the park. You just need to take it easy. One day at a time."

"I know." She sighed. "I just...don't think he likes me very much. I'm totally failing at this."

"You're doing fine. He's twelve. He's lost his mom, we've shoved him into a new house, new school, new life. That's a lot of adjustments to deal with. It's not going to be easy. He has every right to be in a bad mood."

She huffed and looked kind of pained. "How am I supposed to help him? He can't stay in a bad mood for the rest of his life."

"He won't." I chuckled, reaching forward without thinking. To my surprise, she didn't shy away when I gave her arm a quick rub. She was too distracted shaking her head and chewing on her bottom lip to even notice my touch.

I eased back before she did. It felt like a win. She was obviously getting comfortable enough around me to not be hyperaware...or she was just really distracted. I'd take either. She let me touch her arm. It was progress.

"Listen..." I ran my fingers through my hair and gave her an encouraging smile. "Felix is hurting. His anger at you is nothing personal."

"I forgot about him! Of course it's personal."

"And he'll get over it. You made a mistake."

"What if I make another one?"

"You will." I shrugged.

Her eyes bulged and she covered her face with her hands.

"Hey." I chuckled, lightly tapping her shoulder.

She flinched and jolted up to look at me.

I ignored her reaction. "We'll all make more mistakes. It's a guarantee. But we just have to go with it and learn what we can. I'm pretty sure you're never going to forget to pick him up from anything ever again." My eyes narrowed and I studied her with a smile. "Am I right?"

"Most definitely. I'm going to be paranoid about it now. I've already set my watch and phone alarms for tomorrow."

I grinned.

"But that still doesn't solve the problem that I have a boy living with me who doesn't want to be here. He's miserable and I don't know how to help him."

"Those things take time, Cassie. But for now, maybe you could find a way to connect to him, find something you have in common so you can talk about it and get excited together. Can you think of anything?"

"I don't know." She shrugged. "He doesn't seem to like reading or watching movies. All he does is lie on his bed listening to music."

"Music, of course." I snapped my fingers. "That's your in. We know he likes old-school rock. What else does he listen to?"

"I-I'm not sure."

"Find out." I smiled down at her. "Whatever it is, learn to like it. And if you need any ideas, let me know. I love music."

"I remember." She flashed me a brief smile. "Bon Jovi, right?"

I laughed and pointed at her. "What can I say, the guy's a legend...and Felix liked it too."

"I know." She looked mystified as she nodded.

Gazing down at her expression, I couldn't help that tug of affection again. "He's something special, Cassie."

"I know," she whispered, missing the fact I was actually talking about her and that I only said Cassie because I wanted to feel her name on my lips again.

As much as I could have stood there and asked

her out on the spot, it wasn't the right time. I didn't know a whole lot about Cassie Grayson, but from everything I'd observed, I guessed she was a solitary girl. I wouldn't be surprised if she'd never dated, never had a boyfriend...or maybe even a best friend.

Something kept her closed off from intimacy, which was probably why having Felix around was so damn hard. But maybe it was exactly what she needed. That...and me.

Because I wanted to be the guy who opened her up to the possibility of something more in her life. I wanted to see her bloom and figure out that letting people into her controlled little world didn't need to be so bad after all.

EIGHTEEN

CASSIE

Troy was right. Well, about Felix anyway. I'd ignore his comments about opening up in order to set myself free.

Reliving my past? Get real. I was never opening that box...and as if I'd let Troy in on that truth. People didn't take well to hearing about painful, abhorrent things like child abuse. I refused to see his face morph with sympathy or repulsion or whatever feelings he'd process as I laid it all bare.

I closed my eyes and shuddered.

Anyway, this whole thing wasn't even about me.

It was about Felix.

He *was* something special, and I needed to stop freaking out about failing him and start figuring out how to make him happy. Since Crystal left me, I hadn't had to think about anything other than my own survival.

After twelve years, it was going to be a hard habit to break.

Turning off the stove, I left the meat sauce and headed to Felix's room. The door was ajar, and I pushed it open after a soft knock. He was lying on his bed, staring at the ceiling, his legs crossed at the ankles...just the way I'd found him before.

His foot tapped in time with whatever beat he was listening to, his headphones so good he didn't even hear me sneak in.

I approached the bed. He flinched when he spotted me, and then his eyebrows dipped. "What do you want?"

His voice was extra loud because of the music in his ears, but I forced a smile, pretending like he hadn't just shouted at me.

"I was wondering if I could look through your CD collection."

He pulled the headphones away from his ear. "What?"

"Can I look at your CDs?" I pointed to the massive box on the floor.

His face wrinkled with confusion, but he nodded anyway.

"Thank you." Tucking my skirt beneath my legs, I knelt down and started flicking through the CDs.

I didn't know what I was doing really. Looking for a connection, I guess.

The hard plastic cases clicked against each other as I flipped through the titles. Def Leppard, Queen, Twisted Sister, Bon Jovi, Poison, Extreme. There were so many albums, so many artists...so many memories.

Crystal had always loved music. It was her salvation in some ways. When we were kids, Mom always had music blasting in the house. She'd be in the kitchen, singing and chopping vegetables. Crystal would dance around the table, placing knives and forks down with flair. I'd be singing quietly.

I stopped flicking, the memory freezing me for a moment.

I used to sing.

All the time.

The memory suddenly made me realize how quiet my life had been since Mom died. When the police showed up at school to tell us Mom wouldn't be coming to get us...ever again, my insides became an arid desert. Music couldn't exist in a place like that. It hurt too much. I hadn't been able to squeak out a note, and then foster care happened and any hope of bringing it back to life was snuffed out by evil.

"Find anything you like?" Felix's loud question jolted me back to the present.

I glanced up at him, hiding the wretched memories behind a smile. I tried to wash them away with the image of my mother in the kitchen, holding the wooden spoon to her lips and pretending it was a microphone.

I softly snickered. "You know, your mom…and your grandmother…used to adore music. The house was never quiet." My voice petered out as yet another memory hit me.

Mom sitting on the couch while Crystal and I put on a show for her. She clapped and cheered like we were world-famous rock stars, then hopped on stage—the coffee table—and started dancing with us. My bright purple boa swung in the air while I danced, jumping onto the couch, stretching my arms wide and singing with abandon.

Felix swung his legs over the bed and pulled out the headphone jack.

"Ironic" by Alanis Morissette filled the room. I knew it but I couldn't remember how.

"Alanis was Mom's favorite," Felix murmured.

That's how. She used to play *Jagged Little Pill* all the time. I snatched the CD case off the player and looked at the cover.

"I remember." A smile pulled at my lips. Crystal had known every single word on that album. It'd belonged to Mom. I opened the case and looked inside for my mother's name, but it wasn't there.

Running my finger over the blank plastic, I frowned and glanced at Felix.

His eyebrows rose, obviously confused by my silent wondering.

"Is this, uh…" My question trailed away as I suddenly remembered what had happened to Mom's copy. Hard plastic shattered in pieces, the shiny disc snapped in half while Crystal knelt on the floor crying.

"I told you to keep it down!" Davis yelled.

The door slammed shut. I counted to twenty before scrambling off my bed to comfort her. I rubbed her back, unable to say anything as she collected the shards of Mom's precious disc.

He came back that night to *apologize* and the next day bought her a new CD of some current chart topper. She listened to it once to appease him, but then never touched the CD again.

I stared at Felix, wondering how he could possibly be related to that man. Crystal had to be right. The father had to be that random guy from the party.

"Aunt Cassie?" Felix looked so worried. He couldn't be Davis's son. He just couldn't be.

I screamed at myself to smile, hide the memory before he saw it. I didn't want that blackness touching him. Blinking, I placed the CD down and managed a closed-mouth grin.

"Where'd you get this massive collection from?"

He stared at the box, a soft smile lifting his face. "Art."

"Who?"

"He was the guy who looked after us. Mom met him when she was pregnant with me. He took her to the hospital when I was born and paid all our bills and stuff."

I raised my eyebrows. "Was he her boyfriend?"

Felix laughed and shook his head. "He was like eighty."

"Oh." I snickered and returned to flicking through discs, finding the amount of close-range eye contact a little too intense. "Did you live with him?"

"Kind of. He was a caretaker at this massive church, and he arranged for us to move into this little apartment house thing next door. The church let us stay there until Art died."

I'd actually read a little about Arthur. Troy let me look over Felix's file, but it was nice to hear it from Felix himself. He looked kind of sad before pulling in a breath. "But he left us everything he had. He didn't have any kids or anything, and his wife had died before he even met Mom. So we were able to find a little apartment to rent, and I got his CD collection." He ran his hands lovingly over the discs.

"It's a nice memory of him."

"Not just him," he murmured.

I felt like my heart was going to break. Remembering my mom unearthed all that raw pain I'd buried deep, trying to forget how debilitating losing her had been. But I'd had Crystal.

Felix had no one.

Except me.

I swallowed, desperate to put a little sparkle into the conversation. Crystal would have found a way to make Felix laugh or smile.

Chewing my lip, I continued snapping the CDs against each other until I spotted a single that made me laugh out loud. "No way." I pulled it free, staring at the cheesy shot of Hall and Oates. "My mom loved this song."

Felix smiled and took it off me, carefully opening it and swapping out the Alanis CD. A few seconds later the familiar synthesized music started pumping.

Felix tapped his foot to the beat, and I sang, "What I want…"

Memories flooded me as "You Make My Dreams" filled Felix's little bedroom and took me back to a kitchen in Bakersfield. Mom sang into the wooden spoon, Crystal did twirls, and I stood on the chair, singing at the top of my lungs.

My voice rose like I was a kid again, until I became aware of Felix's gaze. I bit my lips together and dipped my head, my skin on fire.

But then something cool happened.

Felix started singing. He knew all the words.

I gaped up at him and he just laughed. "Mom used to make me listen to this song all the time!"

He turned up the volume to ear-splitting and started singing with such gusto his voice broke.

Laughter popped out of me. My body shook with it.

It felt so foreign yet familiar.

Felix tipped his head back, pretending to play guitar, and when the words kicked back in, I started singing along with him, even doing a little dance during the "Oos."

The moment was sweet, pure, and the start of a connection. We spent the rest of the evening going through Felix's collection. He played me all his favorite songs, everything from "Superstitious" by

Europe to "Sweet Child O' Mine" by Guns N' Roses.

The kid really was special, just like his mother…born into an era that didn't fit him.

My heart swelled with affection as I soaked in his passion for music. He looked so like Crystal when he spoke—his gestures, expressions…I even saw a little of my mom in there.

His beauty brought all my sweet memories to the forefront of my brain and chased away the darkness. It made me believe for a few precious moments that maybe we could do this. Maybe Felix and I were going to make it.

NINETEEN

FELIX

"Superstitious" blasted in the car as we drove to school. I'd always loved Europe. It was Art's favorite. "Final Countdown" and "Cherokee" were his top two. We'd rock out to those every time he came over for dinner. Twice a week until the day he died. The thought made me sad, so I leaned forward and turned up the volume a little higher...to honor him.

Aunt Cassie glanced at the volume dial but didn't say anything. The car was practically vibrating but it felt good. I loved that feeling of music swamping me, buzzing out every one of my senses until it was the only thing I could focus on.

We stopped for a red light and Aunt Cassie's finger tapped on the wheel. It was in time with the music. I bet she didn't even know she was doing it.

I grinned. She was actually kind of cool. Watching her sing last night had been pretty funny. It reminded me of Mom. I liked that.

Just before she left my room the night before—while we were listening to "Smells Like Teen Spirit"—I told her my dream of becoming a guitarist in a rock band. She smiled at me like she thought I was cool. I figured if she liked music too, then maybe there was a chance I could survive living with her.

The light turned green. The second we started moving, Aunt Cassie's knuckles turned white, gripping the steering wheel like we'd crash if she didn't. As much as she chilled out with the music, she was still totally uptight. I didn't get it. If driving made her so damn nervous, why'd she do it?

I kept the thought to myself and tried to mentally prep myself for school.

Anything had to be better than the suck-fest the day before. Eating lunch in the corner of the cafeteria with blabbermouth Butler was painful. The guy liked to play chess. That was his favorite thing to do and the only thing he talked about...all frickin' day. Strategy, what each piece meant. Whatever, dude. It was a total mind-kill. I couldn't get away from him fast enough when the final bell rang. Probably one of the reasons I was so pissed off with Aunt Cass for forgetting about me.

But she redeemed herself with the whole music thing, and I forgave her without really saying it.

The car jerked as she braked outside the school. She turned the music down and faced me. "I won't forget you today. I promise."

I shrugged. "It's cool. I know my way home now. You don't have to pick me up."

Reaching out, she hesitantly patted my arm. I missed Mom's hugs. She'd hold on so tight.

"I want to." Aunt Cassie swallowed. "I like picking you up."

I was so tempted to say, "How would you know?" but I figured she'd take the snark personally when I'd only meant it as a joke.

She really did need to loosen up.

"Catch you after school, then."

"Okay." Her lips rose into a smile. It was kind of pretty and reminded me of Mom, so I smiled back before getting out of her bomb and trudging into school.

I saw the messy blonde standing near the stairs. She was studying me again, no doubt mocking the beat-up car I'd gotten out of. I frowned and glanced away, noticing the pretty blonde coming into school behind me.

She walked like she was in high school, books perched on her hip and a mysterious smile on her lips.

"Hey, Ginny." I raised my eyebrows at her, trying to be cool.

"Hi." She smiled, but it was polite and insincere.

I wanted to step in time with her, try to be cool and charming...flirt like a rock star, but she reached the stairs and screams came from the doors as her two girlfriends ran down to greet her. They hugged like they hadn't seen each other the day before.

Messy Blonde—I couldn't remember her name—rolled her eyes, her upper lip curling as she grabbed her bag and walked past them. I paused to watch the three gigglers. With their short skirts and perfect hair, it wasn't a bad view.

A hard slap caught me on the back of the head and I lurched forward.

"What the hell are you staring at?" Mr. Evil Eyes from my homeroom pushed me again, but I caught myself before hitting the ground. "Are you checking out my girlfriend?"

I backed away, not saying a word. The asshole wasn't worth that much effort.

Spinning away, I walked into school, averting my eyes as I passed Ginny. She smelled like strawberries. My favorite fruit.

"Hey!" Dickhead shouted behind me. "I'm talking to you."

I kept walking. Because that was the sensible thing to do.

"You just gonna walk away like a pathetic loser?"

Anger fired up my spine, tensing every muscle along the way.

I could pound his pretentious ass into the dirt.

But I wouldn't.

I couldn't get expelled from another school. I wouldn't let them beat me that easily. Who gave a rat's ass what they thought.

"Come back here, you chickenshit!"

I clenched my fists and started counting.

One...calm the hell down, Felix. Two...don't let them win...

"Oh, I get it," Evil Eyes snickered. "Your poor candy's not good enough. Had to fight your way into our school just so you could see a pretty girl once in a while." Rapid footsteps caught up to me, then rough hands grabbed my sweater and spun me around. "It doesn't work like that here. You don't belong in this school. The only chicks you're worthy of checking out belong on the street."

I tried to wrestle him off me, but he wouldn't let up. So I fought a little harder, shoving his shoulder. "Get off me."

I didn't want to use fists, but if he didn't let go, I wouldn't hold back.

He fought me with a sneering laugh, holding onto my hoodie and giving it a hard yank.

The sound of tearing fabric jerked me still.

"Whoops!" His voice was so mocking. "I guess that comes from buying cheap shit. Like my mom always says, you get what you pay for."

I stared down at the gaping hole in the sweater Mom gave me for Christmas...

And then I just lost it.

My fist cannonballed into the side of his face. He hit the floor and I jumped on him, plowing my knuckles into his cheek until blood spurted from his mouth.

I wanted to kill him.

That asshole just ruined the last gift my mother ever gave me. He deserved to bleed, to cry like the sniveling wimp he was.

"That's enough!" Fuzzy shouting came from down the hallway, but I couldn't register it until strong hands pulled me away.

Evil Eyes wasn't so evil anymore. He rolled over, whimpering like a baby and holding a hand over his mouth.

A crowd had gathered around us, shocked whispers working through the students as I was marched to the principal's office by a gruff-looking teacher. I didn't know his name, but I guessed I wouldn't get a chance to learn it.

I shook him off me and followed him to what would no doubt be an immediate expulsion. I didn't care. I didn't want to stay at this school with a bunch of stupid assholes anyway.

"Sit." The man pointed at a seat in reception.

I slumped onto the padded chairs and fingered the torn sleeve of my sweater, trying to lift it back into place and pretend that Mom's gift was still whole.

Muffled voices came from the office, and then the sniveling asshole was ushered past reception and into the nurse's room. Mrs. Tindal's arm was around his shoulders, and she was murmuring something to calm him down.

She glanced over his head and caught my eye, giving me a stern glare. I turned away from it.

Great, just what I needed, another adult who hated me and thought I was a no-good troublemaker. A poor orphan with anger issues.

They didn't know shit!

Thumping the couch, I shot to my feet and headed for the door.

The receptionist was too busy on the phone to notice me slip outside. As soon as my feet hit the concrete steps, I started to run.

Screw this stupid school.

Screw everybody!

The only person who ever understood me was gone.

She was gone!

I wanted her back. I wanted her to tell me that I was okay. That she loved my fight...that I was a lucky one. But I would never hear her voice again.

Tears burned my eyes as I sprinted out of school. I had no idea where I was gonna go. I just needed to get away.

TWENTY

TROY

It was a quiet Tuesday afternoon at Reynold's. The lunch rush was over and the kitchen staff were no doubt prepping for dinner. I sat on one of the bar stools, catching the drips off my bottle of beer and waiting for Cole.

"Sorry about that." My high school buddy appeared at the end of the bar, pushing up his sleeves as he walked toward me. He leaned his arms against the wood and grinned. "I just had to check on Ella."

"She okay?" I took a swig of beer. It was on the house. I always got my first one free.

I loved that Cole moved out from Chicago. When I'd said goodbye to him after high school, I expected to see him maybe once every couple of years. But now it was about once a month.

Cole winced and squeezed the back of his neck. "She's been a little off color."

My eyes narrowed as I slowly placed the bottle down. My gut was already twisting in a tight knot. Not Ella. She was the sweetest girl in the world and everything to Cole. He couldn't lose her.

I swallowed, struggling to find my voice. "How sick is she?"

His shoulder hitched. "Can't really work right now. Exhausted all the time. Constantly throwing up."

"What's wrong with her?" My voice pitched, worst-case scenarios hitting me on all sides.

"She's pregnant." Cole's worried frown morphed into a sheepish grin. "With twins."

"Pregnant?" I had to repeat the word in order to absorb it. "Twins?"

"Uh-huh." Cole's laughter was breathy, as if he was still trying to believe it himself.

"Well, how far along is she?"

"About ten weeks. It's still early days, but the doctor says morning sickness isn't uncommon." His face bunched in agony. "I don't know why the hell they call it morning sickness. She's sick *all* the time. Poor thing's so little already. It's killing me watching her. Doc says it should be over in a few weeks. I hope it's sooner." He blew out a breath.

My smile grew wide as I studied his expression.

"She's got your babies growing in her belly."

Cole gazed into the bar, staring at nothing while he shook his head in wonder. "Yeah, she does."

"Can't believe you're gonna be a dad."

"Neither can I." Cole's eyes bulged. Turning for the fridge, he grabbed out a bottle of beer and uncapped it. He raised it to his mouth to take a sip, then paused and shook his head again, a half-smile creeping over his lips. "Some days it feels so huge, and other days I can't wait."

"It's a life-changer, man. But you're gonna be awesome."

Cole took a swig of beer then leaned across the bar again. "I hope so." We clinked bottlenecks and both took another swig. Rubbing his thumb over the condensation, Cole stared at the label before glancing up at me. "You know, you'd make a great dad one day too."

"What are you talking about? I already am a dad." I rolled my eyes, thinking about Jimmy and all the times I'd had to step in and play dad when my deadbeat father didn't show up.

"He's lucky to have you."

I shrugged. "He doesn't need me anymore. Look at him. Famous rock star, gorgeous girlfriend, impulses pretty much under control."

We both chuckled.

"So, maybe it's time to start having your own kids, then." Cole wiggled his eyebrows.

"Yeah, well, last I heard, you need a girl for that." I gazed at my bottle, thinking of Cassie and wondering how she'd ever be a mother when she didn't even like being touched.

My mind wandered over her pretty body, imagining what lay beneath her high-buttoned shirts and pastel-colored skirts. Would she ever relax enough for me to find out?

Geez, even the idea of holding her hand would be enough, or giving her a hug. I wanted to hold her, rest her head against my chest and tell her she was safe, that she was doing a great job with Felix...that she had everything it took to love him.

I wanted her to—

"Wait a second..." Cole pulled me away from Cassie. "Have you met someone?"

"What?" I glanced into his narrow-eyed gaze. "No!"

His eyes narrowed even further. Was I seriously that transparent? God help me.

I winced. "Okay. Yes. Maybe. I don't know." I raised my hands. "I shouldn't. She's going through a tough time. I really can't get involved like that, and I don't understand why I'm thinking about her all the time. I just... I want to help. I want to...see them make it."

"What do you mean?"

I sighed and scrubbed a hand down my face. "Her nephew is one of my cases. It'd be inappropriate for me to hook up with his struggling aunt. And besides, she's seriously not ready. There's stuff she needs to..."

Cole crossed his arms and gave me one of his classic half-smiles. "So those are your excuses this time, huh?"

I frowned. "What the hell is that supposed to mean?"

"Well, it's not like you'll get fired for getting involved with her, will you?"

"No. I don't think so, but it would complicate everything."

Cole let out a disgusted scoff. "That excuse is such BS. Life *is* complicated. I don't care who you are. You can't let that stop you from following your heart."

I opened my mouth to argue back. I wanted to cut him off before he launched into his spiel about how he would have lost Ella if he'd let life's complications get in the way.

But the phone saved my ass.

I ripped it out of my pocket, not even checking the number before answering. "Hello."

"Troy, it's Cassie," she squeaked, then pulled in a shaky breath.

Oh no. The last time she'd called me like this, Felix was getting expelled.

I jumped off my stool, hoping my dread was misplaced. "Is everything okay?"

"It's Felix. The school just called me. Apparently he beat some kid up then took off. I raced home to check the house but he's not here. What do I do? How do I find him?"

"It's okay," I soothed her. "I'll be right over. We'll look for him together."

She let out a whimper. "I can't lose him, Troy. I've got to keep him safe."

"We'll find him." I said it with as much

conviction as I could, ignoring the knots in my stomach as I said goodbye and slipped the phone back in my pocket.

"Is everything okay?" Cole's voice was deep with concern.

"Yeah." I rubbed my forehead. "Missing kid. I need to go."

"Do you want me to do anything?"

"No." I headed for the door. "I'll call if I need you. Thanks for the beer."

"Anytime." Cole's voice followed me out the door. I ran away from it, hauling ass to my car and speeding to Cassie's house. I nearly lost one of my kids last year and spent half the night looking for her. It was the worst feeling in the world, and I dreaded having to go through it with Felix.

My lips started muttering prayers before I even pulled away from Reynold's.

Felix was old enough and smart enough to disappear. I couldn't let that happen, not just for his sake...but for Cassie's too.

TWENTY-ONE

CASSIE

Troy turned up faster than I thought he would. Thank God, because I was going out of my mind. Nightmare scenarios of Felix hurt or wounded on the roadside spun out of control into kidnapping, torture, rape. I was near crippled by my imagination.

Tears blurred my vision as Troy and I drove the streets looking for my nephew.

My nephew.

My promise to Crystal.

I had to find him. I had to keep him safe, protect him. This was my chance to do the right thing. I should have fought harder for Crystal. Maybe if I had, she wouldn't have left me.

I wasn't going to let Felix down. I didn't care what it took. I would find him and bring him home...prove to him that I was the best option.

Rubbing the tears out of my eyes, I sniffed and looked through the glass, scouring the roads for any signs of him. We'd covered each street within a four-block radius of my house, then driven toward the school. I'd been on and off the phone with Jane Tindal, Felix's homeroom teacher. She'd asked her husband, Harry, to join in the search, and even the principal had left the premises to look for Felix.

He'd informed the police, and I was freaking out that Felix would be taken off my hands and put into foster care. What kind of aunt drives her nephew to run away?

Wringing my hands, I forced myself to breathe as Troy accelerated up the hill. We were reaching the outer limits of Pasadena, and I started to worry that Felix may have jumped on a bus. We'd have no chance of finding him at all if that was the case. He could be anywhere.

The police would have to get involved, which meant questions, interviews, hours of saying the same thing over and over again. My body went rigid as memories of my twelve-year-old self shaking in front of two towering police officers tried to disable me.

I squeezed my eyes shut, my lips fighting to hold back my whimpers. I couldn't let them out. Not in front of Troy. Felix needed me to stay strong, focused…together.

Snapping my eyes open, I drew in a breath, looked out the window, and shouted, "Stop!"

Troy slammed on the brakes.

"Look." I tapped the window, my heart hammering as I spied the figure in the distance.

It was definitely a kid, but I didn't know for sure if it was Felix until Troy turned down the road and we caught up to a black sweater with a white guitar on the back and a ripped sleeve.

My heart cracked at that one little tear. Crystal had given him that hoodie. He'd worn it every day since receiving it. I knew exactly how precious it was to him, and someone or something had tried to destroy it.

I was too relieved to see Felix alive and well to spare any emotion on anger. All that mattered in that moment was getting Felix to come home.

He glanced over his shoulder as we drew near, then jerked back to face the front and started walking faster. Troy slowed to a stop, and I jumped out of the passenger door.

"Felix! Stop, please."

He didn't. "Leave me alone!"

"I'm not going to do that." I started walking after him, but he just picked up his pace. I didn't want to scare him off, so I forced myself to stand still and keep talking. "Felix, please."

"I just want to go home!" He spun around, his voice savage and raw.

I swallowed and patted my chest. "I'm your home now."

"No, you're not!" He pointed at me. "You're not my mom!"

It was really hard to find a comeback. I wasn't his mother. I never would be. I'd never be enough.

I nearly turned back and asked Troy to step in, but when I glanced over my shoulder he smiled at me and mouthed, "You're doing great." Flicking his chin in Felix's direction, he whispered, "Keep going."

I spun back. Felix was even farther away but his pace had slowed. I raised my voice and called out to him. "Look, I know, okay! I'm not your mom. She was amazing and cool and the perfect person to raise you. And I'm sorry she's gone! I wish she was still here because she'd know exactly what to say and do...and I don't!" I flicked my hands in the air, tears getting the better of me. I pushed through them, my voice wobbling. "But I do know that she loved you and she wanted to keep you safe, so she asked me to take care of you and that's what I'm going to do."

"I don't need you to take care of me!"

"But I want to."

He jerked to a stop, his hands balling into fists. "No, you don't!"

"Yes, I do!"

Looking over his shoulder with a skeptical frown, he shook his head and kept walking.

"Okay, fine! Maybe I didn't at first. My life was set and I didn't want you disrupting it, but the idea of you leaving is killing me. I don't know how it's happened, but you've grown on me. You have this magic power, just like your mom. You've won me over, and I want you to stay. I can't imagine my house without you now." Tears were running freely down my cheeks. I hated crying in front of people. It always felt like I'd lost, but I couldn't worry about my tears. All I could think about was getting Felix into Troy's car and safely home.

Felix was still shaking his head, still walking away. My stomach pitched with desperation as I scoured my brain for the right thing to say. I couldn't think of anything so I just started walking, following him.

"Get lost!" His voice broke when he shouted over his shoulder.

"I'm not going to do that. If you need to walk, then that's fine, but I'm following you."

He huffed, hunching his shoulders and continuing to shuffle forward.

After a few more paces, he let out a loud cry and spun around. "Seriously! Stop!"

"I can't! Felix, I'm not letting you walk away."

He stood there puffing at me, his nostrils flaring.

I didn't know what else to say.

So out of nowhere, I started singing, "Keep on walking that road and I'll follow..."

I don't know why I did it. It just popped out. We'd been listening to "Superstitious" in the car, and it felt like the perfect song for the moment.

Felix went still and blinked at me like I was crazy.

I didn't care.

He'd stopped walking and I took advantage.

Licking my lips, I sang the next line. My voice petered off on the "Yeah..." Felix's chest was heaving, but he still hadn't moved away.

So I sang the next line. When I hit the words "know that you care," he let out a sob and started running straight for me.

My instinct was to move out of the way, but I held my breath and planted my feet. He was two steps away from me when he dropped his bag on the road and wrapped his arms around my waist. Pressing his forehead into my neck, he held on tight and sobbed the tears he should have let out weeks ago.

I didn't know what to do at first. I wasn't great with people touching me, but it only took a moment for my arms to wrap around his body. I clung tight the way I used to when Crystal was having a bad day. She'd tremble in my arms, and I'd pour every ounce of love I had into the hug. Closing my eyes, I rested my cheek against Felix's head and did the same thing.

It was easier than I thought it would be.

I'd closed off that part of myself a long time ago and always figured it'd be too painful to open it again, but cracks were forming in my resolve and a twelve-year-old kid with the heart of a lion was chipping away at my protective coating.

As terrifying as that was, a small part of me knew it was about time.

My life had changed forever, and for the first time since Crystal laid it on me, I felt ready.

TWENTY-TWO

FELIX

I sat in the back of Troy's car, swiping tears off my face and feeling like an idiot. I'd cried so hard I thought I was going to throw up. My head ached with this dull thud that I couldn't squeeze out of my brain.

I sniffed and tried to act like nothing had happened, but the truth was…I'd probably needed to cry. I hadn't let one drop fall since Mom died, and it felt kind of good to get it out. I was just glad only Troy and Aunt Cassie were around to see it.

Running my fingers through my hair, I made a fist then sighed, leaning my head against the window and trying not to think so hard.

Aunt Cassie was on the phone to the school, letting them know I'd been found and would be off for the rest of the day and also the next. I looked at her in surprise, but she gave me a soft smile and winked. As soon as she hung up, she murmured, "I figured we could use a day. Is that cool?"

"It's cool," I mumbled.

Troy hadn't said much as we drove home. He kept looking at me in the rearview mirror though. I ignored him but could feel his gaze on me.

As soon as we pulled into the driveway, I jumped out of the car and headed for the house. I could hear quiet conversation behind me.

"Call if you need anything."

"Thank you so much for…" I glanced back in time to see Aunt Cassie shake her head. She did that when she ran out of words.

"Anytime." Troy smiled at her. His eyes kind of glowed, like he was trying to tell her more without saying anything.

I turned away with a slight frown. Mom never dated. The only guy she let into our lives was Art, and he was like a grandfather to both of us. I wasn't used to some guy smiling at the person who was supposed to take care of me.

Troy was pretty cool, so it wasn't all bad…just unusual.

I asked Mom once about my dad. She told me my father had given her enough love to last her a lifetime, but they couldn't stay together. Apparently it was a magical one-night stand. She told me the story on my eleventh birthday, painted this perfect picture of soulmates who were destined to only touch for a brief moment. I was her reminder of that special night. A precious gift.

It was sweet and everything, but she wouldn't look at me the whole time she told the story, and I couldn't help wondering if it was complete bullshit.

I didn't care. I didn't need a dad. Mom had always been enough. And now Aunt Cassie would fill that space.

I couldn't believe she sang to me. One of my favorite songs and she'd belted it out. It was unlike her, and it gave me enough hope to stop walking. Her voice had been soft and desperate. I could tell how bad she meant it and it… Something inside me snapped and I couldn't keep walking. I just wanted a hug.

Rubbing my forehead, I shuffled to my room, flicking on the stereo and cranking it up as Aunt Cassie arrived at the door.

"Runaway Train" by Soul Asylum came on. We both froze and looked at the stereo.

"Your mom used to listen to this song all the time." Aunt Cassie's face crumpled. "I used to worry that she'd…leave me." Her eyes swam with tears, her little voice showing me how devastating that must have been for her.

My throat restricted, making it hurt to swallow. "Why'd she do it?" I croaked.

Aunt Cassie's lips pursed, but then she pinched her nose and sniffed, cutting off the tears before they could fall. Tucking a loose lock of hair back into her ponytail, she looked at me and forced a smile. "She loved you. She wanted to protect you."

"From who?"

Aunt Cassie's jaw worked to the side. "Our foster parents. They were kind of mean, and if they'd found out she was pregnant..." She shook her head.

"Would I exist if they had?"

"Probably not," she whispered.

"Wow." My eyebrows popped up. "No wonder she always made up stories."

Aunt Cassie's head tipped to the side. "What do you mean?"

"Whenever I asked about her past, she'd always smile and then make up these magical stories. I used to believe them until I started noticing holes. Sometimes the retellings would be different or I'd ask a question that obviously got too close to the truth and she'd clam up, put on some happy music and start dancing."

"She could always bring the sun into any situation."

I frowned and shook my head. "Yeah, but she liked to run. Not the way you run for exercise, but from the truth. She admitted once that she was a runner. You know that fight-or-flight thing?"

Aunt Cassie nodded.

"Yeah, well, she said she'd always fly and you'd stand to fight."

My aunt went still, her eyes glassing with tears as she stared at me. Part of me wanted to know what she was thinking, but I was too afraid to ask. For someone who was so in control, she looked like she was about to lose it, dissolve into a shower of tears.

I quickly kept talking. "She wanted me to be like you." I smiled, hoping to pull Aunt Cassie away from whatever darkness haunted her. "So, I'm really sorry I ran."

Aunt Cassie covered her face with her hands, then brushed them over her head and looked at me. Her eyes still glistened but she was smiling. "You fought first." She reached out her hand. Her fingers were trembling but I took them. She gripped my hand and whispered, "And then you came running back. You're a fighter, Felix Grayson, and your mom would be so proud of you. Just like I am."

Aw, man. She was gonna make me cry again.

Thank God the music changed. "Animal" by Def Leppard pumped out of the stereo and I jumped up, cranking the volume and playing air guitar. I mouthed the lyrics, putting on a show for Aunt Cassie until she laughed.

The sound spurred me on and I went for it, killing the shit from my day and making it better with a little rock 'n' roll.

TWENTY-THREE

CASSIE

I sat on the floor watching Felix jump around the room. His air guitar was amazing. He banged his head, getting into the song and looking like the rock star he so desperately wanted to be. The cracks forming in my shell broke apart a little further.

And an idea grew in my brain.

It was only something small that quickly bloomed into an *I must do this*. I didn't know how I was going to pull it off, but I somehow had to find a way to give my nephew everything he deserved.

*****

The next day as I was prepping for my run, Felix walked into the kitchen and asked if we could go to the beach.

"Um…" I paused, unable to think of a good excuse not to go. "Sure. As soon as I get back we can—"

"Why don't you run at the beach?" He shrugged. "I'll sit in the sand, checking out the hotties while you do your running thing."

"Checking out the hotties?" I raised my eyebrows.

Felix blushed and scratched the back of his neck. "Come on, Aunt Cass, please."

Aunt Cass. He'd shortened my name, and I suddenly couldn't refuse him. "All right." I nodded. "Go grab your stuff and a couple of towels from the hall closet. The stripy ones. I'll meet you in the car."

He nodded like an eager puppy and ran off.

I stayed in the kitchen, chewing my lip and wondering what the hell I was in for.

"The hotties," I muttered and shook my head.

*****

The sky was blue. The sun was warm on my skin. For a mid-January day, it was hot and beautiful. Felix flicked out his towel and took a seat, adjusting his shades and already scanning the beach. Sad for him, but there weren't any hotties on display.

A couple of surfers bobbed on the waves in front of us, and there was an older woman walking her dog. I tried to hide my smile, but relief was making it hard. Felix may have been twelve going on thirteen, but I didn't want him checking out girls already. It felt too young. Too soon.

But what the hell did I know. Until six weeks earlier, I didn't know I'd be playing mom to a kid hitting puberty.

The P word scared the crap out of me. I was too young for this!

Clearing my throat, I shook out my arms and got ready to run. "Okay, so I'll be about an hour."

"I don't know how you do it." Felix shook his head.

I shrugged, jumping on my tiptoes. "I've been doing it since I was thirteen. I was told that running was a good way to..." I shook my head. "Anyway, I kind of got addicted."

"I didn't mean that." Felix snickered. "I meant I don't know how you run without music."

"Oh. I..." I didn't know. Music had left me the day Crystal ran, and I hadn't thought to bring it back in until Felix entered my life.

"Here." He held up a small shuffle. "Take this."

"But what about you? You're just going to sit here with no music?"

"You need to experience running with music. I've got everything I need up here." He tapped his forehead. "It's only an hour. I'll be okay."

I took the device and earbuds. "Are you sure?"

He nodded. "You have to know what you're

missing out on."

I grinned at his wink, then let him turn on the music for me. I put the buds in and jolted.

"Sorry," Felix mumbled, quickly turning the volume down.

"Thanks."

I opened my mouth to ask one more time if he was sure, but he pointed to the pathway. "Off you go."

I snickered and went on my way.

"Can't Stop" by Red Hot Chili Peppers thumped in my ears, the guitar solo working right through my body and injecting me with an energy I'd never felt before.

A smile spread across my face as I ran, my rhythm matching the music. My arms swung and the pavement was lost beneath me as I experienced a new kind of run. With the music flowing through me, my brain didn't have as much space to think. For the first time ever, I ran without feeling like I was running *from* something…someone.

Instead of dodging nightmares, I focused on beats, lyrics, melodies. I made it to the end of the path and turned back. Checking my time, I figured I'd done about three miles and was happy with my pace. I couldn't believe how fast the time had gone. The music was entertaining, and I nearly laughed when "Play With Me" by Extreme started up.

It made me want to dance back to Felix, not run.

I giggled and pushed forward, scanning the ocean as I went. I saw a surfer getting out of the water. His full-body wet suit gloved his muscular frame, showing off how strong and masculine he was. I usually shied away from that kind of power. It scared me. But something about the guy made me look a little longer. He planted his surfboard in the ground and, as the path curved closer to the sand, I got an even better look at him.

He was so hot. Like a romance novel cover model.

I felt bad for checking him out. A guy that gorgeous would already be taken, and I shouldn't be ogling someone else's guy, but he made it really hard to look away. Especially when he unzipped his suit and pulled it off the top half of his body.

His broad shoulders rippled. Drips of water ran from the ends of his hair and down his back. Flicking the longer locks off his forehead, he scrubbed a hand over his face, then glanced my way.

I gasped and tripped, my foot catching on a crack in the concrete.

My hands shot out, catching me before I faceplanted. My knees hit kind of hard, scraping the skin. I hissed and turned over, sitting on my butt to check out the blood. It wasn't too bad. I could easily run back to Felix and patch it up when I got home. The heels of my hands were grazed too. They stung pretty badly, but nothing I couldn't handle. I rubbed them together and felt my cheeks flood with color as *Troy* and his naked torso appeared above me.

"Are you okay?" His large hand touched my elbow and he helped me to my feet, running his fingers down my arm as he crouched to look at my knee.

I stood frozen, wondering why his soft hand hadn't made me flinch. I usually hated being touched.

His fingers were cold from the water but actually felt kind of nice against the back of my throbbing knee.

I needed to move. I couldn't stand here with his hands on me.

So why did it feel so un-scary?

I cleared my throat and shifted away, confused by whatever the hell was going on in my chest. "Um, I'm fine."

Troy looked up at me, his ocean eyes making my stomach tremble. I averted my gaze as he stood, trying not to notice how beautiful his sculpted body was. His abs had shape. If I'd wanted to, I could have traced a line with my finger, all the way from the dip between his pecs to his belly button...to the line of hair that trailed down to the edge of his wet suit.

I blinked and clenched my jaw, hoping my cheeks weren't too bright. Thankfully I'd been running, so I could hide my shame behind that excuse.

Sweat trickled down the side of my face. I brushed it away, suddenly aware of how bad I must have smelled. I took a small step away from him, pulling one of the earbuds free and asking in a jittery voice, "What are you doing here?"

Troy's eyebrows rose and he pointed to his

longboard. "I'm still learning. Not very good yet." I smiled at his self-deprecating expression. "Are you sure you're okay? My car's just behind us if you want me to drive you somewhere."

"No, really. I'm good. It's not that bad."

We both gazed down at my knee and the small trickle of blood that was inching toward my sock. The sweat was helping it along. I grimaced and tucked my foot behind my other one. There I was salivating over the guy, and he was probably being repulsed by my stench and blood.

"Well, I better get going." I pointed over my shoulder.

"What are you listening to?" Troy grinned, nabbing the bud against my shoulder and putting it in his ear.

I didn't even know what I was listening to. My throat grew thick as I gazed up at him.

I loved his smile and those eyes.

"Def Leppard," he murmured. "You've just gone up in your cool ranking."

"My cool ranking?"

"Yeah." He turned his smile to full beam, making my legs want to crumple. "I now think you're cooler than I already thought you were."

"I'm not cool." I scoffed, shaking my head and wondering if skin could actually catch fire if you blushed hard enough.

"You're something special," he whispered. Obviously embarrassed by his candor, he looked down at his sandy feet.

I bit my lips together, my heart racing while my

head told me not to be an idiot. Like Troy Baker would ever be attracted to someone like me. I didn't even want him to be. I didn't need a man in my life...ever. I was happy. Alone.

Not alone, I had Felix.

I didn't need a man.

Men were mean and they hurt you.

But as I stood there staring at Troy's captivating grin, I had to wonder if that was true of all men. I'd made myself believe it for so long...but what if I'd been mistaken?

Troy squeezed the back of his neck, his sharp nose wrinkling as he stared out at the ocean. His cheeks were pink and he couldn't quite get his smile under control. He looked embarrassed...and adorable.

Clearing his throat, he stood a little taller. "So, you don't usually run down here, do you? I thought you were spending the day with Felix?"

"I am. I mean..." I pointed over my shoulder, relieved by the change in subject. "Felix wanted to come to the beach and check out the babes." I winced. "I think he was hoping for bikinis, but..."

"You didn't have the heart to tell him that it's too early in the day for the beauties to be out."

I opened my mouth to speak, but all I could utter was a helpless sigh. "What am I going to do with a boy who's already thinking about girls? I'm so not cut out for this."

Troy's encouraging smile was back in place, reminding me that he wasn't just some half-naked surfer but also the guy who helped me find Felix.

He reminded me every time he was around that I was capable of raising a kid who would soon be a teenager.

"You know, when my brother was going through a really tough time, I bought him a guitar. It kind of gave him something to pour all his energy into."

"A guitar," I whispered. "Felix wants a guitar! I mean, I just had that thought yesterday when I was watching him rock out on his air guitar. I want to get him one and hook up some lessons for him. Do you know how I could do that? I mean, are they expensive? Where could he get lessons?"

Troy's eyes lit while I was talking, and as soon as I'd finished he snapped his fingers and pointed at me with a broad grin. "I've just had a great idea. I know a guy who might be able to help us out." His wink made my heart melt, and then he turned it to a puddle of liquid affection. "How'd you like to give that kid the surprise of his life? Come on, I'll drive you back to Felix and we can start plotting. This is going to be awesome."

I should have kept running, but my head nodded before I could stop it. I didn't need to run anymore that day. I usually couldn't rest until I'd pounded out at least six miles, but as I stood there with blood trickling down my leg and the sweetest guy I'd ever met hovering next to me with those twinkling eyes and that excited smile...I just couldn't say no.

TWENTY-FOUR

TROY

I didn't just drive her back to Felix. I stuck around, helped her dig out the first aid kit from the trunk of her car. I couldn't leave her with blood trailing down her shin.

She let me touch her.

Sure, she was tense and stiff, but she didn't flinch or shy away when I placed my hand beneath her calf muscle and gently cleaned up her knees—one at a time.

Damn, she had the sexiest legs I'd ever seen. They were slender and strong, the muscles beautifully defined from years of running.

I took my time, hoping she wouldn't notice how slowly I worked. Felix was doing me huge favors, hovering beside us and asking Cassie all about her injuries. The conversation then veered toward running with music, and I was all but forgotten as playlists dominated. Distracted by her nephew, Cassie relaxed, and I had that fleeting, unbidden thought that I could do this for the rest of my life—stand there looking after a pretty girl while she chatted to "our" kid. It felt so natural, normal...so nothing that I'd ever thought of before in my life.

I never wanted kids. I'd spent my childhood raising one; I didn't want to do it all over again. But that moment made it seem like something I could try.

And I had to be honest—the idea took me way off guard.

Smoothing the Band-Aid over Cassie's knee, I cleared my throat and lowered her leg.

She glanced up, squinting against the sunlight, and smiled at me. "Thank you."

"You're welcome." My voice was husky. I had to get out of there. I had plans to implement, wistful thinking to avoid.

Cassie loved my idea about the guitar. She actually looked excited, an emotion I hadn't seen on her before. It was pretty.

"Well, I gotta split." I raised my hand. "Things to do."

Cassie's eyes shot to mine, and she gave me a very subtle wink. Again, not what I was expecting. I was the winker, but there she was, blowing my mind and showing me a hidden part of herself that I never wanted her to lock away again.

My heart did a weird double-beat, and I couldn't help smiling once again before reluctantly walking to my car. It was a bizarre dichotomy: I wanted to stay and spend the day with those two, but I also couldn't get away fast enough.

I wasn't used to my heart doing anything more than feeling compassion or sympathy...sometimes a little lust. But this thing it did around Cassie was strong and only growing more powerful, especially when she showed me a slice of something new.

If I could fall in crush with uptight Cassie, unguarded Cassie would knock me clean off my feet. I had to get her talking. I had to help her break those chains and open up even more. Because I wanted her to find a place for me in her life.

But it wasn't my job to do that.

It wasn't about me.

It was about helping her and Felix find their way. Although Cassie loosening up would only help Felix too. I could justify it that way, right?

Clenching my jaw, I forced myself to stroll, not run, to the car. As soon as the door clicked shut behind me, I pulled the phone out of my bag and started making plans to surprise Felix.

My brother's phone rang and a smile stretched across my face as I waited for him to answer.

*****

Jimmy came through.

My insides jiggled with excitement as I bounced up the path to Cassie's front door.

I hadn't spoken to her since the day on the beach, but we'd exchanged a few texts and I knew they were home, Felix blissfully unaware of the surprise we were about to lay on him.

Music blasted from somewhere in the house, "Livin' On A Prayer." It only made my smile grow wider. Man, I loved that kid.

I knocked once, hiding the guitar behind my back while I waited. It didn't take long for Cassie's cautious gaze to appear between the curtains. The second she spotted me, her eyes rounded then started to sparkle.

I winked at her and she disappeared from view. The locks had never been clicked back so fast...and then the door flew open.

"Hey." She grinned.

"Hey." I wiggled my eyebrows and stepped inside, nearly tripping through the door when I noticed she was wearing the necklace I gave her for Christmas. I probably shouldn't have gotten such a rush from something so little, but I did.

She was wearing my necklace.

"I'll go get him!" she called over her shoulder as she rushed from the room, her footsteps fast and jittery.

"We're halfway there..." Bon Jovi's voice powered out of Felix's room, and I started singing under my breath. It was one of my favorite Bon Jovi songs. The volume decreased. I kept singing to myself, only just catching a muffled conversation.

My voice petered off to a light whisper, but I still couldn't hear what they were saying.

Then came two sets of footsteps—one hurried, one slow. Cassie reappeared and a few seconds later Felix shuffled in behind her.

"Oh, hey, Troy." He forced a smile, obviously a little miffed at being pulled out of bed on a Saturday morning. He yawned and scrubbed a hand over his face. "You don't have to worry," he mumbled. "I went back to school for the rest of the week, kept my head down and my knuckles clean. The guy who ripped my sweater has pretty much stayed away so..." He shrugged. "Oh, and Aunt Cass mended the sleeve so I'm all good." Felix waved his hand in the air then looked at his aunt. "Can I go back to bed now?"

Cassie snickered and shook her head. "I don't think you want to."

Felix's eyebrows furrowed then slowly rose as I revealed the guitar case behind me.

His lips parted with a gasp, and he looked between me and Cassie. "What's this?"

Cassie crossed her arms. "It's a gift." She smiled, her eyes glistening with emotion. "We wanted to get you something to help you through."

We—I liked the sound of that way too much.

"A guitar?" Felix blinked and stumbled over to me.

I laid the case down on the floor and popped it open to reveal a red Fender Stratocaster. "It's one of Jimmy's old ones."

"No way." Felix pulled out the guitar like it was

made of solid gold.

Lifting the strap over his head, he nestled the guitar against his body and fingered the strings in awe.

I glanced at Cassie. She was gazing at Felix like she loved him, her eyes glowing with a look of affection that made my heart do that double-beating thing again.

My swallow was thick and audible before I managed to find my voice. "I have an amp in the car."

"And I've arranged for you to start guitar lessons at school. The music teacher's going to fit you in at lunchtime. I figured you'd be okay with that."

Felix's head bobbed enthusiastically. He caressed the strings with an awestruck smile. It was a sweet moment, each of us gazing at the other, unable to find any words that could possibly suffice.

Finally, Felix sniffed then rubbed his finger under his nose. "Thank you," he croaked. "Thank you so much."

Cassie blinked. "You deserve it."

His lips wobbled into a heartfelt smile before he lurched forward and wrapped his arm around her shoulders. She yelped as he pulled her against him, then let out a nervous laugh, leaning her head against his and gifting me a smile.

It was another beautiful moment. A flash of brilliance in the blossoming of Cassie Grayson.

I felt privileged to be a part of it and didn't want

to miss a moment.

My heart squeezed and took off running as I once again wished that these two weren't just another case. I wanted them to be so much more.

TWENTY-FIVE

FELIX

I practically ran to my first guitar lesson. I couldn't help it! One, I was getting to play Jimmy Baker's guitar! And two, I was getting out of another torturous lunchtime avoiding idiots who still wanted to get me back for being a better fighter than them. They'd stopped using physical threats and had shifted to words, which could be just as painful as fists.

Anyway, I was stoked to be hiding away in a music room, just me and a guitar teacher. I couldn't think of a better way to spend my lunch hour.

The door creaked when I opened it, but no one

was there to turn and see me. I glanced around the room, rubbing a hand down my leg and taking a seat near the teacher's desk. There was a music stand set up with a couple of stools. I assumed one of them was for me.

Sitting down, I gently took out the guitar, running my hand over it, still slightly in awe. I'd been messing around a little, strumming the strings with this stupid smile on my face.

Jimmy Baker's guitar. It was un-freaking-believable!

The door creaked, and I spun to greet the teacher.

But it wasn't Mr. Maddison.

"Hey." The girl with the black nail polish and constant stare smirked at me as she walked into the room. Her skull ring had been switched out for a mini vinyl record ring. It was wicked and totally cool, but it didn't curb the fact I wasn't interested in sharing my lesson with a messy-haired chick who seemed kind of weird to me.

My stomach twisted with annoyance. She was carrying a guitar case too. Hers was bigger than mine. She set it down on the desk behind us and popped it open, gently pulling out a bass guitar, the same way I'd pulled out Jimmy's Fender—total respect and awe of her instrument.

Flicking the strap over her shoulder, she took a seat beside me.

I still hadn't said anything. I could feel her gaze on me as I stared at my guitar, running my fingers up and down the strings.

"I'm Summer, by the way...and you're Felix, right?"

I nodded. "Yeah, we're in a few classes together."

"I know."

I glanced up in time to see another smirk. It wasn't a put-down though. She actually looked happy to be sitting next to me. My guess was that a smirk for her was like a normal smile for most people. She just seemed like that kind of chick, oozing this mysterious, cool vibe that didn't really fit at Strantham Academy.

"Nice guitar." She raised her chin at the instrument resting on my lap.

"Yeah, it's a..." I ran my hand over the shiny red finish, wondering if I should tell her it belonged to a famous rock star. Would she even believe me?

Nah. I chickened out. I really didn't need another excuse for anyone at this stinking rich school to hassle me.

I cleared my throat and settled for, "It's a hand-me-down."

She grinned. "They're the best. Pre-loved. Nothing wrong with that." She tapped her bass guitar. "This was my dad's. He used to be in a band when he was in college. He's a fat businessman now, but I like that he used to be cool."

I laughed and it caught me off guard. Biting my lips together, I bobbed my head, trying to play it cool. She snickered and lightly punched my arm.

"Chill out, dude. I think this school sucks too.

Bunch of rich, stick-up-their-ass kids who think they're better than everyone else? Gimme a break. Why'd you think I signed up for lunchtime guitar lessons? Anything for a breather, right?"

I went still and just looked at her for a second. I didn't know how to respond because I felt like I was looking at my new best friend, which was weird because one, she was a girl, and two…I'd never had a best friend before.

The door swung open and fast footsteps hurried into the room. "Sorry I'm late."

Summer and I spun together to check out Mr. Maddison. He was wiping his hands on a napkin. He then swiped it across his mouth and down his beard before throwing it in the trash and snatching up a third stool. He placed it down opposite us then quickly skimmed his eyes over our faces and instruments.

"Okay, good. Sorry we have to do these lessons together, but my schedule's pretty full and it's the only way I can fit you both in."

"I'm cool with it." Summer shrugged.

I grinned. "Me too."

"Great." Mr. Maddison clapped his hands together, giving them a rub. "Okay, let's see what you guys can do."

We spent the next ten minutes chatting about what we already knew, and then he pulled out two chord books that we were to take home and learn.

"Memorize finger positions until it's as natural as breathing. If you want to be brilliant guitarists, you have to practice your butts off." He grinned, his wide teeth looking extra white framed by his dark beard.

I opened the book, laying it on the stand so Summer and I could see the chords. The teacher spent a few minutes focusing on her while I messed around with fingering, finding the G chord first then shifting into D. It was easier to follow the little pictures than I thought it would be, and by the end of the session, I'd managed to strum three chords and change between them.

Mr. Maddison tapped the stand with a little laugh. "I think you're a natural, kid." He took the book and flicked through the pages. "I want you to work through pages five to eight this week. The songs look simple, but don't worry about that. Learning an instrument is like building a house. You get the basics right, that's your foundation, then you just keep adding more and more layers. We'll have you playing rock 'n' roll in no time."

I was smiling so wide my face hurt. "Sounds good."

He chuckled. "Okay, you two, the bell's due to go in about five, so just stay here and mess around until it rings."

Summer and I glanced at each other as he stepped out of the room. Then the door clicked shut and we both started laughing. I didn't know why. I guess we were just high on the music, because as soon as he left we started practicing what we'd learned, grinning at each other when we played a chord together and actually sounded good.

At this rate, I'd be playing like a pro in no time. I'd never been more motivated by anything in my life. I was determined to be as good as Jimmy. Because one day, I wanted to be in a band just like Chaos, and maybe I was sitting next to someone who could join me.

TWENTY-SIX

CASSIE

Felix had been practicing non-stop since Troy gave him that guitar. After six weeks of shutting himself away every afternoon and playing when I went out for my morning run, he was getting really good. He was passionate and therefore progressing at an accelerated rate. His guitar teacher emailed to tell me he was a natural.

I'd never felt pride like it.

The guitar playing had also put him in a good mood, which put me in a good mood. Since singing him into my arms that day, we'd gone from strength to strength. Life at home had become easier. Music filled the house. Felix started to actually eat the food I cooked him. He didn't kick up too much of a fuss when I asked him to do the dishes, and so far the disorder in my structured life wasn't throwing me off balance. Although most days I still didn't feel good enough and the task of raising Felix was so monumental, I felt like we would somehow get through. We could do this.

After years of letting Crystal down, I was finally redeeming myself, looking after her son the way I should have looked after her.

I was determined not to fail my sister...but more than that, I was determined not to fail Felix, because he was growing on me big time, especially that sweet smile.

I grinned back at him as I pulled the car into the drop-off bay outside Strantham Academy.

"You all set?"

"Yep." He reached back for his school bag, hugging it to his chest and pausing to look at me.

"Everything all right?"

He nodded. "I, um...forgot to tell you."

My mind immediately jumped into caution mode. I hated that about myself, but I hopefully hid any kind of alarm behind my smile. "What's that?" My voice was too tight, too twitchy.

Dammit. Why couldn't I be more like Crystal? She was the mother Felix really deserved.

"I started reading Percy Jackson last night."

I gasped, my eyes rounding wide. "You did?"

I couldn't describe the feeling blooming in my chest. He was reading one of my favorite books. It meant so much to me.

"Yeah, it's really good."

"You think so? You like it?" My smile was huge and dominating, but I couldn't help it. His enthusiasm over my Christmas gift had been nonexistent, so the fact he started reading it…that meant more than some kid just reading a book because he felt like it. He was reading Percy Jackson for me, and I wanted to wrap him in my arms and tell him…

I pressed my lips together but couldn't hold back my smile. "I'm so glad."

"I thought you'd like that." He chuckled and gently nudged my shoulder. "Aw, Aunt Cass. You're such a geek."

"I know." I giggled, shaking my head and smoothing back my hair. "Thanks for not minding that about me."

He shook his head. "You're all right, you know?"

I bobbed my head but didn't actually believe him. Patting his arm, I grinned. "So are you."

He snickered and reached for the handle then, stopped and turned back to face me again. He looked hesitant. Biting the inside of his cheek, he studied my face, letting a smile loose and totally blindsiding me with one simple question.

TWENTY-SEVEN

FELIX

"Guess what?" As soon as I said the words, my heart started pounding. I'd never played this game with anyone other than my mom. It felt weird saying it to Aunt Cass, but for the first time since moving in with her, I actually felt it. Like seriously.

"What?" Her smile was tentative, unsure like it always was.

I licked my bottom lip, then grinned. "I love you."

Her smile fell away, her lips parting. Her skin kind of drained of color and her knuckles went white as she gripped the steering wheel and looked out the window. She stared straight ahead, blinking like crazy. I couldn't help a grin as I watched her. She really was weird.

"It's a game… Mom used to play with me all the time."

She whipped back to look at me. "Your…your mom said 'I love you'?"

"Every day." I grinned, warmed by the memory until a weird kind of shyness took me over. Maybe I shouldn't have said anything. Aunt Cass was looking at me with this pale surprise that I didn't understand. Of course Mom told me she loved me. What mother wouldn't?

I cleared my throat and clicked the door open. "Anyway, thanks again for arranging the guitar and the lessons, and just…being cool. I know I said I didn't want to live with you, but…I kind of like it. Thanks for taking me in."

Her mouth opened and closed then pulled into a smile. "Of course. You've become my favorite person. Made it very easy on me. You know I'd do anything for you, right?"

"Yeah." I nodded. "I do now. Thanks, Aunt Cass."

She cleared her throat, her head bobbing kind of fast and jerky. "You know, I…" Her voice seemed to stop working, like whatever she wanted to tell me refused to pop out of her mouth. In the end she sighed and mumbled, "Have a good day at school."

"Have a good day at work." I shut the door and grabbed my guitar from the back before walking into school. It was getting easier each day. The assholes stayed out of my way as long as I didn't make eye contact. Easy.

Summer and I were hanging out every day in the music suite. Mr. Maddison let us use one of the small practice rooms, and we jammed together every chance we got. I was happy. Like actually happy.

I reached the main entrance and glanced over my shoulder. Aunt Cass was still sitting there gazing out the windshield, like she was frozen or something. She looked kind of lost and hopeless. A horn beeped behind her and she jolted, glancing back before accelerating away from the curb like she was in a police chase.

She really was weird sometimes.

Maybe I shouldn't have told her I loved her, but I kind of did. The longer I lived with her, the more I thought maybe we could make this work. She was an uptight freak, but there was definitely some sunshine in there. When she smiled without thinking, she looked just like Mom. I didn't know why she stayed so closed off to everything or what she was so afraid of. I hoped she could figure it out. Because my mom was the most beautiful person ever...and maybe Aunt Cass could be too.

An image of my mother dancing in our tiny living room came to me, flooding my mind and making me hum "Let The Sunshine In." She used to love that song. Her face would practically glow when she sang it, swaying around the room like a hippie from the sixties.

I smiled. I guessed Aunt Cass wasn't the only

weirdo in the family. My smile turned into a soft laugh as I strolled to the music room to drop off my guitar.

TWENTY-EIGHT

TROY

I pushed my office door open and headed straight for the blinds. The day was beautiful and I wanted to let in as much sunlight as possible. Pulling them up, I secured the tie then dumped my bag at the foot of my desk. My calendar was pretty full for the day, but my first appointment didn't start until nine thirty, which meant I had about forty minutes to catch up on emails.

I was definitely behind. I'd been finding it harder to focus on work lately. My mind kept on getting overrun with Cassie. I made excuses to pop by her place to "check on Felix." My plan worked.

I'd been invited over for a few meals, and every time I hung out there, it felt like the most natural thing in the world. I'd subtly probed Cassie about her running and knew her favorite routes. It was kind of stalker-ish, but I'd ended up getting lucky and bumping into her a couple of times and we'd jog together, poor Jovi struggling to keep up. He'd collapse the second we arrived home.

It was weird. I'd never felt like this about a girl before, especially one who was so cautious and closed off. I mean, I could tell she liked hanging out with me. Her smile was a little more open and she seemed to laugh more easily, but was that because of Felix or me? I guessed the reason didn't really matter. Cassie was unfurling like a bloom in spring. It was beautiful and making it impossible not to feel something more than friendly affection.

I still needed to try to break through her barrier. If I could just get her talking, make her feel safe enough to open up and get out some of the things that plagued her, I knew I could help set her free. And I wasn't giving up until I had. Even though Felix was getting close to signing off—his grades were up, he was happy at school, we were making progress in his counseling sessions—I wasn't ready to let them go. I wanted to be firmly in the friend— and possibly more—zone before I had to allocate his case time to another kid who needed me more.

Raking a hand through my hair, I thumped into my seat and started up my computer.

The screen had only just come to life when there was an urgent knocking on my door.

I jumped up, immediately switching into problem-solving mode before even opening the door.

My heart lurched into my throat when I spotted Cassie. Her face was pale, her eyes rimmed red, and the second we made eye contact, she burst into tears. I ushered her in and quickly shut the door. Guiding her to the couch, I grabbed the box of tissues and set them in front of her before taking the adjacent seat and leaning in to listen.

She'd loosened up a little on the whole touching thing, and I could get away with a shoulder squeeze and elbow pat, but in that moment, it seemed wise to give her some space. I'd never seen her cry this big, and I had a feeling that something massive was breaking free. Some ugly truth from her past was going to come out in my office.

As much as I hated seeing her upset, I couldn't help hoping this was the cathartic moment she needed. I braced myself and waited for her to open up.

She pulled in a shuddering breath, swiping at her tears and snatching a tissue out of the box. "I'm not good enough." She hiccupped and dabbed at her cheeks. "Felix deserves so much more than I can give him."

"Okay." I threaded my fingers together, resisting the urge to lurch forward and wrap her in a hug. "What's triggering this? Did you and Felix have a fight this morning?"

"No." She flicked her hands up, then covered her face.

I gave her another minute to whimper and whine. It was killing me. I wanted to hold her, make it all go away, but I just had to sit there, because she needed to do this.

A couple more quivering breaths punched out of her before she found the control to murmur, "He told me he loved me. Said it just before he got out of the car this morning."

Okay. Unexpected that something so sweet could throw her. The inklings I'd been fighting since meeting Cassie started to stir, making me queasy. Did I really want to hear what she had to tell me? A woman afraid of the words "I love you" could mean a whole heap of things, and they weren't good.

But she had to do this.

I gritted my teeth and reminded myself to speak slow and easy. "And that's a problem because…"

"I can't say it back!" She looked at me, her eyes wide and vibrant. "I haven't said those words since…" She started blinking and swallowed, her skin draining of the little color she had left. She looked grey, sick with fear and self-loathing.

Oh, shit. No, I didn't want to hear this.

Her jaw worked to the side. "I don't understand. I…"

She sniffed, then whimpered. The pitiful sound tore large chunks out of me, only increasing that sick sense of foreboding.

"Just take your time." I swallowed. "You're safe here, Cassie. You can say anything in this space and nothing bad is going to happen to you."

Her body shook, and she started so softly I had to strain to hear her.

"I'm guessing you know Crystal and I were in the system."

I nodded.

She stared at me for a moment, obviously trying to figure out how much I knew.

I gave her a soft smile. "There's a little information about Crystal in Felix's file, but it only says she ran away from foster care at the age of fourteen. I don't know why."

Cassie shuddered. "Thank you for not..." Her face crumpled. "Looking into it."

I shrugged. "Crystal wanted you to raise her son. You've never given me a reason to do a background check. You're a wonderful caregiver for Felix."

She shook her head. "I want to be, but..."

"But what, Cassie?" My voice was barely above a whisper. I didn't want to ask, but I had to know. She had to get it out if she was going to move forward. It almost didn't matter that unearthing whatever this ugly truth was would hurt like hell.

"Mindy and Davis McCoy." Cassie sniffed. "They were our foster parents for a few years. At first it wasn't so bad, but then..." Her lips wobbled.

It was basically impossible to ask. But when she went quiet, I had to choke out the question. "Did he abuse you?"

Her expression puckered. "Crystal was twelve when he started sneaking into our room at night."

I closed my eyes, rage and repulsion warring for

top place within me.

"He used to make her say it. Every time he came in, he'd make her whisper 'I love you, Davis' before he started touching her. Sick bastard!" she spat. "Like those three words could somehow clean his filthy conscience." Her expression washed with a look of rage and despair that made my stomach clench. I already knew what was coming, and I didn't know if I'd have the strength to hear it. "The first time it happened, I just… I couldn't believe it, you know. It was like a bad dream, and I kept on trying to wake up, but I couldn't. Crystal was so scared. She knew why he was in there. He got into bed with her and then started whispering, telling her to say it. She wouldn't at first. She was too terrified to say anything, but he got mad and punched her, so she did what he wanted." Cassie swallowed. "And then he raped her. She whimpered and cried the whole time. I should have got up to help her, but I was so afraid that I was next. All I could do was lie there, hiding under the covers."

She started to cry again, her entire body shaking. I wanted to tell her to stop, but I couldn't help wondering if this was the first time she'd ever laid it bare, and I had to let her do it.

My throat was so thick I didn't know how I croaked out my next question. "Do you feel guilty?"

Cassie shrugged. "Some days, but then logic reminds me that I'd just turned eight and I wouldn't have been strong enough to stop him."

Her lips flat-lined, her voice cold and robotic. "She left me with him. Maybe that was my punishment. I spent two years doing nothing to help her and so she abandoned me. Left me alone with the beast."

My eyes were burning. I wanted to find that fucker and kill him.

And how could Crystal just leave her there? I never would have left Jimmy alone in a situation like that.

Anger was making it hard to speak, but I had to ask. "Did he…touch you too?"

She swallowed. The sound was loud in my quiet office. "I wouldn't tell him I loved him. He wasn't getting those words from me." Bitterness gave her voice a hard, unrecognizable edge.

"So what did he do?"

She stiffened, her nostrils flaring as she looked to the floor.

"He beat me." Her voice turned clipped and matter-of-fact. "I'd stay down in the cellar until my bruises healed. Finally I'd be allowed back up…and he'd try again. And so it went for nearly two years. But I wouldn't give in. I didn't care how much those fists hurt. Those words were the only thing I could control." Her chest heaved, a sob suddenly bursting out of her. Covering her mouth with quivering fingers, she met my gaze, showing me a piece of her soul. "And now I can't say them at all! I don't understand how someone who got raped every time she uttered those words could ever say them to anyone again. And then I, who got beaten up for *not* saying them, can't! How am I supposed to love this kid when I don't even know what love is? My mother died when I was six, and then the only person I really cared about left me in the hands of a monster. Felix needs someone who can give him all the things he deserves, and I don't think it's me."

I dropped to my knees in front of her, gently taking her hands and holding them to my chest. "It *is* you, and you know how I know?"

She shook her head, her eyes glistening with despair.

I reached for her face, brushing the tears with my thumb and making my voice as tender as I could. It wasn't hard. I was falling in love with this woman. All I wanted to do was cradle her against me, protect her, save her from the pain.

"I know it's you because you're sitting here crying about how to care for this kid. Love has a thousand faces, Cassie. Your actions over the last few months have made him feel safe enough to tell you that he loves you. That's huge."

She sniffed, her chest shuddering as she tried to calm her breathing.

"You're safe now. When you tell Felix you love him, no one's going to hurt you. Nothing bad will come from it."

Her lips quivered. "I know that in my head, and I wanted to say it this morning, but I just couldn't unearth the words."

"One day you will." I smiled at her, hoping she'd see my conviction. "Talking about this today, as hard as it was, helped you. It's just one more step away from that pain. One step closer to becoming whoever you want to be and being able to say whatever you need to say."

Leaning her face into my hand, she gave me one more glimpse of her heart. It was bright and beautiful. I was almost too scared to believe what I saw, but I couldn't deny it. I wasn't the only one falling. I wanted to kiss her so bad, to do something with the emotions swirling between us.

But she was way too vulnerable in that moment. I couldn't...could I?

Searching her face, I held my breath. Time stood still while I waited but then I felt the shift. It was small and possibly missable, but she leaned forward and I couldn't hold back.

I gently pressed my lips to hers. She flinched at first but then went still, not pulling away, not pushing forward. Her lips were soft. They tasted like orange gloss and salty tears.

She didn't open her mouth. She simply leaned into me, resting her hand lightly on my shoulder and applying her own, hesitant pressure. I smiled against her lips, savoring how epic the moment was. I was kissing Cassie...and she was kissing back.

It was sweet and perfect. A moment filled with hope and possibility.

TWENTY-NINE

CASSIE

I was kissing Troy. My first kiss ever. I expected it to be terrifying, disgusting, intrusive…but it was none of those things. Troy's lips were soft and undemanding, gentle and sweet. He didn't try to shove his tongue in my mouth or take without asking. He just pressed his lips to mine and waited. I rested my hand on his shoulder, resisting the urge to curl my fingers into his shirt. My insides were going crazy. I was kissing a man…and not just any man.

I was kissing Troy Baker—the kindest person I knew. The man I was quite possibly falling in love with.

Horrifying. I never thought I could ever feel something like that, but it was happening and I couldn't stop it. I didn't even want to.

The thought made me pull away. Troy brushed the pads of his fingers down my cheek. Soft and gentle. His breath tickled my chin as he searched my eyes. I couldn't say anything; my voice had been shocked into hiding. The tidal wave of emotions coursing through me had shut down every sense but touch and sight.

He was so incredibly beautiful. So near. So open.

His perfect lips curved into a smile, his eyes glimmering with affection.

There was nothing greedy or evil about him. I could trust this man. I already knew that, but...could I trust him with more? Between him and Felix, every barrier within me was starting to tremble and fall. It made me vulnerable, weak. I expected that feeling to make me want to sprint, but I just sat there, gazing at his smile...unable to move.

A soft knock on the door jolted us both. I fisted Troy's shirt without meaning to, breaths punching out of me.

"It's okay." He chuckled, uncurling my fingers and kissing my hand. His smile was a touch pained as he called out, "Just a minute." Brushing my cheek with the back of his knuckles, he winced. "My nine thirty's here. I—"

"That's okay." I cut him off, standing tall and smoothing down my skirt, quickly taking back any control the kiss may have taken from me. Lightly brushing my lower lip, I had to fight a smile at the buzz firing through my body. I wanted to kiss him again.

Curling my fingers into a fist, I cut the thought from my mind and snatched my bag off the floor.

"I hate the idea of you just suddenly having to leave like this." Troy reached for my hand.

I nearly tucked it in my pocket, but that would have hurt his feelings. I let him take my hand and rub his thumb over my skin. His touch was so confident, his hands large and strong. They could do so much damage, but they wouldn't, because he wasn't Davis McCoy. I could let go at any moment and he wouldn't get mad. I still had control. I was safe.

He didn't know the whole truth though.

I'd never give him that. I saw his face when I told him Crystal had been raped by that monster. How could he possibly love me if he knew I'd suffered the same fate?

I reminded myself yet again that *the night never happened*. That was one door I wasn't opening…one step I'd never take. I could become who I needed to be without unleashing that ugliness on anybody.

I'd given Troy enough of my past.

I forced my eyes up to his face, hoping I was right.

His smile faltered, a nervous flush working across his skin. "Do you want to go out to dinner sometime? We could talk some more."

"Uh…" I swallowed. "I'm not sure if I'm up for

more talking...like that. It's kind of exhausting."

He looked disappointed for a second but then shrugged and grinned. "Okay, well, how about we just go have some fun?"

I hesitated for a second. "You-you mean, like a date?"

He chuckled, his eyes narrowing a little as he studied me. "We don't have to call it that. Why don't we just say a dinner for two, and you can dictate how it goes. Whatever you want to do." He winked. "I won't even kiss ya goodnight, if you don't want me to."

I couldn't help a nervous titter. His smile could unravel me in a heartbeat.

Smoothing a hand over my hair, I tried not to sound too nervous as the last words I expected popped out of my mouth. "Okay. Yeah, we could..." I bobbed my head then breathed, "Okay."

Why was I saying yes?

Because I wanted to go out and have some fun...with a guy. Something I'd never really done.

"All right then." Troy guided me to the door with a hand on my lower back. Damn, it felt good.

I paused at the door and glanced over my shoulder. He was towering behind me, tall and protective. I could get used to that. I gave him a tentative smile. "So, I'll..."

His grin was wide and sweet. "I'll text you this afternoon. We'll work out a time."

"Okay." My voice had gotten kind of breathy in the last hour. Was it the gut-wrenching sobbing or the fact I'd had my first kiss?

"See ya soon, Cass." His husky voice touched me right at the core, and I didn't need to ask myself any more questions.

I'd shown Troy a piece of my wretched soul and he'd kissed me for it. I was breathy because of him and him alone.

THIRTY

FELIX

I knew Aunt Cass was uptight, but she was off the charts as she got ready to go out with Troy. She'd spent the day frenetically cleaning. I helped out by tidying my bedroom enough so that she could vacuum the rug and wash the floors. The house sparkled, and I was almost afraid to touch anything. She'd quadruple-checked I'd be okay, told me over and over that she wouldn't be late, laid out food for me, made sure I was all set with her cell phone number.

"Nothin' But A Good Time" pumped from the stereo in the living room. I tapped my foot to the beat and tried to strum along with the guitar. It was a little hard to keep up, but I *would* get it. I wanted to show Summer on Monday.

"Don't need nothin'…" I mumbled along with the chorus, loving the song. As the second verse kicked in, I grinned and shuffled around the living room, acting like a rock star. The specks on the wooden floor became a screaming crowd. I banged my head, pretending I was dressed in smokin' hot leather and the girls were drooling over me.

The guitar solo began and I got totally lost, my fingers feeling clunky and slow on the strings. Damn, I had some work to do.

I rewound the music back to the solo and listened to it more carefully, focusing on the notes and chords. I then stopped it and went through it again slowly, reworking the pattern until it didn't sound so bad.

A sharp tapping sound rushed down the hall, and I glanced over my shoulder as Aunt Cassie walked into the room. She wrung her hands, then smoothed down her purple dress.

"Do I look okay?"

"Yeah, sure." I nodded, smiling at her in the hopes of wiping the jitters away. She'd be a wreck before Troy even got her out the door.

I thought it was kind of cute that he was taking her out on a date. Aunt Cass kept saying it was just them hanging out for dinner, but she couldn't fool me.

"The heels don't work, right? I mean, I can't even walk in heels, so why am I wearing heels!"

Her voice got kind of high and screechy, which made me laugh. I couldn't help it.

She let out this weird kind of whine that turned into a screamy thing before she spun and wobbled back to her room.

Placing my guitar on the couch, I quietly walked after her. Her door was wide open, her heels kicked off on the floor.

"I don't think I can do this," she muttered to herself.

I cleared my throat and shuffled in. "Why don't you wear those flat shoes you like? You know, the black ones."

"I just thought they might be too boring. I mean, I'm gonna be standing next to Troy."

"So?" I shrugged, digging my hands into my pockets.

"So, he's gorgeous and I'm just… I'm…"

"Pretty?"

"No!" She flicked her hands up. "I'm plain." Her shoulders slumped and she closed her eyes. "I've only gone on one other date in my life, and it was a total disaster. I'm so nervous. I hate feeling like this."

"Everybody does." I smiled, trying to make her feel better. "Look, don't stress. You're gonna be great. The dress is really nice. Let your hair down, put some sparkly earrings in, and you'll look amazing. He won't even notice your shoes."

She glanced up at me, her expression forming a mushy smile that reminded me of Mom.

I looked to the floor and scratched the back of

my neck, not wanting to admit just how much her smile warmed me.

"You really think sparkly earrings will do the trick?"

"For sure." I nodded. "Mom always said that you can never have too much sparkle in this world."

"Really?" Aunt Cass's lips were toying with a grin, I could tell.

I nodded. "Yep. She was convinced sparkles could make people smile."

She grinned.

"Actually, she was convinced a lot of things could make people smile, but sparkles were one of them." I snickered, remembering my mother's conviction. She made it impossible not to adore her.

An unexpected sadness swept through me, stealing my joy for a moment. Man, I missed her so much.

Aunt Cassie cleared her throat and stepped to her dresser. "Well, maybe you could help me pick something."

I could see she was trying to distract me, and I didn't mind so much. We picked through the jewelry box and unearthed some sparkly earrings that kind of dangled. I then had to convince her to pull her hair tie free. Finally, with shaking hands, she let her hair down, brushing her fingers through the long locks and curling one of them around her pinky.

I grinned. "You look cool. I like your hair down."

"Really?" She glanced in the mirror, her expression doubtful. "Why?"

"Believe it or not, you look more relaxed…like you don't have a stick up your butt."

She gasped, rounding her eyes at me.

I laughed. "Sorry, but it's kind of true."

It was pretty funny, watching her stand there, not sure what to say. I think she wanted to tell me off but couldn't quite bring herself to do it.

That only made me laugh harder.

Eventually she rolled her eyes and gave me a gentle nudge with her elbow.

I wanted to tell her I loved her again, smooth things over, but after what happened last time I said it, I wasn't sure I should.

Instead, I smiled at her and hoped it was enough.

She went still, staring at me as a slow grin formed on her lips. "You sure you're going to be okay tonight?"

I groaned. "Would you stop asking? I'm gonna be fine." I walked to the living room and she followed me, so I talked over my shoulder. "I've got food, drink, music, books. I don't need anything else."

"You're welcome to watch a movie."

I shrugged, not really that interested. Heading for my guitar, Aunt Cass stopped me with her hand on my shoulder. Spinning me around, she smiled and said, "I don't know much about kids still, but I get this sense that you're not the average kind."

With a frown, I shook my head, not sure what she was trying to say to me.

Her snicker was light and playful as she pulled me into a tentative hug. "I think it's the coolest thing in the world. I wouldn't want you any other way."

Again my body flooded with warmth, the familiar kind I used to feel when I hung out with Mom. I squeezed back and rubbed Aunt Cassie's shoulder, then pulled away when the doorbell rang.

Aunt Cass stopped breathing, so I rubbed her arm and reminded her she was gonna be great. I answered the door for her.

Troy stood on the porch, tall and cool in his standard leather jacket and jean combo. "Hey, Felix. How's it going, man?"

I grinned, punching his fist before stepping back so he could check out his *not-a-date*.

He caught a glimpse of her and breathed out one simple word. "Wow."

I thought Aunt Cass was going to melt right into the floor. Her cheeks flared with color, and she didn't need those sparkly earrings anymore—her smile was enough to light a city.

Standing by the door, I took it all in, trying not to laugh out loud as I watched them say hi to each other and then leave on their *not-a-date*.

Yeah, right.

Closing the door, I locked it and called out, "I'm in, now go out. Have fun. Sparkle!"

Aunt Cassie laughed and I ran for my guitar,

slumping onto the couch with a whoop before grabbing the remote and cranking up "Nothin' But A Good Time" again.

It was gonna be a good night.

THIRTY-ONE

TROY

Cassie looked amazing. Her hair was down, which I'd never seen before. It was beautiful with a slight wave that curled around her shoulders. Her purple dress was simple and modest but fitted her slim figure perfectly. I couldn't help a touch of pride as I walked down the street beside her. I was with the prettiest girl on the block, and I couldn't stop smiling.

I took her to a hipster diner near Griffin Park. She had the grilled chicken while I wolfed down a plate of pasta. It was so good. We skipped dessert and decided to stroll the street instead, checking out the shops. Cassie seemed in a good mood, so I kept the conversation light and fun. I was smart enough to know she had more talking to do. But the snippets of her dark past she told me in my office had obviously released something. She seemed lighter already.

Part of me knew I had to push for more, but I just wanted to enjoy the night. I wanted to pretend like there wasn't more.

But I knew better.

One tear-fest over such darkness was usually not enough to set someone completely free.

After Cassie left my office, I spent the rest of my day trying to focus on other patients and cases, but I was haunted by visions of an evil man sneaking into Cassie's room and abusing her. She must have only been ten or eleven when he beat her like that. Then locking her in a cellar? I wanted to kill him. What kind of sick asshole raped a kid, forced her to tell him that she loved him. It was twisted and sick. The fact he never broke Cassie showed her true strength. At such a young age being beaten and locked in a cellar. I wanted to cry for her.

I hadn't been sleeping well since finding out, but I was determined to hide it. Cassie was a survivor, and since Felix had come into her life, she was learning how to open up and actually live. I wanted to keep fueling that, give her every good thing, show her that not all men were evil. I wanted to prove I could give her the love she deserved.

"What's this place?" Cassie veered off the sidewalk and into a secondhand book and music store.

I jumped forward and opened the door for her. She gave me a blushing smile and slipped inside. The soft music hit me first, "Heaven" by Warrant. Yes, classic. I loved the place immediately.

Lightly touching Cassie's back, I led her down the aisle of CDs. The walls were covered with posters of '80s rock bands—Kiss, Scorpion, Poison, Twisted Sister, Bon Jovi. I grinned at the big hair and bandanas. Epic. I couldn't believe I hadn't found the place sooner.

The owner caught my eye and I grinned at him. "Great place."

"Thanks." He raised his eyebrows. "There's a stereo over there if you want to play anything."

I followed his pudgy finger and spotted the sound system. "Thanks, man."

Cassie had stopped and was flipping through a few discs. "I wonder if there's anything in here Felix doesn't have yet. Maybe I could buy him something."

"I'm sure he'd love that." I leaned over her shoulder, loving how close she was letting me. She didn't shy away when I slung my arm around her. I kept reminding myself to keep it casual and light.

She grinned, pulling out Def Leppard's *Rock of Ages*. "A little surprise?"

"I'm pretty sure he's already got that one."

Her frown was cute, pulling her eyebrows together. "You're right. His collection's so big. I probably won't find anything he doesn't already have."

"You know, if you're looking to surprise him, I've actually got the perfect idea. I meant to run it by you earlier this week but I forgot."

She turned to gaze up at me, her eyes wide with curiosity.

"Jimmy said if I ever wanted to bring Felix along to one of his practices, he'd—"

Cassie's gasp cut me off. "Really? Oh my gosh, that would be amazing. He'd love that!"

I chuckled and took a risk, squeezing her into a light hug. I couldn't help it. She looked way too cute not to cuddle. She didn't fight me, and when I pulled back she was still grinning.

It felt like a massive win.

"Okay, well, I'll set it up."

"We're free tomorrow." Cassie's nose wrinkled. "That's probably too short notice, right?"

"No, I think we can make that work." I pulled the phone from my back pocket and texted my brother while Cassie went back to flipping through CDs. Glancing around the shop, I spotted the rows of bookshelves and figured we'd probably be here a while. I didn't mind. Hanging out with Cassie in her happy place was just what the doctor ordered. She needed this—joy, smiles, normalcy.

A rage-filled sadness swept through me again as I pictured her curled up on a cellar floor, cold and aching from the bruises on her body. I clenched my jaw and blinked, trying to hide how vivid the images in my head were, how much they hurt me.

I wanted to know how she got away from the guy, but I didn't want to bring him into our evening. That conversation could come up later, once she trusted me enough to let it all out. The fact she'd given me what she had was huge, and I needed to keep building that sense of safety.

As if reading my mind, the next song kicked in. "I'll Be There For You"—Bon Jovi at his best. Perfect. I hovered close to Cassie, watching her out of the corner of my eye while I started mouthing the words. She didn't notice me at first, but then as the song grew more intense, I put in a little more effort and started hamming it up, throwing my all into mouthing the lyrics.

She did a double take but then couldn't fight her grin, a soft laugh popping between her lips as I stretched my arms wide on the chorus. Closing my eyes, I started into the second verse, over-exaggerating the words and pretending I was a rock star from the eighties.

Cassie's laughter grew, and when I opened my eyes her smile was so beautiful I nearly lost my place. Pulling it together, I put my all into the final bridge and chorus, finishing the song with a flourish.

She was still laughing, but she threw in a soft clap and cheer when I took a bow. Standing tall, I stepped right into her space, lightly brushing my fingers down her cheek and whispering, "I will be there for you. No matter what."

Her smile fled, her eyes filling with tears. I leaned forward and pressed my lips to hers before any of them could fall.

And then the music played another romance

card. Before the intro for "Can't Fight This Feeling" had even finished, I placed my arm around Cassie's waist and started swaying to the music. She let out a nervous giggle, then looked over her shoulder at the owner. He was absorbed in a magazine, and it gave her the confidence to turn back and look up at me.

I started mouthing the words to the chorus, and very slowly her hands trailed up my arms. She looked kind of scared, so I winked at her and gave her my best smile.

She responded with a sweet blush and linked her fingers behind my back, finally starting to sway with me.

It was another win, and I couldn't deny that in that moment I felt happier than I ever had. Winding my arms a little tighter around her waist, I pulled her against me. She rested her chin on my shoulder, splaying her hand on my back and holding me like she never wanted to let go.

I was cool with that, because I could see myself holding this woman for the rest of my life.

THIRTY-TWO

FELIX

I was gonna pee my pants. I swear, I was so excited, I was gonna pee my pants.

When Aunt Cass got back from her date with Troy, she floated in the door. I was still working on my guitar solo. I made her listen to it before she could say anything, and when I was done, she clapped then told me the news.

I was invited to a Chaos practice.

A Chaos practice!

I couldn't believe it.

My knee bobbed in the back of Troy's wagon as we wound down a quiet street and stopped outside a sliding gate.

The Chaos mansion. Holy shit!

Troy pressed the intercom. The buzz was loud, and my stomach jumped with butterflies.

"Yo."

"Hey, Flick. It's Troy."

"You may enter."

Troy snickered and rolled his eyes, resting his wrist on the wheel while the gate ground open.

"How'd you know who it was?" Aunt Cass murmured.

"Flick's the only one who'd answer with a yo. He likes to use as few words as possible whenever he can."

Aunt Cass glanced over her shoulder to check on me. "You good?"

I nodded. My head felt like it was being held up by a wet sponge. I was about to meet rock stars.

Troy drove up the driveway, curving around the massive white house and parking next to a row of vehicles. A wide open lawn, green and lush, stretched between the main house and a smaller guest house.

Music was already blasting from the small white building. I slammed the car door closed with a grin, resisting the urge to run down the path and check it out.

"Don't forget the guitar." Aunt Cass smiled at me.

I bit my lip, my face scrunching with doubt. I wasn't good enough to play with those guys.

"Maybe I should leave it in the car." I scratched

the back of my neck.

"Not happening." Troy laughed and grabbed the guitar out for me. He passed it over, and I made him wait three long beats before I found the courage to take it. "You're awesome. Never forget that." He looked me straight in the eye, willing me to believe every word.

I thought of Mom and the way she always said we were lucky. As I trailed Troy and Aunt Cass down the path, I had to agree. I could have been living with a foster family who could take or leave me, but I'd ended up with an aunt who cared enough to make this happen.

I was lucky. I was the luckiest guy in the world.

The thought helped me relax, and when I walked in the door and caught sight of Jimmy strumming and singing into the mic, I couldn't help a goofy grin.

He had his back to us and was playing "Hey Leonardo" to Nessa, who was on the drums. She had a hook attached to her arm, and I couldn't take my eyes off it. She played like a pro, keeping time and crashing the cymbals. She was so good.

Neither of them had noticed us yet. They were obviously messing around while they waited for the rest of the band to show up.

Nessa was smiling at Jimmy with stars in her eyes. She looked totally in love and it made me blush. I couldn't imagine a girl ever looking at me that way.

Troy stepped down into the room and Jimmy glanced over his shoulder, doing a double take and bringing the song to a quick finish. He turned to face us with a huge smile.

"Hey, man. How's it going?" He greeted Troy with an eyebrow raise, then looked past Aunt Cassie to me. His eyes narrowed slightly when he saw the guitar case in my hand. It made me want to squirm, but then his face broke into a grin that told me I was all right.

I swallowed and inched a little closer to the practice area.

Nessa was out of her seat and bounding around the instruments to give Troy a hug. He lifted her off her feet and kissed her cheek.

"Meet my friends, Cassie and Felix."

"Hi." Nessa's smile was pretty. Damn, she was way hotter close up.

My palms were no doubt sweating when I shook her hand. I hoped she didn't notice.

"So." She crossed her arms and gazed at me. "You're the genius guitar player."

"What? No, I'm not..." I shook my head and had to clear my throat to be able to keep talking. "I'm still learning."

"Troy told me you were kick-ass." She tipped her head at him, then poked her tongue out the side of her mouth. "You want to show me what you can do?"

"Uh..." I looked at Jimmy, who was smirking at me. His forearm was resting on his guitar. He was so natural, casual...just like I wanted to be.

My eyes then flicked to Aunt Cass. She gave me an encouraging smile and mouthed, "You can do it."

I cleared my throat...again! The room felt hotter than it did before.

"Come on, man. Give us a song and we'll have a jam." Jimmy raised his eyebrows.

Footsteps entered behind me, and I spun to spot Ralphie and some girl I didn't recognize. Her smile was sweet and friendly.

"Hi." She waved her fingers. "I'm Ronnie. Nessa's sister."

"And my girl." Ralphie wrapped his arm around her shoulders and kissed her forehead before loping over to me. "You must be Felix, right? Welcome to band practice."

"Um, thanks." I licked my bottom lip and tried for a smile. I must have looked like such an idiot.

"So, you wanna unlock that bad boy and play a little something while we wait for Flick and Jace?" Jimmy asked me again. If I didn't do something soon, I was going to win the World's Biggest Moron award.

I forced my head to bob and quickly laid the guitar case down on the kitchen counter, ensuring I took extra care when taking it out. I wanted Jimmy to know I wouldn't do anything to hurt his guitar. Flipping the strap over my shoulder, I started to tune it. My fingers were trembling as I adjusted the pegs. Ralphie tuned up with me, easing my nerves and encouraging me to move a little closer.

Nessa's sister took a seat on the couch, waving her hand for Aunt Cass to join her. My aunt shuffled over, looking about as nervous as me.

Gripping the neck of the guitar, I inched into the practice circle. Nessa was back on the drums and eyeing me expectantly.

"So, what do you want to play?"

"Uh…" I scratched the back of my neck. "Do you guys know 'Black Betty'?"

Nessa's face lit like a Christmas tree and she let out a whoop. "The boy's a rocker!"

She started thumping the bass pedal and brought me in with a quick beat. I came in on time, strumming the right chords. As the song quickly built, Jimmy joined me, adding in the more fiddly complicated bits. I couldn't stop grinning as I played with them…and then Jimmy started singing.

I swear, I entered heaven.

Jimmy's fingers on the strings were magic to watch. And I loved the way Ralphie bobbed his head and hit the fat bass strings. It made me wish Summer was with me. She'd be drooling.

Nessa couldn't stop smiling as she played the drums. She actually started laughing when the fast part started. She and Jimmy rocked out, and I lost my place, too in awe of their talent to do anything but stand there gaping.

I wanted to be just like that. Part of a group where they were so in sync they could play whatever, whenever. I could tell by the way they interacted that these guys were family.

Nessa finished off the song with a short solo then threw her stick in the air, catching it again before slamming it on the cymbals.

Troy whistled and Cassie clapped. Ronnie let out a cheer, and all I could do was stand there grinning.

THIRTY-THREE

CASSIE

I'd never seen Felix so happy. He practically floated out of the practice when it was done. A guy called Flick had shown up during "Black Betty" and stood there looking impressed. Too bad my nephew stopped playing halfway through the song. But the awe on his face... I wish I could have captured it. I kicked myself for not taking a photo. I'd never had to be that person before, the one who pulled out her camera to capture memories. I didn't have any memories worth capturing. But now I did. And I needed to start cherishing them.

Getting Felix off to school the next day was a

breeze. Since starting guitar lessons, he seemed happier to go, but I was pretty sure he spent lunchtimes hiding from those bullies who tried to take him down his first week. A hot rage still whistled through me every time I thought about them. I was secretly glad Felix had pummeled that kid. He deserved exactly what he'd gotten. Relief that Felix was strong and feisty enough to stand up for himself was an understatement. I never wanted him to be terrorized the way I'd been. The thought of something like that happening to him made my stomach surge with bile.

But I didn't have to worry. Felix was a fighter and I hoped he always would be. When I dropped him off that morning, he practically skipped into school. He said he couldn't wait to tell his class what he'd done over the weekend.

"I've met Chaos in person! I've played with them! I'm going to be cool now."

"You're cool already," I reassured him.

Jimmy's precious guitar would no doubt be on full display, and I couldn't wait to hear about it after school.

Traffic was lighter than usual, probably because Felix got ready so much faster than normal. He couldn't wait to get out the door. I ended up being a couple of minutes early to work, and rather than rushing in and getting started, I decided to sit back and read a few more pages of Crystal's diary. I'd been working through it over the past few weeks. Just a few pages every now and then. Some entries were pretty heartbreaking, and I had to be in a good headspace in order to cope with them.

Crystal wrestled with some pretty dark demons. She was haunted by groping hands, violation, and pain. She felt dirty, unworthy, like she was somehow to blame for what he did to her. Logically, I think she understood that she wasn't, but a broken soul can be more powerful than logic. It can wipe all common sense from the mind.

Pulling out the worn book, I found my place and smoothed the page back. Every now and then I'd read a passage that made me warm, like the entry about her naming Felix after the cartoon cat we both adored. She said the name reminded her of me. I, of course, bawled my eyes out over that one, but they were tears of sentiment, not pain.

I steeled myself, deciding that no matter what I read, I would not cry. As I sat in the car that morning, I was going to read something that would uplift and motivate me.

"Help me out, Crys," I muttered.

Felix is perfect. He is sweet and beautiful.

He's only been in this world three months and he's making me a believer.

Art tells me every day when he visits that I'm a wonderful mother. He tells me God loves me and that I have everything I need to raise this boy.

It's hard to believe him sometimes, but I've just watched my son fall asleep in my arms. He's soft and perfect, with his round cheeks and delicate eyelashes. The way he smells. Everything about him is so innocent, so trusting. Everything about him is pure and good.

Is this what love is supposed to look like? Memories of Mom grow stronger each day and I think I'm right. Love is supposed to be like this.

I will protect this baby with my life. He will never know darkness like I have. He will never have to question his worth.

So...if I'm constantly questioning mine...what will that teach him?

I need to be strong. I need to make him believe that life can be wonderful. But I'm scared that I don't know how.

His sweet, sleepy murmurings are keeping me company as I write this.

I'm safe right now, in this little apartment. No door will creak in the night. No one is going to make me do something I don't want to. Felix is safe from harm.

So...maybe I have to admit that Art is right. Stars do shine in the darkness and the ocean after a storm is calm and peaceful.

The darkness inside me is so strong though. I don't know how I'll beat it. Will he haunt me forever?

I feel like I've made it through the storm, but will I ever find peace?

Can I teach Felix how lucky we are?

Can I be strong enough?

Will I ever be clean enough?

Tears lined my lashes. I squeezed my eyes shut, and the tears trickled down my cheeks. I shouldn't have read another passage just before work.

Swiping the tears away, I sniffed and pulled myself together, shoving the diary back into my bag.

I understood every one of her fears. I understood why she ran.

Crystal broke out to give Felix a chance, and that boy helped her believe in beauty again. He unearthed all that was buried by Davis's brutality.

He was doing the same for me, cracking me open with his unguarded smiles and sweet sense of humor, his undying passion for music. He kept giving me reasons to smile...to laugh. He'd reawakened my love of music, forced me out of my shell so I could see the world properly again.

I had to wonder if it hadn't been for Felix whether I ever would have let Troy in.

I wouldn't even know Troy if Felix hadn't been dropped into my life.

I had so much to thank Crystal for. And as I sat in the car, preparing for a day of work, I realized that maybe I *had* forgiven her for leaving me.

A soft smile tugged at my lips as I gazed at nothing yet saw everything.

My insides were piled high with boulders, but between Felix, Troy, and Crystal I was learning to push them away, to discover who I could be. There were still a few rocks I wasn't willing to move—the darkness beneath them was too terrifying—but I felt lighter, and it made me wonder how far I could really go.

Life with Felix seemed to be getting easier. We'd made it through the storm, and maybe there was a chance to find peace.

My tears dried up completely as my smile grew.

Hope flittered inside me, making me want to giggle. It was a new, giddy feeling that could potentially be addictive. I wasn't used to such freedom, and although it scared me a little, it inspired me more.

THIRTY-FOUR

FELIX

I shouldn't have strutted into school, but I was in such a good mood I didn't really notice. I felt light and free. The guitar in my hand was like a gold medal and I was the champion. I couldn't wait to see their faces when I told them what I'd been doing.

I hoped Ginny would finally notice me. I smiled at her every day. Sometimes she smiled back, other days she ignored me, and every now and again she'd snicker.

Today she'd give me a full beam. I just knew it.

Walking into homeroom with confidence, I

paused at my desk, listening in on the conversation around me. I didn't usually bring Jimmy's guitar into class. I hadn't had the guts to tell anyone who it belonged to... but not anymore.

I glanced over my shoulder at the groups around me. Summer sat alone at the back. She raised her eyebrows at me, and I gave her a quick smile. She was totally cool with her weirdness and the fact no one wanted to hang out with her. I tried not to chat with her too much in class, but I'd never outright ignore her.

Her feet were up on her desk, crossed at the ankles. She wore her black combat boots, so different from Ginny, who stood at the front in skinny jeans and pink high-top Converse. I cleared my throat and approached.

My heart was racing big time, but I wouldn't let that stop me.

I'd spent the day before jamming with Chaos. I was the coolest guy in the entire room.

"Hey, Ginny." My voice cracked, which made her snicker. I nearly backed out then. I probably should have, but I didn't want to. I had the perfect opportunity to impress her.

She glanced at her giggling girlfriends before giving me a tight smile.

"I, um..." I pointed at the guitar on my desk. "I wanted to show you something."

"Oh, yeah?" She crossed her arms, her pale eyebrow arching.

Man, she was pretty.

I smiled and walked to my desk, flipping the

guitar case open and pulling out the Fender. I ran my hand lovingly over the strings. "I got this as a gift from Jimmy Baker."

"Jimmy Baker?" She looked doubtful. "You don't mean the Jimmy Baker from Chaos, do you?"

"Uh-huh." I smiled and nodded like an eager puppy. "His brother's a...friend of...mine." I shrugged. Close enough. Troy was my friend. "Anyway, he arranged for me to have one of Jimmy's old guitars, and then yesterday I got to go to a Chaos practice."

Ginny's eyebrows popped up in unison. The three girls behind her looked skeptical.

"No way," one of them muttered.

"I swear! We played 'Black Betty' together!"

"That's not one of their songs." Her other friend had taken the word scorn to a whole new level.

I scowled at her, then turned my attention to Ginny. "We were just messing around. They asked me what songs I'd been working on and I chose 'Black Betty' and we totally rocked out."

"I've never even heard of that song. Black what?"

"Black...Betty. Ram Jam? 1977?" I gazed past Ginny's shoulder and noticed that every eye in the class was suddenly on me. The only friendly pair belonged to Summer. Her eyes were wide with surprise and wonder. She knew exactly what I was talking about and she thought it was awesome.

I wanted the look on her face to be on Ginny's face. But it wasn't.

"Look, I really doubt Chaos would play some

241

freaky little song from the seventies. Your story's kind of lame." She looked down her nose at me, making me feel like some stupid jerk who was lying to impress her.

"It's not a story! It's the truth!"

"Yeah, right." Dickhead #1 stepped up to the plate, his top lip curling. "Stop being such a wise ass, Grayson. Like you've met Chaos."

"I did," I growled.

"Whatever. There's no way this is Jimmy Baker's guitar." He snatched it out of my hands.

"Hey! Give that back!" I lunged after it, but he spun away from me and leaped onto one of the desks, pretending to be a rock star. He banged his head and twanged the strings, being way too rough.

"Stop it!" I roared, jumping onto the desk beside him and trying to wrestle it out of his hands. He shoved me off him and I stumbled back, cracking my elbow and landing on my ass. It frickin' hurt but I was too horrified to feel a thing because, just as I stood up, Dickhead raised the guitar and smashed it down on the floor like an out-of-control rocker.

"No!"

But he kept going, smashing it down until the base ripped away from the neck and the only thing holding it together were a set of loose strings.

"You fucking asshole!" Summer screamed. She tore through the room, jumping on Dickhead's back and trying to stop him while I raced across to get in my own punch or two.

I didn't even make it. Mrs. Tindal walked in, and her holler put a quick stop to everything.

The room froze as she gaped wide-eyed at the scene. "What is going on in here?"

Summer slid off Dickhead's back and straightened her shirt while I dropped to my knees and picked up the broken guitar.

I wanted to cradle the thing and start blubbering like a baby. I was close. I could feel myself starting to let go, especially when Mrs. Tindal approached, her footsteps soft and even.

"Felix," she said quietly. "Do you want to tell me what happened?"

I sniffed and shook my head. "Doesn't matter. It's broken."

"Ryan smashed up Felix's guitar!" Summer snapped. "Stupid asshole has no respect for how much these things cost."

"Oh, don't you worry about that." Mrs. Tindal bored Dickhead with a look that made him shrink just a little. "I'm sure Mr. Parker has enough money to buy Felix a new one."

"I don't want a new one." I stood up, my voice sharp and loud. "This was Jimmy Baker's guitar. Nothing could ever replace it," I spat, turning a dark glare on Dickhead.

"That's...that's not true." He pointed at the broken instrument. "As if Jimmy Baker would give a guitar away to some—"

"That's enough!" Mrs. Tindal cut him off. "Now all three of you will accompany me to the principal's office where we can sort this out." She flicked her head and started walking for the door. I glanced over my shoulder at Summer. She gave me a sad smile and trailed behind me.

Ginny was at her desk, studying her nails and refusing to look up when I passed her.

THIRTY-FIVE

TROY

I couldn't stop humming to myself. Jovi pranced around my feet, his fat body swaying as I poured him some water and placed the bowl on the floor. He lapped it up—noisy and sloppy. I laughed and patted his rump before heading for the bathroom. I was sweating profusely after my jog. The weather was heating up, and a decent shower before heading to Hamilton Elementary was a necessity. I was due to do school visits for the rest of the day.

Stripping off my wet shirt, I dumped it in the hamper and was about to flick on the shower when my phone started ringing. I immediately thought of

Cassie. She'd been on my mind constantly, and I picked up the phone with a grin that only faltered when I spotted the caller.

Jane Tindal—Felix's homeroom teacher.

"Hey, Jane. How's it going?"

"Hi." Her voice was quiet, slightly sad, and it put me on high alert. "Is Felix okay?"

"Not really." She sighed. "He's in with the principal right now."

I winced. "What happened?"

She huffed and whisper-barked, "One of the idiot boys in my class broke his guitar. He was messing around and being a turd, and Felix is absolutely gutted. He said the guitar belongs to Jimmy. Is that true?"

My insides fired with hot anger, and it was an effort to grit out the words calmly. "Yeah, it's true. When I told Jimmy about him, he wanted to help out. Felix even got to go to a band practice yesterday. He was so happy."

"Aw," Jane sighed. "You're killing me. Why are kids so mean? That arrogant little shit has money to burn, and sweet Felix with his quiet smile and..." She let out a disgusted huff. "I can't believe I have to remain so impartial. Some kids are so hard to like and others are incredibly easy to love. It's impossible not to have favorites, but I teach them both!"

"Jane." I smiled. "I can hear your frustration."

"I'm just so mad on Felix's behalf. You should have seen his face, Troy. He looked ready to burst into tears. He's been through so much already and things have been picking up for him. He seemed happy, more settled...and now this happens."

"Don't worry. We're gonna give him every reason in the world to bounce back."

Jane softly laughed. "You're a good man. I'm glad you're in his life right now. He needs a father figure."

Her words hit me right in the chest. *Father figure. Is that how she sees me?*

Damn, that's exactly how I felt. The anger coursing through me, the hurt at what Felix was no doubt feeling as he sat in the principal's office. I wanted to march in there and make it all better. I wanted to be the father he never had. I wanted to take on the role again.

The thought surprised me a little. After raising Jimmy, I figured I'd never want to do it again, but what did you know...

"He doesn't know I'm calling you. He's so ashamed about the guitar getting damaged that he's too afraid to tell you, but I thought you should know."

"He's such a sweet kid," I murmured, the ache inside me only intensifying.

"I know, right?"

"He's not going to get in trouble for any of this, is he?"

"Definitely not. I may not have been standing in the room, but I heard the smashing, and I knew the second I walked in what had gone down. The only consequence Felix has to suffer from this is the broken guitar, and I'll be pushing to get a reimbursement for him."

"Thanks, Jane. This is why I wanted him in your class. He needs someone who's got his back."

"I'm doing my best to watch out for him."

"You're doing great. Thanks for everything."

She said a soft goodbye and as soon as I hung up, I dialed my kid brother. It felt weird to be calling him for help. It was usually the other way around. We went through a patch where the only time I ever talked to him was when he needed something.

I snickered and lifted the phone to my ear.

"Hey, broski," Jimmy answered after two rings.

"Little brother, I need your help."

Jimmy snickered. "Wow. Things have really changed between us. Not sure how much I'm liking the role reversal."

I shook my head and tried to sound upbeat, but when I started telling him what that shit had done to Felix my voice turned gruff and snappy.

"That little fucker!" Jimmy shouted, then paused and started talking to someone in the room. I assumed it was Ness. "...smashed my guitar!"

I heard a gasp, then Nessa was in my ear. "Is Felix okay? Who the hell is that little shit in his class? I'm happy to go down there and shove a drumstick up his ass! Just tell me where he is!"

I didn't have time to deny Nessa what she wanted. As much as I loved the idea, I couldn't condone it.

Jimmy took the phone off his girl and started speaking to me again. "As you can see, we're pretty pissed. What do you want us to do?"

"Well, for one, Felix's teacher told me he's really embarrassed about the whole thing. He thinks you're going to be mad about the guitar."

Jimmy scoffed. "It's just a guitar, dude."

"Yeah, but to him...it was Jimmy Baker's guitar. The first instrument he'd ever had the chance to really play."

"I didn't think about it like that," Jimmy murmured. "I've still got the guitar you gave me. No one's allowed to touch that thing except me."

I couldn't help a fleeting smile. My voice softened. "He's pretty heartbroken, but knowing Felix he'll try to be stoic about it. He probably won't even tell his aunt."

"Oh, you mean that chick, Cassie? She looks way too straight-laced to be hanging out with a kid that cool."

"Hey," I snapped. "She's awesome."

My firm reprimand was met with a long beat of silence, and then Jimmy took the conversation so far off course I wasn't sure how I'd bring it back around. "Wait a second. Do you like her?"

"It's..." I sighed. "Jimmy, can we stay on point, please."

"No way! You're in love with a pastel-wearing...librarian!"

I groaned and looked to the ceiling. If only he knew that she actually *was* a librarian. He'd never let me hear the end of it.

"You haven't dated a girl in months. And when I say months, I mean *months,* and now you're falling for a chick who doesn't even look like she fits into your world."

I scowled, wishing Jimmy could see my face. "What are you talking about? For one, how the hell do you know who I date and secondly, what world? How does she not fit into mine?"

"She looked so uptight I was surprised she could walk properly. I bet her house fucking sparkles. She probably—"

"Stop!" I cut him off. "You don't know anything about her, so drop the judgments. She's one of the nicest, bravest people I know." My voice grew husky with emotion. "You don't know what she's been through, and the fact she can even take Felix on is huge."

Jimmy went quiet, and for a second I thought the line had gone dead.

"Jimmy?"

"Wow. She's really gotten under your skin."

"Happy to have her there."

"Are you sure? If she's been through shit, she's gonna have baggage."

"I can deal with baggage. You've dealt with baggage and look how great you and Ness are."

"Dude, we've known each other since we were fourteen. I don't know if we would have made it through without that history. She's been my best friend for years. How long have you known this Cassie chick?"

"About three months," I mumbled.

Again, Jimmy took too long to reply, and when he did, his voice was uncharacteristically cautious.

"Just be careful, man. You're the best person I know and you deserve someone who can love you. She just didn't seem that...open to me."

His soft warning cut me off at the knees. I didn't want to have that conversation. I didn't want someone coming in from the outside and giving me a new perspective. I cared about Cassie. In fact, I was pretty sure I loved her. I wanted to be her knight in shining armor. I wanted to heal her, see her shine, and make her believe in the safety of love.

But what if Jimmy was right?

It didn't matter how much I loved her if she wasn't able to love me back.

"Anyway." Jimmy cleared his throat, his voice upbeat after shitting all over me. "I'll talk to the guys and we'll come up with something to make it up to Felix. I'll be in touch, okay?"

"Yeah," I sighed. "Sure. Thanks."

"Hey, you know I love you, bro. I wouldn't make you feel like shit if I didn't care about you."

I raised my eyebrows. "Thanks. I think."

"I'll call you later, okay?"

I nodded and then hung up without saying more. Dropping my phone onto the bathroom counter, I watched it slide into the empty sink. Jovi padded into the room, his claws tapping on the shiny tiles.

Looking down at him, I gave him a sad smile, wondering if my visions of a happy family were no more than just a dream.

THIRTY-SIX

CASSIE

Work went okay. In spite of my tears earlier in the day, I'd driven home feeling upbeat. Felix had texted me at lunchtime and told me he wanted to walk home. I said that was fine. I was proud of him for growing up and told myself nothing bad could happen to him on the way home.

Parking my little car, I glanced at the house, my eyes narrowing slightly when I opened the car door and heard music blasting. Not just blasting, but shake-the-earth loud. With a guilty frown, I glanced around the neighbors' houses, hoping no one was home. Noise control...or the police...could be knocking on my door any minute, asking me to turn it down.

I ran up the front path and quickly unlocked the door. Flicking it closed behind me, I dropped the keys on the side table and raced into the living room.

Alanis Morissette was belting out "Right Through You," her tone angry, the guitar music sharp and aggressive. Felix was in the living room, playing air guitar and banging his head. His dark locks splashed around his face, and when he stood straight, I caught a glimpse of his blotchy cheeks.

He'd been crying.

My heart stuttered and then thumped a dull beat as I gently walked past him and lowered the volume. He faltered, kind of tripped, and ended up flopping onto the couch. With the volume down, Alanis became a soft backing vocal to our conversation.

"What happened?"

He sighed and I perched on the edge of the couch, close enough to rub his shoulder. "Bad day?"

"Total shit."

I swallowed, still not sure if I was supposed to pull him up on his language. What would Crystal have done?

Words from her diary flickered through my brain, and I tried to think about how I could turn his bad mood around and show him how lucky we both were to have each other.

"Is there any particular reason why, or are you

just missing your mom?"

"It's not even about Mom!" he snapped, lurching up and resting his elbows on his knees. His hair was getting longer and covered the side of his face as he stared at the carpet.

His leg bobbed erratically.

"Sorry, it's just you were listening to Alanis, and I thought…"

He huffed and stood, pacing over to my bookshelf and softly mumbling, "One of the guys at school smashed Jimmy's guitar today."

He was speaking so quietly it took me a second to register what he'd said, but when I did, I shot from the couch and practically bellowed. "What! When? Oh, the school is hearing about this!" I straightened my blouse and marched to the phone. "What's his name?"

"They already know," he called after me. "Mrs. Tindal came in at the end and helped me sort it out. I spent half the morning in the principal's office. He's making Dickhead pay for the damage, so I'll be able to buy a new guitar but…" His shoulders sagged.

"It's not the same."

"Nope." He shook his head, looking ready to cry again.

Dammit. I hated bullies so much. Who the hell did they think they were?

"Why didn't the school call me?"

"I asked them not to." He shrugged. "I didn't want to ruin your day."

"You wouldn't have." I walked back to him. "I

want to be there for you."

"How am I going to tell Jimmy?" His voice cracked.

I rubbed his shoulder. "Hey, don't worry about that. I'll call Troy and see if he can help us out."

"I don't want them to be mad at me."

Bless this kid. He was the sweetest thing on the planet.

"They won't. It's not your fault."

"I was showing off!" He stepped back, his expression crumpling. "I never take my guitar into class! But I wanted them to think I was cool. I told them about Chaos, but no one would believe me."

It was killing me. My heart hurt so badly for him.

I so desperately wanted to say the right thing to make it better, but all I could come up with was, "That sucks. Seriously. I wish I had something wise to say. I'm sure your mom would've had just the right words."

He scoffed and shook his head. "She'd tell me not to worry about what others think of me."

"Well, I guess that's kind of true. Would she say anything about kicking that little shithead's ass?"

Felix snorted, then started laughing. "Aunt Cass! Watch your mouth!"

"Oh!" I laughed back. "So you're allowed to swear and I'm not?"

"It just sounds weird coming from you. You're always so…good and sweet."

My shoulder hitched, and I gave him a bashful smile. "Sometimes there's nothing like a good swear to break the tension, am I right?"

"Fuck yeah," Felix muttered, then quickly bit his lips together.

I gasped, my eyes bulging for a second.

But then we both looked at each other and burst out laughing. Without even thinking about it, I stepped forward and grabbed him into a hug. I wanted to tell him I loved him. I even opened my mouth to say it, but an image of Davis's ugly face brushed through the back of my mind. Like a noxious weed it choked off the words, so all I could do was stand there, holding this adorable kid and hoping that the warmth in my chest was in fact a pure, healthy love...and that Felix could feel it oozing out of me.

THIRTY-SEVEN

TROY

For some weird reason, I felt nervous approaching Cassie's house. I'd done it so many times before, but Jimmy's comments had really thrown me. I couldn't stop wondering if he was right. Was I destined to love this woman and never have her love me back? She'd finally opened up a little, but what if she never did again? Would she ever let me in enough to become part of her little family with Felix?

My stomach bunched and jittered as I played with the vision in my head. What if I was walking up to *our* house? I'd stroll in the door, Felix and

Jovi would be playing in the living room together, Cassie would be singing to herself as she pottered around...maybe cooking dinner. I'd hang up my bag and go in there to help her. We'd prepare dinner together, stealing kisses by the fridge and chatting about our days while music played in the background.

It all sounded so idyllic...so out of reach.

The only place I'd ever come home to was either empty or filled with tension.

I couldn't help a heavy sigh as I knocked on the door, completely forgetting my reason for being there.

The lock flicked and Felix appeared. His pale brown eyes rounded and then he looked to the wooden floor. "Hey, man."

It was so unlike him not to smile and welcome me in, but after the day he'd had...I totally got it. Then it occurred to me that he was probably unaware of Jane's phone call. He didn't know that I knew.

My lips lifted into a gentle smile when he glanced back up at me. "Jane...Mrs. Tindal called me earlier. I know about the guitar."

Felix winced.

"It's not your fault. You don't need to feel bad."

"That's what I said." Cassie appeared behind Felix. Her eyes seemed calm and light considering what her nephew had been through. I'd been expecting a little more angst and panic, but she stepped up behind Felix and laid her hand on his shoulder before welcoming me in.

My heart skipped with hope as I stepped into the house, my smile growing even wider as I took in Felix's miserable face and knew I was about to make it all better.

"So, I've got something to show you." I pulled my phone out of my pocket and brought up YouTube. The clip had only been posted an hour ago, and it'd already had 2254 views.

With a chuckle, I passed the phone to Felix.

He pressed play and watched Chaos's message...recorded just for him.

His nervous frown lifted to become an awestruck smile. Cassie watched over his shoulder, her face melting with gratitude when she looked at me.

"Thank you," she mouthed.

I winked and gazed back at her, loving the glimmer in her eyes and the way the light fell on her face from the skylight above. It made her glow, highlighting her beauty.

"This is amazing!" Felix jumped forward and hugged me. "Thank you so much."

"I thought you could play it to your class tomorrow. Figure out who you want to take with you."

Felix bobbed his head, thinking as he pressed play and walked into the living room to watch it again.

Cassie looked up at me and took me by surprise. "Do you want to stay for dinner?"

"Yeah." My voice was a husky whisper. "Can I help you prepare anything?"

She hesitated, crossed her arms, and gazed into the kitchen. I could see quite clearly it was her domain, but then she glanced over her shoulder and surprised me again. "Sure. That'd be great."

With a slightly dopey grin, I followed her through the archway and caught a glimpse of the dream I'd had walking up her path. The only thing missing was Jovi. I'd have to bring him with me the next time I popped over with good news.

*****

The meal was spent figuring out a time to buy Felix a new guitar. I told him I was free on the weekend and if he was lucky, I might be able to rope Jimmy into joining us. He nearly choked on his enchilada. I laughed as he coughed and spluttered out "yes!" repeatedly.

Cassie and I shared a quick glance across the table...and continued to do that all evening. By the time Felix went to bed, I felt like I'd studied her from every angle I could. From the soft curls in her hair to the dip in her lower back, the curve of her butt down to the shape of her ankles. I loved her shape. She was short—well, compared to me—and her muscles were strong and lean from all the running she did. I wanted to trace them, feel their firmness under my fingertips.

As she carried two mugs into the living room, I couldn't take my eyes off her. I couldn't stop picturing her naked.

Forcing my eyes away, I shuffled on the couch

and reached for the mug.

"When Love and Hate Collide"—one of my favorite Def Leppard songs—was oozing out of the stereo, creating a low-key ambiance. It felt like the end of a date night.

"Thanks." I placed the mug on the coaster and leaned back, trying to look casual and hide my desire.

"I so appreciate everything you've done for Felix." Cassie took a seat beside me, resting on her leg and seeming relaxed. "I don't know what I would have done without you, Troy."

Her words, the way she said them, warmed me to the core. I loved her eyes, the way they studied me. Her lips, the way they curved into just a hint of a smile.

"You guys make it easy on me." I grinned. "I really care about you, Cassie. I love seeing you smile. I'd do anything for you." I swallowed, emotions getting the better of me.

Did I admit how I really felt?

Was it too soon?

Would I scare her away?

She rested her hand over mine, giving it a light squeeze and gazing at me with a strength of affection I hadn't seen before.

Moving slowly, I shifted closer, studying her as I closed the space between us. She didn't shy away but didn't move forward either. I went in, pressing my lips against hers. She remained still for a long beat, but eventually her fingers crept up my arm, pausing at my shoulder. She almost felt like she was shaking as her lips gave way, becoming pliant and welcoming.

I ran my arm down her side and rested it against her hip. I kept it there, testing the waters. She didn't move away so I took another risk, running my tongue along her lower lip.

She drew in a quick breath and went still. I expected her to pull back, berating myself for moving too fast. But then she leaned in. Although her lips trembled, I could sense her need to explore, so I opened my mouth again, offering her a little more...and she responded.

Our tongues brushed together. She tasted like the berries we'd had for dessert. The sensual, sweet flavor stirred my desire even more. I wanted to melt against her, feel her beneath me, kiss every inch of her smooth skin, hear her cries of pleasure.

It was an effort to push the thoughts from my mind, to take things slow...especially when her fingers scraped through the back of my hair. She was getting into it. Letting go.

I tightened my arms, running my hand up her back and palming her shoulder blades before gliding up her neck. Gently pulling her hair tie free, I dropped it on the floor and buried my fingers in her luscious locks. I wanted to fist them, gently tug her head back and trace her neck with my tongue, but I kept warning myself to slow down.

And every time I did, she'd do something else to stir me.

With a soft moan, she shifted closer, pressing her body against mine. I could feel her breasts squishing into my chest. I wanted to squeeze them, explore their shape, lick her nipples.

Images fueled my fervor and I dove into her mouth, swiping her tongue hungrily. She seemed to meet my desire, pulled by a force neither of us could control.

Should I take it further?

The phone in my pocket stopped me from finding out.

The sharp ring made Cassie jerk away from me. Her cheeks flared red, her eyes bulging as she wiped her lips. It was like she'd just come out of a fog and suddenly realized how hard she'd been kissing me.

I grinned at her, wishing I could ignore the call. But it may have been one of my cases. Reluctantly pulling the phone from my pocket, I checked the number. "It's my mom. I'll call her on my way home."

I switched off the phone, but it was too late to start something new again.

Cassie had scooched back to her end of the couch. She was tying her hair up, and I swear I could see the pulse pounding in her neck.

"That was nice," I murmured, a lame effort.

"Uh-huh." She smiled but it was wobbly and unbelievable. Her fingers trembled as she rubbed her stomach. Noticing my gaze, she blushed and murmured, "I'm sorry. I've never done..." She bit her lip and looked to the floor. "This is all so new to me. It's slightly terrifying."

"It's okay," I whispered. "We don't have to do

anything you don't want to."

"But that felt so amazing." She ran a finger over her lips. "I want to—" Her expression crumpled—pained and embarrassed. "I don't know how much further I can go. I've never…and you probably want… I just don't…" Her voice trailed off as her eyes filled with tears.

"Hey." I shuffled along the couch, running my hand down her back—nothing more. I forced my hand to rest on her spine, even though I wanted to pull her against me. "I'm not going to lie and say I don't want you. You're beautiful. You've captured my soul. I want to love you in every way I can. But it's whatever you need, Cass. I'm not in a hurry. If it's all right with you, I'm planning on sticking around for a while." I winked, hoping the tension would drain out of her, but she still sat rigid, contradicting the words coming out of her mouth.

"You've captured me too, and I really want to…try."

She was making me soar.

But the tremor in her lips told me not to push it. Brushing my lips across her forehead, I rested my chin on her head and whispered, "How about you come over this weekend. We can have a meal for two…and then do whatever you feel like." I leaned back, capturing her face and rubbing my thumbs over her cheeks. "We don't have to rush this. I'm not going to pressure you into doing anything you're not ready for. You're the boss on this one, okay? No demands from me."

Her smile was grateful, and I could have melted

right into her gaze. She may not have been able to say "I love you," but I swear I could see it.

As much as I wanted to kiss her, I didn't push it. Instead, I stood. "I think I should get going."

"Okay." She seemed reluctant for me to go, but it was the right thing to do.

"I might see you this weekend, then." I winked again and she blushed, biting her lips together.

Man, she really was nervous. Fair, I guess. Anyone's first time was a big deal, but I had a feeling that Cassie's first time would be monumental, thanks to a beast who tried to beat something out of her that was never his to take.

Cassie's virginity would be a gift, and I was going to treat it as the most precious thing I'd ever been given.

THIRTY-EIGHT

FELIX

Going to school the next day was an effort. I wanted to stay in my room and listen to music all day, but then Aunt Cass reminded me about the Chaos video and then took it a step further, torturing me out of bed with "When The Going Gets Tough." She played it on repeat, turning up the volume each time until I shouted into the kitchen, "I'm up, already!"

She laughed but continued singing as she made us breakfast.

It was hard to eat. Even though I had the chance to put Dickhead and his idiot friends in their place, my stomach was filled with nerves.

What if they thought the YouTube clip was fake or something?

What if they smashed my phone?

I wrapped my fingers around it and wove down the Strantham Academy corridor. A few whispers followed me, so I kept my head down and kept shuffling forward. It sucked that I had no guitar to practice with at lunchtime. I had no idea what I was gonna do...probably go anyway and just watch Summer mess around on her bass. It was better than wandering around the schoolyard like a loser.

Stepping into class, I gazed around at the students who were already there. Ginny was sitting on the desk in front of mine, swinging her legs and giggling with her pretty girlfriends. It still kind of hurt that she wouldn't believe me yesterday. In fact, the only person who did was Summer.

I glanced down to the back of the room and caught her eye. She raised her chin at me and did that half-grin she does. I smiled back, realizing that any fantasy of asking Ginny to join me was complete bullshit. Only one person in the entire class stood up for me yesterday, and she was the only one I'd be inviting.

Narrowing my eyes, I walked straight over to Ginny, dumped my bag by her feet and pulled out my phone.

"I know you didn't believe me yesterday about the whole Chaos thing, so I thought you should see this."

I unlocked the screen and pressed play on the video that was ready and waiting.

"Hey, guys. Chaos here." Jimmy smiled.

It took less than five seconds for me to be surrounded. Every kid in the class clambered around me, leaning over each other to look down at my phone.

"This is a shout-out to our boy, Felix. It was great having you at practice the other day, man. You killed it on the guitar."

"You're a true rock star." Nessa made the rock 'n' roll sign with her hand. "So, we'd like to invite you back for another jam session. Bring a friend along if you want."

Flick leaned in and pointed at the camera. "But not that little shithead who broke Jimmy's guitar."

Ralphie laughed. "Yeah, you tell that butt weed from 7JT to stick it. We only want cool people hanging out at our practices." The smile dropped from his face and he looked at the camera, his warning clear.

I felt a shift behind me and glanced over my shoulder to see Dickhead shrinking with a shame-faced frown.

"We'll catch you again soon, Felix." Jace grinned and waved at the camera. I heard a swooning sigh behind me and noticed one of Ginny's friends bugging out as Chaos said goodbye.

"Wow," she breathed into my ear. "That is so cool." Her eyes danced and she looked at me like she never had before. "You know, I totally adore Chaos, right?"

"Me too!" Ginny glared at her friend, then put on her sweet eyes for me. She even twirled a lock of hair around her finger when she smiled at me. "I'd love to meet them."

"So?" I leaned away from her, shoving the phone back into my pocket and wrestling my way out of the circle. Summer was standing back. She'd heard the whole thing but had yet to see it.

She smirked and gave me a thumbs-up. "Nice one," she murmured when I got close enough to hear her. "Shithead and butt weed." Her snicker was like music. "My day has officially been made."

"You want to come with me?"

She froze for a second, did two big blinks, and then whispered, "What?"

"To the Chaos practice. You wanna come?"

"You're inviting me?" She pointed at herself.

"Yeah." I shrugged. "You're the only person who'll appreciate it and—"

She let out this girly kind of squeal and wrapped her arms around me. The whole class ooed and started jeering. To be honest, I was kind of taken off guard, but I went with it, giving her a light squeeze around the waist before she pulled back.

Gripping my shoulders, she shook me and did this little happy dance.

So I finished my sentence. "And you're a good friend."

Her eyebrow arched, her excitement contained once again behind her cool facade. "I think I'm your only friend."

"Ditto," I retorted, and she agreed with a nod.

"I've just been waiting for someone cool enough to hang out with." She shrugged and then winked at me.

The bell rang and I turned for my seat, not missing Ginny's disappointed frown and the icy glare she shot Summer.

I snickered and shook my head, making sure she saw how pitiful I thought she was.

Her cheeks flared red, and she spun to face the front.

It was weird. When I first arrived at this school, I thought she was the prettiest thing I'd ever seen. But she didn't seem as sparkly as she used to.

Glancing over my shoulder, I caught Summer's gaze and grinned at her.

She grinned back, confirming it officially. I had a new best friend, and she was most likely the coolest chick I would ever hang out with.

THIRTY-NINE

CASSIE

It was the weekend.

Saturday evening, to be more precise. The day I said I'd go over to Troy's for another date. The day I kind of implied that maybe we could have sex.

I mean, I wanted to. Troy and I had been hanging out a lot. He called or texted every day, just to check in—a sweet little gesture that made me smile. I waited for it and felt like I could fly when I saw his name pop up on my screen.

I cared about him. Truth was I probably loved him. I was just too afraid to admit it to anyone.

It was hard to hide my jitters as I dropped Felix

off at Summer's house. Troy and Jimmy had taken him out that morning to pick a new guitar. Felix was in heaven and couldn't wait to show his new friend. I did the right thing and walked him to the door, met Summer's parents, had a little chat with her mother and walked back to my car feeling like a real mom. It was a weird sensation, but also kind of nice.

Felix would be safe at Summer's place, and I'd pick him up at ten that night.

I glanced at my watch as I pulled up to Troy's apartment. It was six twenty. I was ten minutes early, but I figured he wouldn't mind. Pulling in a slow breath, I trembled up the stairs, reminding myself I could do it.

Troy was a good man. He wouldn't hurt me, demand anything from me. I could do this monumental thing with him and it'd be okay. I had nothing to fear.

I wanted to sleep with him. The sensation of kissing him felt divine and I wanted more, but the rock covering the darkest part of me quivered and rattled as I walked to his door. I was determined to control it, to remind myself that I was worthy of this moment, that the night I wanted to pretend never happened would not destroy this moment for me.

I was not a worthless cellar rat. I could live a normal life. I could be caressed by a man. I could say the words "I love you" and not get harmed for it.

I didn't have to unearth my past or bring Davis

into Troy's apartment with me.

Easier said than done.

My finger shook as I pressed the buzzer.

Jovi started barking, and I heard his scampering paws. I'd seen him several times over the past few weeks. Felix adored him and I was adjusting. When Troy opened the door, I crouched down and said hi to the happy bulldog. His stumpy tail wagged as I patted his head. I'd never given him so much attention, and he was relishing every second of it.

In truth, I was probably doing it to avoid direct eye contact with Troy. I was so nervous I wanted to throw up.

"He's loving you right now." Troy laughed and ushered me in the door.

I finally found the courage to glance up. Troy's smile was sweet enough to melt into, and I scolded myself for being so uptight. He was amazing on so many levels. I was where I was meant to be.

"Felix play guitar all afternoon?" Troy asked when I followed him into the living room.

I grinned. "He's going to play that thing until his fingers bleed, I swear. He's so in love at the moment."

Troy laughed. "You should have seen him when he was trying to choose a guitar. He hung off Jimmy's every word."

"It's so nice of your brother to look out for him like this." I patted my chest. "I can't tell you how much it means to me."

"It means a lot to me too." Troy's voice was thick with emotion, which just reinforced how much I wanted him to be part of team Felix and Cassie.

The thought froze my voice box, and all I could do was stand there gazing at Troy and loving everything about him.

He approached me slowly, taking my hand and kissing my knuckles. I blushed and stepped forward, closing the gap between us. He brushed his thumb across my cheek, then kissed my ear.

"I have dinner ready," he whispered.

"I think I'm too nervous to eat," I admitted, too afraid to look up at him.

He tipped my chin. "I don't want you to be nervous. Let's just make this a dinner for two and we'll see how things unfold, okay?"

I bobbed my head, forcing myself to breathe. His hand rested on my lower back as he led me to the table. I took a seat, and Troy started chatting about his day. He told me a funny story about Jovi, which got me laughing. He then asked me about my run, which got me talking. Before we ate the pineapple and soy glazed salmon he'd made, he lit some candles and set some music playing. It was all slow ballads from the eighties and nineties—so Troy. I loved it.

We had vanilla ice cream with fresh raspberries and chocolate sauce for dessert. By the time I'd licked my spoon clean, I felt relaxed and happy. It was easy to forget my nerves as I laughed at his humor and smiled at his compliments.

We talked about Felix for a while, acted like an everyday couple having an everyday conversation about their kid.

It wasn't until the music shifted to "When I Look Into Your Eyes" that Troy's voice trailed off and he just stared at me, telling me he loved me, telling me he wanted me without uttering a word.

"I think I'm ready," I whispered.

He didn't say anything, but his gaze went a touch gooier. I could have melted right into it.

My heart took off racing as his finger trailed delicate patterns over my wrist. He took my hand and pulled me to my feet. His arm was strong as he glided it around my back and danced me toward the bedroom. He paused in the doorframe, leaning me back against the wood and kissing me. It was soft at first but then grew with fervor as I dipped my tongue into his mouth.

He squeezed my hip, moaning softly, then pulled back and rested his forehead against mine. "I want you to be sure."

"I'm sure." I swallowed and looked at him.

I wasn't. The rock inside me, the one keeping my darkest secrets at bay, was rattling. I closed my eyes, willing it to stay in place. I could do this with Troy. I could be a normal person.

Desire pulsed through me. I wanted him. I wanted to experience this with him.

"I love you, Cassie. I'd never do anything to hurt you."

"I know," I whispered.

My heart was thundering, telling me two different things. Fear and desire were at war. I had to let desire win.

Squeezing the back of Troy's neck, I rose and planted my lips on his. He took my permission and lifted me off the floor, carrying me into his dimly lit room and placing me on the bed.

I lay down, my insides trembling as he ran his fingers softly down my side.

If I could just keep my lips on his, everything would be okay.

His touch was feather-light, skimming my thigh before palming my butt and giving it a gentle squeeze.

And then his lips left mine.

They brushed my chin and started kissing my neck, working over my shoulder. He pushed the fabric away, my bra strap slipping out of place, and the rock that had been keeping me safe for the last ten years flew off.

Ripping fabric.

Screaming.

Pain.

Blood.

It all came back in a rush so fast I thought I might choke.

I squeezed my eyes against the torment, willing myself not to lose it.

Troy felt good. He was kind. He wasn't going to hurt me!

His fingers continued to gently pull the fabric away from my skin, slowly undressing me, drawing patterns with his tongue as he explored and tried to make me feel good.

But all I could see was an ugly face, glazed eyes.

All I could feel was the fear pulsing through me as my nightgown was ripped off my body.

"No! I don't love you!" I screamed, but Davis wouldn't listen.

He reeked of liquor, his eyes unfocused as he murmured, "Crystal" and pulled me off the bed.

I fisted the back of Troy's hair, trying to dodge what came next.

I'd been pretending it hadn't happened, denying the truth ever since I left the hospital after that abhorrent night. But when Troy shifted on the bed and nestled himself between my legs, I couldn't do it.

A memory of pain so hot and intrusive tore through my center. I let out a guttural scream. "No! Get off me!"

FORTY

TROY

Cassie's scream scared the shit out of me.

I jumped off her, my eyes bulging as she kicked and flailed on the bed.

"Get off me!" she screamed again, but she wasn't talking to me. Her eyes were distant and glazed. "Stop! Please! I don't love you."

The words choked out of her, broken by gut-wrenching sobs. She curled onto her side and whimpered, crying like a little kid.

I shuffled right to the end of the bed, knowing better than to touch her.

My eyes stung with tears. Every emotion from

rage to horror to repulsion rocketed through me. I wanted to kill Davis Fucking McCoy. And I *didn't* want to hear the details, but if Cassie didn't get this out, it'd just go right back inside her and fester like it obviously had been for the last decade.

"I'm not going to touch you." I kept my voice soft but firm. "You're safe here. No one is going to hurt you again. Ever."

My words seemed to calm her, so I kept talking in a quiet, even tone.

"I know you don't want to do this, but you need to get it out. So, you cry for as long as you need to, and I'm just gonna stay right here. I won't move. I'll wait. I'm here to listen when you're ready to talk."

And then I did just what I said I would.

I waited.

I stayed on my knees at the end of the bed, watching her cries slowly peter out. Finally she let out a slow breath and whispered, "I'm sorry."

I wanted to tell her not to apologize, but she sat up and wiped her cheeks then kept going.

"For nearly two years, I managed to avoid it. He'd beg me to love him, and I'd never say it. So he'd beat me, hoping I'd give in. I never did." She licked a tear running past her lips. "But then this one night, he got drunk…really drunk…and obviously decided he didn't need his victim to love him after all."

Her lips began to wobble, and my stinging eyes filled with tears.

"I begged him to stop, but he wouldn't. I

screamed as loud as I could...but no one came to help me."

My throat was getting so swollen with emotion, so thick it was nearly impossible to swallow.

"When he was done, he just left me there on the floor. I was in so much pain, and it would have been so easy to curl into a ball and just cry forever. But the thought of him violating me again was so abhorrent that I ran out of the house. I was naked and blood was running down my legs, but I ran down the street screaming until I bumped into these college kids." She pulled in a hiccupy breath. "They were walking home from a party. Davis was chasing me, but they hid me behind them and called the police. He kept shouting that I was his but..." She shook her head.

My heart was cracking open. I could picture it all so clearly, and I couldn't process my pain fast enough. Her fear was so vibrant I could practically taste it.

"Social services put me in a safe place. The police arrested Davis." She dipped her head, her voice weak and defeated. "He killed himself in prison, but...he still owns me."

I shook my head. "No."

"Yes, Troy!" Her head shot up to face me. "He does! He will haunt me forever. Why do you think I have to run every day? Why can't I share this experience with you and not think about him?"

"We don't have to sleep together to be together. I just want to love you."

"How can you, when I can't give you all of

myself?"

I shook my head, refusing to buy into that crap. "He *doesn't* own you. You're a fighter. You wouldn't let him win then, and you're not going to let him win now."

"He did win!" she screamed. "Don't you get it? I took beatings for months to avoid being raped but he did it anyway. He stole the only thing I had left!" Her face bunched and she squeezed a hand over her eyes.

Having to sit back and just watch her was killing me. I wanted to pull her onto my knee, convince her that it didn't have to be that way.

"I can't be your girlfriend, Troy. You deserve better than me."

"That's not true," I whispered. "You *are* the best. You're the only woman I have ever fallen in love with. We'll work through this together."

She sniffed and joined me in the head shaking. "I can't. I'm sorry. I won't put you through it." Pulling her clothes straight, she stood from the bed and tucked her hair behind her ears. She probably wished she had a hair tie so she could gather it back. "You want someone clean and whole and healthy."

"No, I want you." I reached out for her, my voice adamant.

She backed away from me, nearly crashing into the wall behind her. "Don't, Troy. You have to let me walk away."

"I don't want to lose you." My forehead creased. "I love you, Cassie."

Her gaze was etched with sadness. "But I'll never be able to love you...and that's why you should let me go. You deserve better." Her voice cracked and she zipped out of the room.

I stood up and followed her to the door. "Please, don't do this. We can work through this. We can talk it out. You can—"

"Talking is not going to save me from this!" She spun, her eyes wild.

"It can. You just need to—"

"No!" she practically screamed. "I can't change what happened! And reliving it again isn't going to make any difference. I won't put you through it. Let me go, Troy. Just let me go." Her voice broke and trailed off as she grabbed her bag and shot past Jovi, who was asleep in his bed.

She was crying again, and having to stand there and let her leave was the hardest thing I'd ever done. The door clicked shut and my knees gave out. My head was filled with images of a young Cassie running down the street, bleeding and terrified.

The tears that kept filling my eyes but not falling finally spilled free. I just went with it. I hadn't cried in years, but it was the only thing left to do.

FORTY-ONE

FELIX

Three weeks later...

The car was kind of quiet...a major buzzkill considering it was my birthday. Finally a teenager, I should have been celebrating big. But it was hard to get happy when the people around me were so sad.

I didn't know what went down, but Troy and Cassie had a big fight and she wasn't talking to him anymore. She told me over and over again that she wasn't mad at Troy, but he must have done something. Her eyes have been red and puffy a lot more than usual, she's been super tidy, running for close to ninety minutes every day, and her clothes looked baggier. I only noticed that a few days earlier, but it made me even more worried.

She was trying to put on a brave face and everything, stay in control the way she liked to, but she'd lost her smile. She just looked…defeated.

I sighed and scratched my head, glancing at Troy then back out the window.

He looked kind of sad and tired too.

I spent the first week pissed off at him. The second week I had to call and ask him to stop sending flowers to Aunt Cass. She cried every time a new bunch arrived. But in the third week, when he'd texted me offering to drive me and Summer to a special Chaos practice at the stadium they'd be performing in, I had to cut the guy some slack and say yes. Aunt Cass didn't have to know. She was out running and thought I was spending the day with Summer. She had a birthday dinner planned, which I knew was a major effort on her part when it was obvious all she wanted to do was hide in her shell.

Troy was a good guy. He never got mad, just stayed calm and quietly persistent. I had to give him some credit.

Summer sat in the back, staring out the window, obviously trying to pretend the car was bright and happy like her place always was. The buds in her ears were probably helping. Her head moved to the beat and I tried to guess what she was listening to.

I loved going to her house. Her parents were cool, funny, easy to be around. Her mom never minded me popping over. Summer's dad had set up the garage as a practice area, and we jammed in there for hours.

"So, uh…" Troy cleared his throat when he noticed me glance at him again. "How's school?"

"Yeah, it's going good. Getting easier."

"And…home?"

I rolled my eyes. "Seriously, dude, I don't know what to tell ya. She's running a lot and looking sad all the time."

He sighed, his shoulders drooping.

"Can't you guys just…work it out? She was so happy before."

"We all were," he mumbled. "I wish I could do more, say the right thing. Make this all better. I call her every day trying to make amends, but she just won't talk to me."

I huffed and shook my head, frustrated by the whole thing. "I don't know what happened between you guys, but Aunt Cass seems pretty determined to shut you out. I just wish you could make her change her mind."

"Me too, buddy." Troy clenched his jaw, his lips dipping into a really sad frown.

The car went even quieter after that, if it was even possible. I wanted to fiddle with the stereo and get some tunes pumping, but Troy looked so sad I couldn't do anything but sit there.

Thankfully we pulled into the stadium a few minutes later, and Summer started fangirling before we even got out of the car. Ralphie was standing next to his truck, making out with Nessa's little sister. I'd forgotten her name. Veronica, maybe?

Summer tapped the window. "It's Ralphie. It's Ralphie!"

"Calm down," I snickered. "Act cool."

"Yeah, yeah, cool. You're right. I'm cool." She blew out a breath. "I'm totally cool."

She was pretty adorable sometimes. I slid out of the car and pulled out her bass case for her. She stayed close as we walked up to Ralphie.

His girlfriend said hi first. "How y'all doin'? It's nice to see you again." She gave my shoulder a squeeze and kissed my cheek, then gave Summer a hug after I'd introduced her.

Ralphie shook Summer's hand and then started asking her about the bass guitar she was holding. Summer blushed bright red and talked faster than she ever had before.

Veronica giggled and Ralphie just grinned and led us into the stadium while Summer launched into the story about her father's college band.

"Hey, Felix, my man!" Jimmy spread his arms wide, his loud voice booming through the microphone and echoing throughout the arena. "Happy birthday, dude!"

I grinned, feeling more and more confident.

"How's the new guitar working out for ya?"

"Yeah. Really good." I climbed the stairs at the side of the stage. Jace kicked into a drum solo that drowned out my next sentence.

Summer was talking to Veronica while she carefully took out her dad's bass. Ralphie said something that made her blush again.

I pulled out my guitar, flipping the strap over my head and feeling a sudden attack of the nerves.

Nessa said something to Jace that killed his solo. I glanced up in time to see his eyebrows rise, and then he started up with a sick beat that made Nessa laugh.

"Oh, you think you're so hot, don't you?" She spread her arms. I couldn't stop looking at the tattoos decorating her stump. "You want me to come back there and show you how it's done?" The expression on her face was pretty funny. Cocky Nessa was kind of cute.

I grinned and flicked the hair out of my eyes when I stood.

Jimmy leaned over to me and whispered, "Small but feisty. Damn, I love that woman."

It was hard not to blush. The expression on his face told me just how much he loved her.

"She's your girlfriend, right?" I cleared my throat, wondering if I should have asked. Rumors have been rife for months, and in the last interview I saw, Jimmy wouldn't say either way. They liked to keep it pretty private, which was why I nearly fell off my feet when he leaned super close and told me a secret hardly anyone else knew.

"She's actually my wife." He wiggled his eyebrows. "We got married in Vegas at Christmas." He lifted his arm, showing me a tattoo on the inside of his wrist—*forever her true love*. "She's got a *his* one just like it. They're kind of like our wedding rings."

"Wow."

"Don't tell anyone though, okay? Not even Marcus and Troy know."

"Then why are you telling me?" I whispered, my eyes bugging out big time.

He nudged me with his elbow and grinned. "Because you're like an honorary Chaos member."

"I am?"

"You jammed with us, man." He winked. "Now, close your mouth before someone asks what we're talking about…and tune up."

I bit my lips together and dipped my head, focusing on tuning my guitar. My fingers were kind of shaking. I couldn't believe it. Honorary member? It was freaking insane. I had no idea why Jimmy liked me so much. I was a little nobody, but he'd taken me under his wing like a younger brother. He'd pulled me into his family.

Thanks to Troy.

I glanced up and spotted the big guy on the edge of the stage. He was talking to a man in a suit. I didn't know who he was. Maybe it was Chaos's band manager or something. I wasn't sure. Anyway, Troy seemed to know him. The shorter blond guy said something that was obviously supposed to make Troy laugh, but all he could muster was a closed-mouth smile. It was tight and unconvincing.

I wanted to make it real again.

I wanted Troy to hang out at our place. I wanted

to be like a family. Since his falling out with Aunt Cassie, things hadn't been the same. I wanted Troy to stay in my world forever, just like Jimmy. And I wanted him to stay in Aunt Cassie's world too. She was better when he was around. We all were.

I'd let it ride for nearly a month, thinking there was nothing I could do about it.

But maybe there was.

FORTY-TWO

TROY

It'd been a month since Cassie had fled my apartment, and I was missing her like crazy. Seeing Felix on the weekend only drove home how miserable I was. I'd called and left a message on her phone, telling her how much Felix loved the practice. I thought it might be enough to pull her out of her funk, but she hadn't replied.

I clenched my jaw, picking up my phone and resisting the urge to text something inane and undemanding. Just a little check-in so she knew I was thinking about her.

Sitting on the couch, I gazed at the screen,

wondering what I could say that I hadn't said already.

Jovi snuffled at my feet, nudging my ankle with his nose and looking for a pet. I patted his head while I slumped on the couch, staring up at the ceiling.

My dining room table was covered with files. I'd used my job to gain access to the case files of Crystal and Cassie Grayson. I knew as much as social services did. I knew their single mother was killed in a car accident and the girls had been placed in foster care. I'd tracked their progress, discovering that Crystal had disappeared from the system when she was fourteen.

The McCoys had reported her disappearance, but the police had never found her.

Crystal had left Cassie with that monster, which of course fueled a whole new barrage of emotions. If my calculations were right, she was most likely pregnant when she ran off, begging the question of who Felix's father was. There was no name registered on Felix's birth certificate.

I despised the idea that Felix might have McCoy blood running in his veins, but comforted myself with the fact he was one of the sweetest kids I'd ever met. He had too much of his mother in him to ever turn into a sick bastard.

And he had Cassie.

Unlike me.

I closed my eyes, trying to wipe the images of her haunted face from my mind. The picture in her file, the one taken just after she left the McCoys, nearly did me in. Her eyes were so big and defeated, so dead, like the only way for her to process it all was to bury the trauma deep enough to forget it'd ever happened.

According to her file, she'd had counseling, but I had a suspicion the person working with her couldn't get through. As soon as she was out of harm's way, Cassie went into denial, shutting away the horror and taking control of every aspect of her life.

And I'd unearthed the trauma all over again. So she was back on the defensive, locking up her feelings in order not to lose it.

It sucked.

I so wanted to make it right. Fix it for her.

But Cassie wouldn't return my calls, reply to my emails...accept my flowers.

Hearing Felix's quiet voice when he asked me to stop sending them was like a punch in the gut. How could I make Cassie understand that I just wanted to be with her? I didn't need more than her company, conversation, and sweet smile. Sure, I was a guy and sex would be great eventually, but we'd get there...together.

But she was convinced I deserved better than her. Part of me wanted to give her a light shake and beg her to believe that she was worth so much. That Davis didn't have to own any part of her.

Damn his sick, twisted mind...his evil soul. He deserved to die in that prison. I hoped he suffered on the way out.

I hated that he still haunted Cassie.

Thumping the cushion, I scared Jovi. He jumped up, barked, and then scampered for the door, his stubby tail going crazy. Before he even reached it, someone knocked.

The hopeful thought that maybe it was Cassie soared through me and I leaped off the couch, running for the door and swinging it back with a smile.

It wasn't Cassie.

It was a courier.

"Sign here, please."

I did as I was told and took the box. Rubbing my thumb over my address, I stared at the letters until my eyes lost focus. The return address indicated what would be inside.

The parcel was for Cassie.

I'd found mint condition copies of the Lord of the Rings trilogy. They were first edition and cost a bomb, but I'd happily paid the money. Seeing her face when she opened them would be worth every penny.

Fantasy novels were her go-to collection. It made sense—heroes defeating wicked beasts. She probably didn't even understand that her obsession subconsciously stemmed from an inner desire to beat the man who had wounded her so badly.

I wanted to grab my keys and rush over there. A gift like this would make her so happy. It'd be enough for her to let me in, surely.

I had my wallet and keys in my hand when my phone rang. I checked the screen and was tempted to ignore the call. But it was Jimmy, and when had

I ever been able to ignore a call from him. He might have needed me.

"Hey, lil' bro." My voice probably sounded too tight, but I had somewhere to be. "What's up?"

"Nothin'. I was just checking in."

I paused on my way to the door, slightly confused. "What?"

Jimmy sighed. "I noticed you've been kind of down, and I wanted to see if you were okay."

My eyebrows rose. It was impossible not to feel just a touch surprised. "Wow, Jimmy. Things have really changed between us."

My brother snickered. "Gimme a break, man. I don't like seeing my brother moping around over a woman."

I rolled my eyes and muttered, "Yeah, so not sure how much I'm liking the whole role reversal either."

I could sense Jimmy's smile and it irritated me.

"You can talk," I snapped. "You moped around for weeks when Ness took off."

"Yeah, and you called me repeatedly to make sure I wasn't drowning in a bowl of self-pity."

I clenched my teeth. "I'm not feeling sorry for myself, okay?"

"You're feeling something."

"Yeah, it's called heartache. The woman I love doesn't think she's good enough for me, and she cut me out like that." I snapped my fingers.

Jimmy took a second to respond, and when he did, his voice was quiet and so rich with emotion I almost didn't recognize it. "You know, man, Nessa used to say shit like that to me. I spent hours trying to convince her how awesome she was but nothing worked. She just wouldn't see herself the way I did. And trying to make her believe it only frustrated me and kind of pushed her away. In the end, she was the only one who could deal with her demons and close the space between us." He sighed. "As impossibly hard as it is to do, I think you need to just back off and give Cassie some time to figure it out...on her own."

My shoulders slumped and I closed my eyes. "I need to fix this, Jimmy. I miss her so much." My words came out husky and dry.

"I get it."

The way he said it made me believe him, and so I took on the role reversal, for once acting like the younger brother. "How do I get her back, man?"

"You leave her alone...and let her come to you."

The idea shattered me. I hated the thought of sitting back and doing nothing.

"I know that feels like death to you. You're the guy who swoops in to calm the storm and make it all better. You've helped so many people, but you can't fix everything. And I know this one is really close to the bone, and I wish I could fling her over my shoulder and drop her at your door. But you know as well as I do that it won't work. She's got to deal, and you need to give her space to do that."

I scrubbed a hand down my face and fell back against the wall. "Shit, Jimmy. When did you get so damn smart?"

"Ah, well, I was raised by an awesome guy. He

taught me a lot."

I couldn't help a small smile. "Thanks, bro."

"Love you, man. Stay strong. If she's as amazing as you think she is, then she'll knock on your door one day. I know it."

"Yeah." I nodded and said a soft goodbye before hanging up and shoving the phone back in my pocket.

A big part of me wanted to ignore Jimmy's advice. He was my kid brother; what the hell did he know?

But in spite of my doubts, I turned away from my door and walked back into the living room. As I neared the dining room table and stared down at the files, I had to face the fact that Jimmy was probably right. Forcing myself on Cassie, no matter how great my gifts were, could potentially push her even further away.

It went against every grain in my body. I was used to being the hero, the mediator, the one to help people heal, but maybe the best thing I could do for Cassie was leave her alone.

Razor blades sliced right through me as I tucked her epic gift onto my bookshelf before returning to the table to slowly pack away the files.

I didn't know how long my resolve would last, but I chose not to text or call her. She obviously wanted radio silence. It made me feel like a failure, but I guess I couldn't fight a battle that wasn't mine.

All I could pray was that one day, she'd find the ability to defeat the wicked beast once and for all…and make her way home to me.

FORTY-THREE

FELIX

So I had big plans to talk to Aunt Cass.

And it took me two weeks to find the right moment to do it. She'd been keeping to herself—running in the mornings, cleaning in the evenings. At dinner time, she kept the conversation all about me, school, Summer, guitar. I'm not sure if she heard any of my answers, because her eyes seemed in a constant state of glaze.

I remembered Mom looking like that. Not very often. Just occasionally she'd go really quiet and look like she was in another world. A place filled with sadness and regret.

I'd ask her if she was okay, and she'd snap out of it right away. Her smile would be instant. She'd pull me into a hug, tell me I was lucky and that she loved me.

Aunt Cass wasn't doing that. When I asked her if she was all right, her body would snap straight and she'd nod, her words fast and clipped. "Of course I am."

It was kind of depressing. I wanted the Aunt Cassie back who said "shithead" and laughed with me, sang along to my rock 'n' roll, smiled when I walked in the door.

The Aunt Cass I was living with looked completely lost.

When I opened the door that afternoon, she rushed out of the kitchen, her eyes wide with fear. "Where've you been? I thought you were walking straight home from school. I was worried."

"Sorry." I frowned. "I-I texted you."

"Oh." Her shoulders sagged and she pulled her phone out of her bag, checking my message with a sheepish frown. "Sorry. I didn't even think to check my phone." She rolled her eyes, obviously feeling stupid and annoyed with herself.

"It's okay. I didn't mean to worry you." I slipped the bag off my shoulder and put it in the basket by the shoe rack.

"I guess I expected to come home and find you here. It freaked me out a little when you weren't."

I wanted to tell her she could have just called me. I was surprised she hadn't thought to do it, but maybe I wasn't. She'd been kind of flaky and out of focus, like her brain was filled with something that shouldn't be there.

I stared at her face, my smile sad as I took in the dark smudges under her eyes. The sudden fear that maybe she was sick crippled me for a second. I couldn't watch her die. Seeing Mom fade away had been too much. Not Aunt Cassie too.

My eyes rounded with fear, and I whispered, "You're not sick, are you?"

"What?" She touched her chest, my expression obviously alarming her. She reached for my shoulders and gave them a squeeze. "No, of course not. I'm healthy. I run. I just... I'm not sleeping well."

I narrowed my eyes, watching her carefully before mumbling, "So it's heart sick, not body sick?"

She crossed her arms, unnerved by my observation. Smoothing a hand over her pulled-back hair, she looked away from me and forced a bright tone. "Anyway, where've you been? Hanging out with Summer?"

I worked my jaw to the side and decided it was finally time to act on my big plans. "Actually, I was with Troy."

"Troy?" Her head jerked back. "Why?"

Because I wanted to check on him, see how he was doing. Hang out. I missed him big time!

I didn't say any of that. Instead I shrugged and mumbled, "I called him after school to see if I could take Jovi for a walk, and he said yes and then came with us. It was fun."

She swallowed, lightly touching her throat and nodding. "Good. That's…good."

Oh no. She looked ready to cry again.

"You miss him, don't you?"

Her eyes filled with tears, but still she shook her head.

Liar.

I frowned and gave her a pointed glare. "Why do you keep ignoring him? Is it really helping anybody? You're miserable. He's miserable. I don't get it!"

She closed her eyes and took a calming breath.

"Felix, there's things you don't understand." She swiveled into the kitchen and tried to walk away from me…so I followed her.

"Maybe not, but when you and Troy were together, you were happy. I was happy. We were becoming like a family. Now you've just cut him off! And I might not understand all the reasons behind that, but I'm smart enough to know what makes sense. And you and Troy together makes sense."

She placed her hands on the counter and leaned forward, like her legs couldn't hold her up anymore. "It's too hard," she whispered.

"So you're just gonna turn your back on something good because it's too hard? That's bullshit, Aunt Cass. You're supposed to be the fighter, the strong one, but all you've done lately is run. Why are you running from something that's good?"

"Because I don't deserve it!" She whipped

around to face me. "I don't know how to do this!"

"Yes, you do!" I fought back, remembering the same conversation I'd had with my mom when she told me the chemo hadn't worked. I'd yelled and screamed, telling her she wasn't allowed to leave me. That I couldn't make it on my own.

She'd touched my tear-streaked face and given me the kind of smile I'd remember forever.

"You can do this, Felix. You can do anything. You're strong enough to figure a way forward. You're brave enough to make the most of your life. Don't let this beat you, baby. You keep fighting for the things you want."

My jaw shook as I opened my mouth and rehashed a speech that had never left me. "You can do anything you want. You're strong enough to figure a way forward. You're brave enough to fight for the things you want. Don't tell me you don't deserve it. If Troy loves you and you love him, then you deserve each other! It's that simple!"

My chest was heaving by the time I finished my spiel. I didn't mean to yell at her like that, but it just all came out of me—strong and passionate.

Aunt Cassie slumped back against the counter, gaping at me with wide eyes. A couple of tears trickled down her cheeks. I didn't know if they were my fault or not, and I didn't want to watch her cry again, so I spun on my heel and headed for my room.

Flopping onto my bed, I gazed up at the ceiling. Damn, I wished Mom was there. She'd know exactly what to say to make things better.

FORTY-FOUR

CASSIE

Felix's speech kicked my ass.

His words ran around my brain in a never-ending tornado. He was so impassioned as he stood there in the kitchen, telling me not to overcomplicate things.

I wanted him to be right.

If Troy loves you and you love him, then you deserve each other.

If only it were that simple.

I wanted to love him...all the way. But how could I do that without Davis getting between us? My nights had been haunted by dreams that were twisted and weird—me naked in Troy's arms morphed into visions of being raped on a cold bedroom floor. The pain. The humiliation. The shame. I'd buried it deep for so long, and having it rise up again was suffocating. I'd never faced that night, really thought it through, relived it.

The first few weeks after leaving Troy's apartment had been hell.

But as the days passed, I seemed to have found my control again. Not my joy, but my ability to function without feeling like I was being shoved through a shredder.

I still didn't feel good enough for Troy though.

What if I freaked out on him again? What if I could never be normal?

His texts and calls telling me he didn't need sex, that he just wanted to be with me, weren't the truth. How could he possibly mean that?

Couples made love. That was normal!

He deserved a woman who could love him with abandon. He needed to kiss, lick, moan, cry out in ecstasy. I'd be a plank of wood in his bed—frigid and afraid.

He hadn't called in a couple of weeks, but Felix had said he was miserable.

Still?

I figured he'd moved on.

I didn't think I ever could. Loving Troy had happened without my say-so, but I couldn't imagine feeling like that about anybody else.

I missed him so much.

Tears flooded my eyes. Sitting up, I reached for

a tissue, but the box slipped off my nightstand. I tutted and switched on my lamp, crawling out of bed to retrieve the box. It'd landed next to Crystal's diary, which I had tucked out of sight.

It felt too close to the core to read again, so I'd made myself forget about it.

With a sniff, I snatched it up and flicked it open near the middle. I didn't know what I was looking for. I just skimmed random passages until one caught my eye, drawing me in with an opening sentence that froze the air in my lungs.

I've had a revelation—I can make a choice.

Pastor Mike preached about starting anew this morning. That nothing from our past can bind our future. God's mercies are new every morning.

It got me thinking.

If God doesn't hold on to the past...then why should I?

Art tells me every day that God loves me. Felix shows me every day that maybe that's true. Because how does a worthless wretch like me deserve such a precious child?

So this is what I've decided, and this is what I'm going to tell myself every day until I believe it.

I am enough.

I am clean.

I am whole.

My past no longer matters. I will not let it bind me, own me, or shame me. Davis took what did not belong to him. He forced me to say words I never meant. I have lived with that guilt and shame for too long. I've let him hold on to me...

BUT NOT ANYMORE!

I'm making a choice.

I reclaim the girl I once was. I reclaim my beauty, my innocence, my purity.

I am loved by a pure heart, and therefore I have what it takes to love back. I can say "I love you" and something good will come of it.

I couldn't breathe. It was like she'd written the words just for me.

But they'd been for her.

She'd done it. She'd made a choice and she'd beaten the beast in a way I'd never been able to.

Gripping the book, I forced myself to finish reading the entry, then went back to the top and read the whole thing through again.

"I am loved by a pure heart." I read her words aloud and kept going, speaking her last line in a clear voice that sounded loud in the quiet room. "I don't feel it right this second, but I *will* one day. I'm choosing to start anew. I'm choosing to win."

She'd underlined the last two sentences and gone over the letters until they were thick and bold on the page—a clear sign of determination.

A tear dropped onto the corner of the paper. I quickly smudged it out, not wanting to ruin my sister's precious diary.

Gently closing it, I placed it on my nightstand and covered my mouth. My jaw was trembling and tears continued to spill from my eyes.

Emotions were coursing through me—strong waves ready to knock me to the floor. I stood up before they could, refusing to fall again, refusing to be taken out.

Sucking in a breath, I grabbed my watch, checked the time, and muttered, "Screw it."

I didn't care that it was two o'clock in the morning. I needed to run.

Changing into my gear, I left a note for Felix on the off chance he woke and couldn't find me. Then I crept out of the house, locking the door and pressing play on Felix's shuffle before jogging down the path. I took a route I was familiar with, pounding through the darkness at a quick pace. Street lamps lit my way with an eerie glow that would normally freak me out, but the urge to run overpowered it.

I tried to focus on the music but couldn't stay with any song for more than half of it.

Crystal's and Felix's words—written and spoken—barged through the melodies and lyrics, trying to work their way into my soul. Trying to make me a believer.

I swung my arms a little harder, tuning back into the music, but it didn't work.

I was being spoken to, and I'd be an idiot to ignore it.

Running up the hill, I turned onto the wooden staircase and raced up to the lookout. It was my halfway point, and I always stopped to admire the view.

A light rain had started to fall, a soft sprinkling that wasn't enough to make me return home. It felt more like a cleansing shower than anything.

Could it be?

Could I really be cleaned of the filth inside me?

Gripping the railing, I gazed out at the twinkling lights of LA. They sparkled and glimmered, looking magical and romantic in the darkness.

Light in the darkness. It did exist.

Crystal had found it, and I wanted to as well.

It was time to make a choice.

The wood dug into my palms as I squeezed a little tighter. The soft rain sprayed my skin—a fine mist that was slowly growing heavier.

I licked my trembling lips and whispered, "I am enough. I am clean. I am whole."

I closed my eyes and dipped my head.

"I am enough!" I said the words with more force. "I am whole. I am healthy! I am strong!" I shouted. "I can do this!"

Going very still, I took a deep breath and let the nightmares in. I forced my quaking limbs to stand there and relive it...all of it. The cold cellar, the bruises, the fists, the pain, the dreaded night where he stole the one thing I'd fought so hard to protect.

I was a trembling mess by the time I was finished. But as that last thought of me cowering behind those irate college kids while they kept Davis away from me finally flicked past, I whispered the words, "It's done. No more."

With a fearful swallow, I then forced my mind to a new place that was pure and clean...and normal.

I pictured myself on Troy's bed, naked and

exposed. I imagined his hands gliding over me, his tongue on my skin. I brushed my fingers over his bare shoulders, clutching them as I spread my legs beneath him. I closed my eyes and forced myself to imagine what it'd feel like to have him push inside me, move on top of me, creating a friction that was supposed to breed pleasure, not pain.

Tears burned my eyes and I gripped the railing, willing it to hold me up.

The rain was falling a little harder, melding with my tears. I wanted to stand there and let everything be washed away—all my fear and hesitation.

Looking up to the sky, I spread my arms wide and welcomed the raindrops. They splashed into my eyes and pinged off my face, dribbling down to my neck and shoulders.

A song I'd never heard before started playing in my ears. It was unlike most of Felix's music. This song was gentle with emotion, the kind that made my heart listen.

I went still, dropping my arms and sagging against the railing. The music flooded me, rising up in my chest and inspiring me.

"Can you turn my black roses red…"

Troy expanded in my mind, and the thoughts I'd been forcing suddenly flowed freely. His hands were soft and tentative, wanting to please, comfort, ignite. He'd show me what real love looked like because he *did* love me.

And I loved him.

I was *capable* of loving him.

As the music stirred my soul, I whispered into

the cold night air, "I can do this."

Slapping the railing, I headed straight back down the stairs. The music drove me through the rain, and I ran all the way to the only place I was meant to be.

FORTY-FIVE

TROY

Someone was pounding on my door.

Jovi had already scampered out of the room and was barking. His claws scraped the wood as I stumbled into the living room. I squinted at the clock as I passed the kitchen.

It was three o'clock in the morning.

If it was Jimmy, I was kicking his butt to the curb. I didn't care what kind of shit he'd gotten himself into.

Knock-knock-knock!

Jovi barked then growled, his stumpy tail going nuts.

"It's okay, buddy," I mumbled, scrubbing a hand over my face and raking the hair out of my eyes. Moving him aside with my foot, I opened the door and felt the air whoosh out of my lungs.

Cassie stood at my door, water droplets running down her face. She was saturated, her running shirt clinging to her body as she stood there puffing.

I blinked a few times, trying to work out why she was there. My mind churned with scenarios, but she disintegrated them all when she looked me in the eye and whispered, "I love you."

My heart flipped, and I clutched the door. It took me a minute to process the enormity of what was happening.

Cassie had just said three little words that terrified her...and she'd said them to me.

"I love you." She said them again, then stepped into the doorframe and planted her lips on mine.

There was only one thing to do—wrap my arms around her and kiss her back.

Her lips were cold from the rain. Her wet clothes stuck to my bare chest. Goose bumps rippled over me, but I held on anyway. Jovi wanted in on the action, but I nudged him away with my foot. I was holding Cassie, kissing her.

She'd just told me she loved me.

Gripping my face, she kissed a little hard, tipping her head to swipe her tongue into my mouth. She kept pressing her hips against me, indicating exactly what she wanted. She was hungry, determined...and trembling.

I pulled back, holding her at arm's length to

check her face. I looked deep into her wide brown eyes and whispered, "What do you want, Cass? There's no hurry here. I told you, I—"

"I need to do this with you," she interrupted me. "I need to know I can be normal. The reason I ran away from you is because you deserve to be with a woman who can give you everything. I couldn't do that before, but I'm ready now. I'm ready to give you every last part of me…because I'm miserable without you. Because I love you."

I held her face, slightly in awe of what was happening. She'd said it three times in five minutes. It was like a living, breathing miracle. I didn't know which words to fill the silent space with. I didn't want to screw it up by speaking. I just wanted to gaze into those eyes and see her conviction.

"I've made a choice, Troy. I won't be haunted. I will not be controlled by my past anymore, and you're the first step in proving it. I'm standing here wet and sweaty. I look disgusting, but—"

"You're gorgeous and I love you." I decimated the space between us, lifting her into my arms and pouring every ounce of love into a kiss that was our new beginning.

When I'd backed away from Cassie and chose to cut all contact, I'd had to accept that I'd lose her for good. But there she was, in my arms, asking me to be her first step on a brand new road.

I'd never felt more humbled and honored in my life.

FORTY-SIX

CASSIE

Kissing Troy was easy—his tongue was warm and pliable, the light scrape of his stubble intoxicated me. I loved the feel of his lips on mine. Being encased in his arms felt safe...doable.

Taking things to the next level was a different story, but it was one I had to write. I wasn't leaving Troy's apartment until I'd given him my all, proved to both of us we had a future together.

I pulled away, brushing the mussed hair off his face and hoping my voice didn't quiver too much. "Let's go to your room."

His face bunched, his eyebrows dipping into a

pained frown. "Are you sure?"

"Yes." I nodded. "I'm sorry I had to push you away. But since I left, I've done nothing but miss you." I brushed my thumb over his mouth. "I want a life with you. It doesn't matter if I'm a little scared right now. You have to let me try again. Because if I can do this, then maybe we can be like a normal couple. We can be a family."

"We don't have to have sex to be a family."

"You keep saying that, but you know it's not true. People in love make love. That's how it works." I rose to my tiptoes, brushing my nose against his and whispering, "I want you. I want us to be in love."

I didn't have to say more. With a kind smile, he took my hand and led me to his room. I stopped in the doorway, biting my lips together. My stomach pulsed with nerves. I crossed my arms, willing myself to stay together.

Troy turned to look at me, his eyes crinkling at the corners. I rested my head against the frame, admiring his muscular torso. He was like a piece of art, worthy of display in a flashy museum. Far too good for the likes of me.

I snapped my eyes closed and whispered under my breath, "I'm enough."

With a thick swallow, I inched into the room. Jovi padded in behind me, but Troy clicked his fingers and pointed for the door.

"Jovi. Bed." The bulldog whined. Troy just shook his head. "Bed."

His doe eyes looked to me for backup. Poor

thing, I was too nervous to do anything but wince at him.

He drooped his head and shuffled out the door. I closed it behind him and turned back to face the man I loved.

Troy had moved to stand by the bed. His hands were resting in his pajama pockets, pulling them just a little farther down. I could make out the line of hair above his manhood, and my insides burned with desire.

I wasn't used to the sensation, but I knew I wanted more of it. I took another step closer.

Troy looked relaxed where he was, which made it easier to strip off my shirt.

I dropped it behind me then peeled off my pants, sneakers, and socks.

I was down to my underwear and feeling vulnerable. Troy stood back—watching, waiting. His eyes were asking me what I wanted, but I couldn't speak.

With trembling hands, I undid my bra and dropped it on top of the sopping pile of running clothes, then wiggled out of my underpants.

Nerves pulsed through me, and it took a deep breath and more courage than I thought to look up from the floor.

Troy smiled, waiting until we made eye contact before dropping his pants.

My lips parted, and I couldn't help staring at him...all of him. He didn't seem to mind my gaping perusal. Everything about him was so calm and unhurried.

"How do you want to do this? Should I guide you or…"

I bit my lip. "Do you know what you're doing?"

I figured I already knew the answer.

Troy's smile was slow and sweet. "If you're asking if I've done this before, then yeah."

It was tempting to ask how often, but the answer would no doubt throw me.

"What do you want me to do, Cass?"

I blinked, and pointed at the bed. "You sit. I'll, um…come to you."

"Okay." He sat down and stretched his body out, linking his hands behind his head and grinning at me. "You come to me whenever you're ready." He waved his hand up and down, indicating my naked body. "I could sit here looking at this all night, so really, no hurry."

His wink was adorable and sexy, breaking the debilitating tension holding me back. My cheeks flared hot as I giggled and padded across to him.

Scratching my elbow, I worried my lip and wondered what to do next.

My lips trembled as I rested my knee on the edge of the bed then spread my legs over Troy's lap. He adjusted himself on the pillows, lightly holding my thighs and staring at me.

I tried to smile, but it didn't really work. Troy stayed still, doing no more than resting his hands on my legs. I reached forward and traced my finger over his lips and down his chin. I made it all the way to his collarbone before palming his chest and moving to his arm, gliding my hand all the way down until I rounded his wrist. Taking his hand, I lifted it slowly to my breast, giving him permission to explore.

He lightly massaged me, not taking his eyes off my face. I took his other hand and put it to my other breast, losing my breath when he skimmed my nipples with his fingertips.

It felt so good.

Fiery tingles shot between my legs, desire drawing a hot line from my heart to my core.

Lurching forward, I ran my tongue across Troy's lips. He opened his mouth to me, twirling his tongue around mine while massaging my breasts. It was a heady rush. When I pulled back for air, he glided his hand around my back, holding me steady and looking into my eyes.

"I'll stop whenever you want." He held my gaze until I nodded; then he leaned forward and drew my nipple into his mouth.

I tipped my head back, closing my eyes and scraping my fingers through his hair. I held him to me, relishing the sensations rocketing inside as he took his time, kissing and sucking my tender skin.

My heart was thundering, my breaths quick and erratic, only increasing when I felt his erection skim my inner thigh. I fisted his hair, nerves battling it out with a heady desire.

I wasn't quite sure what to do and faltered when I tried to line myself up.

Troy pulled back from my breasts, stopping me quickly. "Wait." He grabbed my arms, holding me up. "I don't want to hurt you. I need to know you're ready."

The tender look in his eyes was enough to make me dissolve.

"How do you know if I'm ready?" I whispered.

"Do you trust me?"

I nodded.

Settling me over him, he made sure I was secure on my knees and then slowly put two fingers in his mouth, moistening the ends before reaching between my legs. I didn't know what to expect, so when he gently ran his fingers between my legs then pushed them inside me, I let out a surprised gasp.

"I can stop." He went to pull out.

"No!" Gripping his shoulders, I shook my head and begged, "It feels good. Don't stop."

He gently smiled at me and kept going, touching me, arousing me…the desire building to a crescendo that couldn't possibly get any more intense. But it did. My first orgasm tore right through my center, rocketing up my body. I let out a lusty cry, gripping his shoulders and quivering.

Troy caressed my inner thigh with his moist fingers then asked, "Do you want to keep going?"

"Yes," I breathed.

My shaking limbs probably contradicted me, but my need to prove something had shifted to a craving for Troy. I wanted to meld our bodies together, feel him sink inside me and become a part of who I was.

He wrapped himself quickly—maybe worrying that I'd change my mind in the short time it took him.

But I wouldn't. I was determined to do this.

Even more than that...I *wanted* to.

As soon as he was ready, I tipped my hips, his erection teasing me. With his deft fingers, he lined us up and I sank onto him. A soft sigh escaped my lips. I didn't know if it was a breath of relief or desire, but as he filled me, I was struck by an overwhelming sense of completion.

I wasn't done yet though.

Troy placed his hands on my hips and gently guided me, helping me find our rhythm. He smiled, telling me he loved me as we rose and fell together. I held on to his shoulders, unable to bite back my moans. It felt so amazing; my entire body was buzzing. The sensations taking hold of me were like nothing I'd felt before. Again, they built until I thought I might burst.

Troy groaned, his eyes glazing as he dug his fingers in and thrusted a little harder.

I gasped and gripped his shoulders, watching his face as he lost himself in an orgasm. It turned me on, firing rockets through me all over again. I crashed down on him and we tumbled together, both crying out as he came inside me.

Wrapping his arms around my waist, he pulled me against him, kissing the top of my breast before resting his head on my shoulder. "I love you, Cass. I love you," he whispered against my neck, palming my back and securing me into his life.

I rested my cheek on the side of his head, playing with the ends of his hair and softly starting to sing. I have no idea why I did it, but "Head Over Feet" by Alanis Morissette came to me, and it said everything I needed to. So I just…sang it, holding him close to me and telling him how he'd won me over with nothing but his good soul and patience.

He was the only man for me, and finally, I'd had the courage to claim him.

As I sang through the song, Troy shifted, lifting his head to look me in the eye. I smiled and kept singing.

I actually finished the whole song, something that should have been awkward and weird, but it wasn't. My breathy voice set the perfect tone, and he drank me in, absorbing each word as it left my mouth.

"It's all your fault," I ended with a grin.

He chuckled and came for my mouth, kissing me as soon as I'd finished. I sank into the feeling, knowing how safe it actually was.

He was still inside me, our bodies relaxing together. It was like floating back to earth on a feather, lazily whispering on the breeze before settling softly on the warm green grass. I wanted to curl up beside him and fall asleep in his arms, but I had to get back to Felix.

I'd done what I'd come to do.

I'd be back to do it again.

Troy was part of my life now. We were on our way to becoming a family, which made it a little easier to leave him.

Brushing my thumb across his stubble, I said it again…this time with a confident smile. "I love you, Troy Baker."

"And I love you." His eyes gleamed as he leaned forward and kissed my nose. "And I'm looking forward to saying that to you over," he kissed my lips, "and over," he kissed my neck, "and over," he kissed my shoulder, "again."

I giggled, cupping the back of his head as his lips traveled down to my breasts and he set my body sizzling all over again.

EPILOGUE

FELIX

Two months later...

The stadium loomed large, and my stomach jumped into unexpected knots.

Unexpected? Who was I kidding? I was about to do something huge! I was surprised I could even function properly.

The rumble of the expectant crowd fueled my nerves.

I glanced at Aunt Cass, who was walking hand in hand with Troy. I'd finally convinced her to buy a pair of jeans. Her friend from work, Aubrey, took her shopping, and she came home looking like Aunt Cass version 2.0.

Now when she stood next to Troy, they kind of matched. He was in his standard leather jacket and looking pretty casual, considering what he had planned for the night.

I bit my lips together to hide my smile. He'd come to see me four weeks earlier. He'd needed to talk man-to-man. I'd been kind of mystified to be honest, but as we walked Jovi to the dog park he asked me how I'd feel about him moving in.

I'd been cool with it. Since he and Aunt Cass got back together, he'd practically been living there anyway. Most nights were either dinner at our place or his. Moving in made sense.

But then he told me how he wanted to go about doing it…and I'd tripped over the dog.

Jovi yelped and scampered away, but when I rolled onto my back, he returned, resting his paws on my chest and panting excitedly. All I could do was squint into the sun and ask Troy, "Will Chaos be okay with this?"

He nodded. "I've already checked."

I bit my lip the way Aunt Cass always did, then broke into a smile. "Do you think I can do it?"

"I know you can, man. I wouldn't have asked you if I didn't." Troy reached out his hand and I grabbed it, letting him pull me to my feet. He patted my back then dragged me into a side hug. It was the first time I'd ever felt like I had a father. Art was always a grandpa figure. Troy felt like a dad, and if I did this for him, he'd be the closest thing I'd ever have to one.

"Okay." I nodded. "I'll do it."

Troy grinned. "I love you, kid."

I paused, gazing up at his face, seeing how much he meant it. My throat swelled with emotion, but I finally managed to choke out, "Love you too."

So there I was, walking in the back of a huge stadium with my guitar in one hand and a jittery smile on my face. People were already lined up to get in for the opening concert of Chaos's second national tour. They'd done one last year and were about to kick off a summer tour that took them all over the country to promote their new album.

I couldn't believe I was going to be part of opening night.

We reached the door where I had to say goodbye to Aunt Cass and Troy. Security would then take them through a private entrance to the front part of the stadium where they'd have the best view of the concert. I'd be able to look down and see her watching me.

Her arm came around my back and she kissed my cheek, oblivious to why I was really doing this. She thought I was playing a short solo in the middle of one of the songs. She had no idea.

"Hey, Felix." She grabbed my shoulder as I started to turn away.

I glanced back at her.

"Guess what?"

With a little snicker, I winked at my aunt. "It's okay. You don't have to say it. I've known since the second you sang me back home."

Her nose wrinkled, her eyes shining with tears. "I'm saying it anyway." She pulled me into a tight hug and spoke right into my ear. "Your mom would be so proud of you, but maybe not as much as I am." Pulling back, she held me at arm's length and gave me a watery smile. "I love you."

I blushed and dipped my head. "Thanks, Aunt Cass."

With a quick head bob, I hid my nerves behind a bright smile and walked through the door. Chaos were in their designated room. Some chick was powdering Nessa's face, another applying eyeliner on Ralphie. Veronica sat on the stool beside him, giggling. He reached out and tried to tickle her, but she just squeaked and jumped out of reach, laughing a little harder.

Jimmy spotted me in the mirror and waved me farther in.

"Nice to see you, lil' bro. How you feeling?"

"Nervous," I admitted, laying down my guitar case and setting up.

"You're gonna be great." Nessa sounded so convinced.

"Don't sweat it, man." Flick slapped my shoulder. "You just have to remember to never give a shit what people think of you. If you play for this band, it means you're fuckin' perfect."

Nessa and Ralphie laughed in unison, and I remained clueless to their inside joke.

I just shrugged and put on a smile, pulling the guitar strap over my head and giving the strings a light strum.

The door flew open, and Marcus, their manager, walked in with a blonde who kind of looked like him.

"Hey, guys," he said brightly. As soon as he spotted me, his face broke into a wide smile and he came forward to shake my hand. "Nice to see you again, Felix. Welcome along."

His handshake was firm and confident. It was kind of impossible not to like the guy. He was so friendly and nice all the time.

"This is my sister, Felicity. She's working on a journalism paper for college and is writing an article about tonight's show."

"Hi." I waved at her.

She wiggled her fingers at me. "Call me Fliss." She grinned. "When you're not too nervous to talk, that is."

I gave her a bashful smile and hid behind my growing bangs.

"So." Marcus clapped his hands together. "We're all good to go?" He pointed his finger at each band member, checking in with them.

They all nodded while Fliss took notes on her iPad.

Marcus glanced over his shoulder at her, murmuring something I couldn't hear. She nodded but didn't say anything.

"Okay, ten minutes, guys." Marcus clapped his hands again, then strode out of the room.

Fliss kept her eyes on the iPad and kept tapping.

I went back to tuning my guitar and trying not

to throw up. Then the makeup lady came over to me and started rubbing stuff on my nose and cheeks.

"Don't scrunch your face," she murmured.

I tried to relax, then started praying the eyeliner wouldn't be uncapped. Gripping the neck of my guitar, I scanned the room, distracting myself with watching Chaos.

Jimmy and Nessa shared a secret little conversation while Ralphie and Veronica stole another kiss. They obviously weren't as secret about their relationship as Jimmy and Nessa were.

Flick stayed on the edge of the room, watching the two couples before rolling his eyes and making some derogatory comment to Jace.

I didn't quite catch it, but it made Jace snicker and Fliss's head pop up. Her eyebrows bunched into a tight frown as she glared at Flick.

He caught her gaze and faced it head-on. "You got a problem?"

"Sexist much?"

He adjusted his ever-present beanie and walked into her space, a smirk growing on his lips the whole time. "Hey, blondie, if you can't handle my sexiness, then you just better move on out of the way."

She let out a disgusted scoff and stepped back. "You are such a jackass."

His smirk disappeared behind a dry glare and a heavy dose of sarcasm. "Geez, Fliss, I'm so excited that you're joining us on tour this summer. It's going to be so much fun."

Her eyebrow rose in time with her middle finger. Then she spun out of the room, nearly crashing into a guy with a headset.

He jumped out of the way and looked into the dressing room with a confused frown.

Flick waved his hand dismissively. "Time to go?"

"Yeah." The guy nodded. "Suit up."

Flick barged out of the room first, cracking his knuckles as he went. I looked back in time to see Nessa grin. "This should be an interesting summer."

Jimmy groaned while Ralphie snickered.

"Looks like Flick may have met his match." Nessa wiggled her eyebrows and skipped over to me. Throwing her arm around me, she planted a kiss on my cheek. "See you on stage soon, big guy." She patted my belly with her stump. "Use those nerves as energy, okay? Don't think about what you're doing. Feel it." She patted my chest. "We already know you can sing and play, so that's not even an issue. The song should flow from here. It'll sound a million times better if it does."

"Got it." I tried to smile but could only manage a lopsided grin.

Nessa squeezed me into a hug. "This is going to be beautiful. She'll love it."

I hugged her, then hung back as the rest of the band filed out the door. I had to suffer twenty backstage minutes before my turn. Waiting would be a special type of torture.

At least that's what I thought until a smiling face

appeared in the doorway.

"Summer!" I was so happy to see her I didn't even think about lurching across the room to pull her against me. The guitar was between us, but it didn't stop her clinging to my shoulders and hugging back. "Oh, man, I'm so happy to see you."

"Sorry I'm late. I was supposed to be here when you arrived, but Mom was late getting ready and then traffic..." She pulled back in time for me to see the end of her eye roll. "Anyway, I'm here and I'm not missing this epic moment."

Having her there was just what I needed. She distracted me with her funny chatter until the guy with the headset came back to collect me. He said Summer could watch from the side. The nerves I'd managed to ignore kicked back in, exploding in my stomach and making me want to pass out.

"You can do this." Summer took my hand, giving it a little squeeze and then hanging on to it as we walked to the stage.

Thousands of people packed out the stadium, and I could hear their roar thundering through the air. It only ignited me, making me feel a heady rush of excited and petrified.

We slowed to a stop at the edge of the curtain. Jace was finishing up his drumroll and Jimmy was talking into the mic. He and Nessa kicked into a little banter. They were about to introduce me.

"Oh, shit," I murmured.

"Don't worry. Just enjoy it." Summer grinned at me. "It's an adrenaline rush, man. Just go with it."

With a quick swallow, I pulled her into a hug

and whispered in her ear. "Thanks for being my best friend."

She pulled back and lightly punched my arm. Her cheeks were so red I could see them glowing even in the dim light. "Just get your butt on stage and kick ass, okay?"

I grinned.

She winked. "Thanks for being my best friend too."

We stared at each other for a second, and I got this warm buzz in my chest.

Then Jimmy said my name. "My man, Felix!"

TROY

The crowd let out an almighty roar, and my heart started pounding. This was it. The moment I'd been planning since Cassie came back to me. That morning we'd made love had been nothing but confirmation. I drove her home, walked her to the door, and kissed her goodbye. As I shuffled back to my car, I knew it would only get harder and harder to leave her...and so I figured I may as well become a permanent feature in her life.

But simply telling her that felt way too unromantic for the epic way she made me feel, so I decided to pull out all the stops and get my brother and Felix involved.

Felix cleared his throat into the mic and adjusted his guitar strap. "H-hey, LA."

The crowd cheered and Cassie grabbed my arm, giving it a squeeze. I grinned down at her. She looked so nervous and alive at the same time. She was practically glowing with pride.

"I, um…" Felix scratched his neck. "I wanted to thank Chaos for letting me play this song for you."

Jimmy patted his shoulder and gave him a big brother smile.

So then I started glowing with pride too. Seeing them up together on the stage like that was an extra gift on top of the one I was hopefully going to get in a few minutes.

Nerves skittered through me, and I glanced down at Cassie again, praying she'd hear my heart.

"I'd like to dedicate this song to my Aunt Cass. She rescued me when my mom died, and I'm so grateful for everything she's done."

Cassie gasped and covered her mouth. Tears were already brimming in her eyes. She'd be a write-off as soon as she knew the song we'd chosen.

"But this song isn't just from me." Felix looked to where he thought we were standing. With the bright lights in his eyes it was impossible for him to see us, but it didn't matter. He was doing exactly what we'd planned. "Aunt Cass, this song's from Troy too. We love you."

He stepped back from the mic and strummed the first few chords of "Hole Hearted" by Extreme. The crowd let rip with a huge cheer as Felix got into the song and Jimmy stepped forward to join him.

Cassie looked up at me, finally catching on that something was a little different. I grinned at her, pointing to the stage when Felix started to sing.

She gasped again, a huge smile dominating her face. I wrapped my arm around her shoulders and pulled her against me. She fit perfectly, and it boosted my confidence. This was meant to happen. All the little threads that were broken and torn ultimately brought us together…created a family out of three lost souls.

Felix killed it, nailing the harmony he'd practiced with Jimmy. When "Hole Hearted" came to an end, the cheers rose to deafening. And then the spotlight swung around to face me.

It was the easiest thing in the world to drop to one knee and pull out the ring Felix and I had chosen only a week before.

The crowd's cheering only escalated when Cassie and I appeared on the screens. I didn't look to check; it was only an assumption. In that moment I only had eyes for Cassie.

Taking her hand, I pressed my thumb into her palm and hoped my voice didn't shake too bad. The cheering was so loud I basically had to yell my proposal.

"I know it's quick. I know it's the last thing you're expecting, but I love you, Cassie Grayson. You fill my heart to overflowing, and I want to be your husband. I want to look after you, to love you, to make you laugh, to hold you when you cry. I want to be a family with you. So…will you marry me?"

CASSIE

I was so numb with shock I could barely breathe, let alone speak.

But the answer was an easy one.

I nodded, and Troy slipped the ring on my finger.

The crowd went ballistic, and Chaos kicked into a quick rendition of "Hole Hearted," playing the final chorus while Troy stood and lifted me into his arms. I held his face and kissed him. Tears streamed down my cheeks, but they were fueled by an inexplicable joy.

The spotlight flew back to the stage, coating us in darkness again. I wrapped my legs around Troy's waist and kept making out with him.

I couldn't believe I was going to marry such an amazing man.

I couldn't believe I had gone from a woman trapped in a world of order, too afraid to even be touched. And there I was, in a packed stadium, becoming the fiancée of Troy Baker after watching my amazing "kid" perform like a rock star.

I was smart enough to know that life was never perfect. Keeping my past at bay was going to be a daily decision and sometimes an all-out battle, but I wasn't riding the roller coaster on my own anymore. I had a family again, people to love and who'd love me back.

I was healthy, I was whole, and I was rich in all

the things that mattered.

Crystal had been right all along...we were the lucky ones.

THE END

Thank you so much for reading *Hole Hearted*. If you've enjoyed it and would like to show me some support, please consider leaving an honest review.

KEEP READING TO FIND OUT ABOUT THE NEXT SONGBIRD NOVEL...

The next Songbird Novel belongs to:

Nixon & Charlie

RATHER BE

Is due for release in April 2017

But while you're waiting for their story, keep an eye out for the second Chaos novella…

COMPLICATED

Flick is used to women swooning at his feet—have a little fun, a little sex, and they can be on their way.

He isn't used to hanging out with an intelligent, opinionated feminist who has a major chip on her shoulder. Felicity "Fliss" Chapman is going to be his biggest buzzkill on the summer tour. He can either go out of his way to avoid her (pretty hard when they're sharing a bus) or he can try to pull the stick out of her ass and show her what a good time looks like.

Fliss never wanted to go on the Chaos summer tour, but after being publicly dumped and humiliated by her college sweetheart, she's ready to get out of town for a while.

But she doesn't count on Flick being such an ass (like all men except her father and brothers). She's determined not to let his sexy little smirk get under her skin. All guys do is burn her and walk away from the ashes. She won't let herself become another victim of the cocky musician.

Too bad neither of them knows that sometimes love can take down even the most resistant souls. As these two go into battle they unwittingly start to break down each other's barriers, stirring a whole new pot of complications neither are ready for.

This novella is an exclusive story for my newsletter subscribers only. If you'd like to receive the story in February 2017, then please sign up to become a Songbird Novels Reader.
You'll also receive a free copy of Angel Eyes (Chaos novella #1) when you sign up.
http://eepurl.com/1cqdj

You can find the other Songbird Novels on Amazon.

FEVER
Ella & Cole's story

BULLETPROOF
Morgan & Sean's story

EVERYTHING
Jody & Leo's story

HOME
Rachel & Josh's story

TRUE LOVE
Nessa & Jimmy's story

TROUBLEMAKER
Marcus & Kelly's story

ROUGH WATER
Justin & Sarah's story

GERONIMO
Harry & Jane's story

.

NOTE FROM THE AUTHOR

Dealing with such a sensitive subject matter made this a really challenging novel to write. I was blessed enough to grow up in a very loving home with parents who treated each other with love and respect, and who showed me every day what honest, healthy love looks like. It breaks my heart to know that not every child gets this same courtesy. I believe it is the right of every human being to be raised in a loving home. But unfortunately it doesn't happen.

Because I have not experienced Cassie's horrors firsthand, I had to base all my writing on research and what I imagined it must be like. I wanted to be respectful in the way I constructed this story. Hopefully I have been.

Cassie and Crystal are amazing women, and I know there are others out there who are just like them. They have my utmost respect and admiration. The human spirit is strong and can overcome so much.

I hope this story has inspired you in some way. Love does have a thousand faces, and watching Cassie and Felix figure out how to live together and love each other was precious to write. Troy is one of the sweetest, most patient characters I've ever written. He reminds me of my dad, with a heart too big for his chest and a true compassion that is often rare.

I hope you enjoyed seeing characters from previous Songbird Novels in this book, and I look forward to writing the final book soon. It will be very strange saying goodbye to a series that has kept me going for nearly three years. Thank you for your love and enthusiasm towards these books. It will be a bittersweet end to a very long journey. :)

xx
Melissa

Keep reading for the playlist and the link to find it on Spotify.

HOLE HEARTED SOUNDTRACK

(Please note: The songs listed below are not always the original versions, but the ones I chose to listen to while constructing this book. The songs are listed in the order they appear.)

MY FAVORITE WASTE OF TIME
Performed by Owen Paul

DON'T LEAVE HOME
Performed by Dido

THE LUCKY ONES
Performed by Brothers3

IF THAT WERE ME
Performed by Melanie C

SEMI-CHARMED LIFE
Performed by Third Eye Blind

YOU GIVE LOVE A BAD NAME
Performed by Bon Jovi

BORN TO BE MY BABY
Performed by Bon Jovi

WIND OF CHANGE
Performed by Scorpion

IRONIC
Performed by Alanis Morissette

YOU MAKE MY DREAMS
Performed by Daryl Hall and John Oates

SUPERSTITIOUS
Performed by Europe

RUNAWAY TRAIN
Performed by Soul Asylum

ANIMAL
Performed by Def Leppard

CAN'T STOP
Performed by Red Hot Chili Peppers

PLAY WITH ME
Performed by Extreme

LIVIN' ON A PRAYER
Performed by Bon Jovi

LET THE SUNSHINE IN
Performed by Army of Lovers

NOTHIN' BUT A GOOD TIME
Performed by Poison

HEAVEN
Performed by Warrant

I'LL BE THERE FOR YOU
Performed by Bon Jovi

CAN'T FIGHT THIS FEELING
Performed by REO Speedwagon

HEY LEONARDO
Performed by Done Again

BLACK BETTY
Performed by Ram Jam

RIGHT THROUGH YOU
Performed by Alanis Morissette

WHEN LOVE AND HATE COLLIDE
Performed by Def Leppard

WHEN THE GOING GETS TOUGH
Performed by Billy Ocean

WHEN I LOOK INTO YOUR EYES
Performed by Firehouse

BLACK ROSES RED
Performed by Alana Grace

HEAD OVER FEET
Performed by Alanis Morissette

HOLE HEARTED
Performed by Extreme

To enhance your reading experience, you can listen along to the playlist for HOLE HEARTED on Spotify:
https://open.spotify.com/user/12146962946/playlist/2lB2wiwqx8TjWOtlhEaKAj

ACKNOWLEDGEMENTS

Thank you so much to everyone who had input in producing *Hole Hearted*.

My critique readers: Cassie and Rae. Your insights were so helpful. Thank you for always giving me so much time and making me think about how I can make the story the best it can be.

My editor: Laurie. Thanks for another job well done.

My proofreaders: I love you guys. Thank you for your time and attention.

My advanced reading team: You guys are seriously the best!

My cover designer and photographer: Regina. You are magic.

My fellow writers: Inklings and Indie Inked. I love that after all this time, I can still check in with you guys for advice and encouragement.

Songbirds & Playmakers: My daily interactions with you guys are so much fun and you make this job so amazing.

My family: I needed extra love and

encouragement while working on this project. Thank you for always being there with your loving words and warm cuddles.

My maker: I'm so incredibly grateful for the life you've given me. Thank you for my family and the constant love you've poured into my life. Thank you for taking my past and giving me new mercies each day.

OTHER BOOKS BY MELISSA PEARL

The Songbird Novels
Fever—Bulletproof—Everything—Home—True
Love—Troublemaker—Rough Water—Geronimo
Coming in autumn 2016: Hole-Hearted

The Space Between Heartbeats
Plus two novellas: The Space Before & The Space
Beyond

The Fugitive Series
I Know Lucy — Set Me Free

The Masks Series
True Colors — Two-Faced— Snake Eyes — Poker
Face

The Time Spirit Trilogy
Golden Blood — Black Blood — Pure Blood

The Elements Trilogy
Unknown — Unseen — Unleashed

The Mica & Lexy Series
Forbidden Territory—Forbidden Waters

Find out more on Melissa Pearl's website:
www.melissapearlauthor.com

ABOUT MELISSA PEARL

Melissa Pearl is a kiwi girl living in Hamilton, New Zealand. She trained as an elementary school teacher but has always had a passion for writing and finally completed her first manuscript in 2003. She has been writing ever since, and the more she learns, the more she loves it.

She writes young adult and new adult fiction in a variety of romance genres—paranormal, fantasy, suspense, and contemporary. Her goal as a writer is to give readers the pleasure of escaping their everyday lives for a while and losing themselves in a journey...one that will make them laugh, cry, and swoon.

MELISSA PEARL ONLINE

Website:
www.melissapearlauthor.com

YouTube Channel:
www.youtube.com / user / melissapearlauthor

Facebook:
www.facebook.com / melissapearlauthor

Instagram:
instagram.com / melissapearlauthor

Twitter:
twitter.com / MelissaPearlG

Pinterest:
www.pinterest.com / melissapearlg

CPSIA information can be obtained
at www.ICGtesting.com
Printed in the USA
LVOW10s2253140217
524297LV00001B/163/P